"You said you're unconventio...

As if she didn't know. Tess couldn't think of anyone she knew who'd dare to wear a designer jacket with a ratty T-shirt.

Ben picked up a cookie and dropped a quarter into her money can. "Well, I prefer white satin sheets on my bed and red silk undies on my ladies. I don't suppose you're wearing red underwear."

"If I was, I wouldn't be likely to tell you."

"I don't see why not. I'd show you mine if you asked."

Tess felt her cheeks turning the same shade of crimson as her briefs. "Are you trying to come on to me?"

"Trying? I thought I *was* coming on to you."

He polished off the first cookie and selected another, dropping a second quarter into the can. "Stop frowning like that. Anyone watching us would think we weren't friends."

"We *aren't* friends," Tess pointed out. "We aren't even what I'd call acquaintances. And the cookies cost thirty cents."

Dear Reader,

Welcome to the Silhouette **Special Edition** experience! With your search for consistently satisfying reading in mind, every month the authors and editors of Silhouette **Special Edition** aim to offer you a stimulating blend of deep emotions and high romance.

The name Silhouette **Special Edition** and the distinctive arch on the cover represent a commitment—a commitment to bring you six sensitive, substantial novels each month. In the pages of a Silhouette **Special Edition**, compelling true-to-life characters face riveting emotional issues—and come out winners. All the authors in the series strive for depth, vividness and warmth in writing about living and loving in today's world.

The result, we hope, is romance you can believe in. Deeply emotional, richly romantic, infinitely rewarding—that's the Silhouette **Special Edition** experience. Come share it with us—six times a month!

From all the authors and editors of Silhouette **Special Edition**,

Best wishes,

Leslie Kazanjian, Senior Editor

P.S. As promised in January, this month brings you Curtiss Ann Matlock's long-awaited first *contemporary* Cordell male, in *Intimate Circle* (#589). And come June, watch what happens to Dallas Cordell's macho brother as... *Love Finds Yancey Cordell* (#601).

ELAINE LAKSO
Forever Young

Silhouette Special Edition

Published by Silhouette Books New York

America's Publisher of Contemporary Romance

For Alan, Harvey and Ed,
who so willingly
came to the aid of a damsel,
and disk drive,
in distress.

And for another mother named Dorothy,
who also has a heart of gold.

SILHOUETTE BOOKS
300 East 42nd St., New York, N.Y. 10017

ISBN: 0-373-09592-9

First Silhouette Books printing April 1990

Printed in the U.S.A.

ELAINE LAKSO,

also known to romance readers as award-winning Laine Allen, claims Mary Stewart and John D. MacDonald as early influences on her writing. Originally from California, Elaine has traveled extensively in Europe, living briefly in West Germany, and now makes her home in upstate New York. She is an avid tennis player and voracious reader. "I'll read anything," says the author, "including cereal boxes!" A lover of "good food, good wine, romantic movies and just about any kind of music," she is also the happily married mother of two active children.

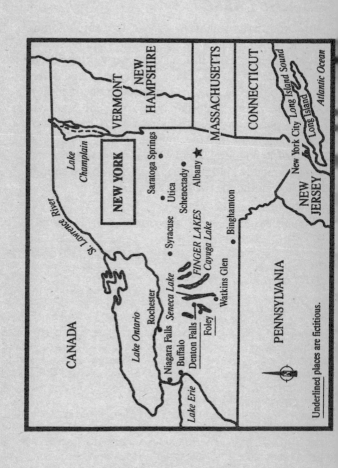

Chapter One

All she needed was a miracle. Not a large one, Tess conceded, adding cinnamon to the other ingredients she was assembling in a large bowl. A small one would do. A little more time, a little more money and a little more understanding on the part of the bank's loan officer were all she needed to get her mother's bakery back on its commercial feet again.

Tess knew she could do it. Never mind that she owed enough to New York State Gas and Electric to rival the national debt. She had no doubt whatsoever that she could turn the small cookie shop she'd inherited into a thriving enterprise. She hadn't spent five frenzied years living and working in the shark-infested waters of Manhattan without learning *something* about survival.

Not that you'd recognize it from looking at her today. Leaning back against the flour-laden counter, Tess wiggled her injured ankle experimentally and sighed. Lord, what a nuisance it was. And what an idiot she had been.

Convinced that the little feline she'd agreed to "kitty-sit" was too young to extricate itself from the high limb it had insisted on exploring, she'd shimmied up the tree, slipped and chinned herself—twice—then embraced the bush at its base before she concluded that if God had meant woman to fly, he would have given her wings—and an engine, as well.

It was probably a miracle she hadn't broken her neck instead of just the branch, Tess acknowledged. That's why she hadn't yet given up all hope of financial solvency. If miracles were being dispensed in her area, there was always the possibility she might receive just one more....

Hopping on one foot like a flamingo, Tess added chopped walnuts to the bowl in front of her, then spooned portions of dough onto a clean cookie sheet. Even barring miracles, she decided, there was still hope. Like her mother before her, she believed in the power of positive thinking. In spite of the alarming number of bills she'd managed to accumulate in the eight short months since she'd reopened the cookie shop, she was certain that there was likely some ridiculously obvious solution to her current financial dilemma. Unfortunately, she had no idea what it could be.

The problems she was having with her physical well-being, however, were much easier to handle. All she had to do the next time she was even *tempted* to act out a Superwoman fantasy was say "never again." Favoring her tender right ankle, Tess limped to the huge black stove at the rear of the shop. She removed a batch of fragrant oatmeal-spice cookies from the hot oven and slid in another panful to bake. "Never, *ever* again," she added, forcing the ill-fitting oven door closed with her good leg before resetting the timer.

Tess put down her potholders and frowned as she spotted a glossy red Porsche sliding into the Handicapped parking space in front of her shop. She wasn't going to put up with any more nonsense concerning the parking spot in front of her store, either. Since she'd moved back to rural Upstate New York it had become abundantly clear to Tess that the disabled, having little to depend on in the way of public transportation, necessarily drove many types of vehicles.

Turbocharged sports cars, however, weren't usually among them.

Keenly aware of the difficulties her handicapped customers faced—partly because her father had been permanently disabled and forced to take early retirement due to an injury on the job—Tess's view of the parking slot was distinctly protective.

Tess brushed flour off her jeans, which had a rip in one knee, courtesy of her cat-rescuing mission, and waited for the driver to take note of the sign and move on. Instead she heard the roar of the engine cut off. She watched the occupant climb out of the Porsche.

Tall, dark and outrageously attractive, he was dressed in jeans and a stylishly oversized gray and black jacket that was probably as outlandishly expensive as it was obviously designer made. Beneath it, he wore a black T-shirt with the words Beam Me Up, Scotty. There's No Intelligent Life Here emblazoned in white across the front.

Definitely not your average Denton Falls male, Tess conceded. He also wasn't visibly handicapped.

Tess folded her arms across her pink sweater as the man stretched languorously, like a cat making itself comfortable in a forbidden chair. Turn around and look at the sign, she silently commanded.

Two seconds later, he did.

Tess shook her head as he shoved his hands into the tanker-sized pockets of his blazer and glanced briefly at the blue and white sign. Then, apparently intent on sunning himself, he leaned back against his car, tilted his high-cheekboned face toward the sky and closed his eyes.

Tess blew her bangs off her forehead in exasperation. This was the second time today that a perfectly healthy male specimen had parked in the Handicapped zone. And it was still only 10:45 a.m.

Almost glad at the opportunity to vent a little frustration, Tess headed for the door. She didn't care how wealthy he was, or how attractive. She was going to give him a piece of her mind.

"Considering how badly he seems to need some brains," Tess murmured to herself as she exited the store to confront the man, "this shouldn't take too long."

He'd wanted to lie back and catch a few rays for so long, he could almost taste it. His eyes slitted against the October sun, Ben Young was in the process of doing just that when he caught sight of the attractive brunette marching toward him. No, not marching, Ben swiftly corrected himself. Limping in high dudgeon.

Heaven only knew *why* the slender woman approaching him looked ready to commit homicide, but at least she was coming after him without any obvious weapon in hand. However, from the deadly look on her otherwise appealing face, Ben acknowledged her tongue was probably all the weapon she needed.

Wondering what he could possibly have done to earn the wrath of a female he was certain he'd never met, Ben smiled as he took in her firmly set pink mouth, the small but distinctive nose that verged on pugnacious, the slightly squared chin set for battle.

The possibility that she'd like to do something of a physically damaging nature to him didn't bother Ben in the least. It intrigued him. He'd been fending off concern for so many months, anger was a refreshing novelty.

Deciding to stay put for the moment, Ben stretched his shoulders. After nine hours in the Porsche he felt like a lizard with its skin on too tight, but he wasn't complaining. He'd be the first to admit he was lucky to be alive. Of course, he realized with mild amusement, that situation might change any second now, if the murderous glint in those tawny brown eyes was anything to go by.

Swiftly approaching the man who appeared to be in robust good health, Tess checked the Porsche's license plate once again just to be sure. She'd battled for months to get that particular spot designated for the handicapped, and she wasn't about to back down after those long hours spent attending frustrating city council meetings.

Satisfied that there was no wheelchair symbol on the white, red and blue plate, Tess opened her mouth to lay the man waste.

Before she could utter a word, the driver straightened and looked straight at her. "Hello, love. Something I could do for you?"

Momentarily disconcerted by the smoky quality of his voice, Tess stopped and stared mutely at him. He had the most amazing eyes, she thought fleetingly. Darkly lashed, neither green nor gray, they were piercingly direct in a very unsettling sort of way.

They were also brimming with intelligence.

Tess swiftly eliminated obtuseness as an excuse for his actions and girded herself for battle. "You could move your car," she suggested politely.

Seconds passed, during which Tess suspected that she and her tenuous calm were being summed up with annoying accuracy. "Why?"

Tess refrained from rolling her eyes. Why? the man asked, when he was lounging next to a sign big enough for a party of ten to picnic on. Knowing she tended to overreact when it came to this particular subject, she fought to sound reasonable. "Because this spot is needed by others less fortunate than yourself."

Tess prayed for patience as he contemplated her damaged jeans, then her bandaged ankle. "You can have it in a minute," he offered. "I won't be here long."

By "here," Tess assumed he meant Denton Falls. He clearly didn't belong in the small, conservative, Finger Lakes community she called home, Tess reflected, any more than she had fit into the dog-eat-dog atmosphere of corporate Manhattan. Everything about him was too sexy, too flashy, too...too everything, Tess concluded.

The product of a strict but loving upbringing, Tess was a firm believer in "Everything in moderation." Even a bat could see *moderation* wasn't in this man's vocabulary.

Neither, apparently, was *chivalry*.

"I wasn't referring to myself," Tess retorted. "Can you read?"

Folding his arms across his T-shirted chest, he gave her a smile that was as lazy as it was maddening. "Last time I checked."

"Good." Tess indicated the posted sign. "What does that say?"

He glanced briefly at the sign, then back to her. "Handicapped Zone."

Tess ignored the way her neck was beginning to prickle under his frank appraisal and waited. When he didn't speak again, she prompted, "So?"

He raised his eyebrows. "So?" he repeated.

So much for giving him the benefit of the doubt, Tess decided. Either the man was giving her the business or he was, indeed, denser than a two-by-four. "So, that means the physically disabled, not the mentally deficient."

To her consternation, he didn't look the least bit abashed. In fact he looked distinctly amused. "Have I just been insulted?"

"No," Tess cooed. "Described. Are you going to move your car, or am I going to have to call the police?"

Seemingly undisturbed by her threat, he calmly gazed to the left, then the right. "There's no public phone on this block," he pointed out obligingly.

"Unlike you," Tess told him, "I don't mind walking more than five feet. There's one inside my store."

He glanced over her shoulder toward the row of retromodernized turn-of-the-century shops behind her. "The bakery?"

"The bakery," Tess confirmed, eyeing in open disapproval the bristle of beard on his lean cheeks, then the flamboyant jacket.

Slouched indolently against the red car, he considered her in turn, skimming his slate gaze over her pink-and-white frilled apron and settling on her French-braided hair. "What if I told you your bakery was where I was heading when you accosted me?"

Refusing to respond to the appealing huskiness in his voice, Tess gave him a level stare. "I'd still ask you to move your car."

"You would, wouldn't you?" Smiling faintly, he cocked his dark head to one side. His clean thick hair shone like polished ebony in the sun. "Do you treat all your customers like this?"

"Only when they park where they're not entitled. And for your information, the pub doesn't open for another hour."

He looked puzzled. "What's the pub got to do with this?" he asked.

"The pub is where you were really heading when you parked here—" Tess contemplated him in open challenge "—isn't it?"

"You don't believe I was coming to the bakery?"

"In a word, no." Tess waited for him to climb back into the Porsche.

Instead he grinned at her. "You're very opinionated, aren't you?"

"I'm not opinionated." Tess felt her cheeks flame with indignation. "I'm in the right. And you are in—"

Tess frowned as he turned and reached into the car. She eyed the long slender object in his hand and adamantly shook her head. "That's not going to work," she told him.

This time he looked genuinely blank. "What's not?"

"The cane. I've seen that ruse before," Tess explained. "The college kids around here use gimmicks like that all the time. Two of them even brought crutches once. Some people," she added meaningfully, "will do anything to keep from having to walk around the block."

His smile, if possible, became even more maddening. "I think I've just been insulted again. You're a very determined woman. What can I say?"

Aware that they'd already attracted at least two onlookers, Tess deadpanned, "How about goodbye?"

To her dismay, he laughed out loud. It was a soft, velvety sound that reminded Tess of sinfully rich chocolate.

"There must be something I can do or say to redeem myself," he persisted, apparently a lot less bothered than she was by the fact that they were fast becoming a public spectacle. "How about this?" Once again, he reached back into the sleek car.

Tess's patience slipped a notch. "Look here, I don't think you're getting the message...." The rest of the sentence died on her lips.

Tess stared at the printed sign in his hand. Her brown eyes took in the stylized wheelchair and the boldly lettered words Temporary Permit. For the first time, Tess peered around the concrete planter of wilting pink and purple petunias he stood behind. Her gaze traveled down the length of his jeans to his feet. One of them was wearing a well-polished black boot. The other was encased in a walking cast.

"There's no need to look quite so stricken," he said as she stared at it in silence. "The doctor assures me I'm going to live."

The soft drawl brought Tess's eyes reluctantly up to meet his. He was watching her in amused interest—no doubt waiting to see if she could put her other foot in her mouth, Tess realized.

A judicious person would probably jump right in and make a swift apology, she acknowledged. Of course, if she were a judicious person she likely wouldn't have insulted him in the first place. And if he were a judicious person, he wouldn't have given her the business the way he had.

Feeling mildly guilty but not overly repentant, Tess decided she might as well get it over with. "I'm sorry." She tried to sound contrite. "I suppose under the circumstances you have a right to be annoyed—"

"I don't get mad." He smiled pleasantly. "I get even."

His drawled response sent an unexpected flurry of butterflies loose in Tess's stomach. Wondering fleetingly how a man with a late-model Porsche "got even" for being verbally abused on a public thoroughfare, Tess smiled wanly. "If there's anything I can do to make amends—"

"I'm sure there is." His deep voice was bland as butter, but for some reason the comment struck her as positively rife with innuendo.

"Like what?" Tess took a small step backward as she spoke.

"A little late for caution, don't you think?" he chided.

Tess supposed he was right. Hoping levity might ease the situation, she said. "I've already apologized publicly. What more do you want? A printed retraction in the *New York Times*?"

"Well..." he appeared to consider her tongue-in-cheek offer "—apologies are well and good, but I think the nature of this offense calls for some sort of compensation, don't you? After all, you did imply that I was mentally deficient."

That was putting it tactfully, Tess reflected. She'd more or less called him stupid. And lazy.

Pondering the error of her ways, Tess felt another frisson of alarm as he purred, "What did you say your name was again?"

She hadn't said, and he knew it. "Tess."

Reluctance positively riddled her voice, but Tess couldn't help it. The instant he'd said the word *compensation*, a sudden vision of creative litigation and impending bankruptcy had danced before her eyes.

He tsked in mild reproval. "Such an informative woman. Tess what?"

Tess wondered if she dared fib. "DeSain."

Something about her response caught him by surprise, Tess was sure of it. The sparkle in his eyes grew brighter.

"You mentioned the bakery was yours." It was all Tess could do to breathe as he took in her seen-better-days jeans. "Do you run it? Or own it?"

Aware that their small audience had dispersed, Tess fought another battle with her conscience before confessing, "I own it." Technically, of course, it was only forty-nine percent hers since her friend and mentor, Dorothy, had put up over half the money to get the shop out of debt. But somehow this hardly seemed the moment to drag Dorothy's good name into the discussion.

"Goo-o-od." Obvious satisfaction percolated through the word.

Telling herself that her imagination was working overtime, Tess considered him at length before asking, half jokingly, "Should I be calling my lawyer?" She figured she might as well find out now if the man was seriously contemplating suing her for public harassment or aggravated embarrassment or some such nonsense.

To her relief he shook his dark head. "I don't think that's going to be necessary, do you? I'm sure we can work something out between us. Shall we go inside and discuss it?" He latched on to her arm before she could answer and started leading her, gently but firmly, back to the shop.

Feeling fairly certain that she wasn't heading for court, but not yet wholly reassured that she was out of trouble,

Tess tried to ignore the firmly muscled forearm beneath the sleeve of his blazer. He could tease her all he wanted. From this point on, Tess vowed, she was going to be cool and self-controlled. But most of all, she was going to keep quiet.

Sure that she could show at least a semblance of composure, Tess nodded graciously as he opened the door and motioned for her to precede him. The aroma of charred cookies met them.

"Oh, Pele, for heaven's sake!" Tess hobbled to the smoking black monstrosity of a stove that she'd nicknamed Pele after the Hawaiian goddess of the volcano, because of its habit of fiery destruction. Grabbing a potholder, she yanked out the sheet of burned cookies. She let out a soft moan as she mentally calculated the monetary loss before she dumped the charcoal mess into the garbage.

"Do you always give inanimate objects names?"

Prickling at the purr in his voice, Tess turned around and discovered herself the object of male bemusement. "Doesn't everyone?"

She waited for him to ask why she'd named the stove after a soccer player, as at least four other people had already done.

Instead he smiled. "Pele's certainly appropriate, at any rate. I haven't seen that much smoke since Mount St. Helens erupted. You're a very sassy woman, aren't you, Tess?"

Surprised he'd recognized the significance of the name, Tess lifted an incredulous eyebrow. "*I'm* sassy? What do you call a man who wears a Beam Me Up, Scotty T-shirt and baits women he doesn't even know?"

"A Trekkie with a death wish?" He grinned at her look. "Mind if I sit?"

Leaning slightly on his cane, he looked perilously close to collapse, Tess suddenly realized, though he was clearly doing his best to disguise it. She wondered if that meant he took to pity with the same lack of enthusiasm as she. Suspecting he did, she placed a chair in front of him.

He settled himself on it, as pain briefly tightened his mouth. "Thanks."

"You're welcome."

The smile lines around his eyes deepened at her terse response. "For a minute, there, I thought you might hit me with it."

"I considered it," Tess lied.

"Did you, now?" He laid his cane on top of the small circular table. "What stopped you?"

"Possible litigation," Tess countered.

His slow smile sent a warm wave of awareness washing over her. "I'm not going to sue you," he assured her, stretching his long, jeaned legs in front of him. "I have all the money I need."

Tess believed it. Even with only one boot he looked well-heeled.

"What do you want, then, if not my life savings?" Tess thought she'd better ask. It never hurt to be too careful, in her opinion.

Whoever he was, he obviously didn't share her "Better safe than sorry" philosophy.

His smoky voice dropped to a husky purr. "Well, since you asked..." He watched in open amusement as she fought to remain silent, then finished with annoying blandness, "How about some cookies, Tess?"

Reminding herself that he was probably suffering more than he was letting on, Tess responded politely, "What kind of cookies would you like?"

He looked as if he knew *exactly* how close she was to throwing them at him, cast or no cast. "Pecan chocolate-chip are my favorite."

They were also her favorite. Not sure why having that or anything else in common with him should bother her, Tess hobbled to the sink and quickly washed her hands.

"What happened to your ankle?" he asked as she placed a plateful of cookies on the table in front of him, then took refuge behind the counter. "Get up on the wrong side of bed?"

Tess decided to ignore the last half of the question. "I fell out of a tree. What happened to you?"

"Would you believe an outraged female attacked me?"

Tess gave him a long look before delivering judgment. "Yes."

"I thought you would." He bit into one of the cookies and gave a nod of approval. "Very tasty. Just like the ones Mom used to make."

"Thank you." The sudden heat rushing into her cheeks at the unexpected compliment reminded Tess that she wasn't above flattery.

She obviously wasn't above being seduced in broad daylight, either.

Unable to breathe or to think clearly when he flashed her that smile, Tess briskly flipped open a clean white paper bag. "How many would you like?"

He didn't even hesitate. "All of them."

All of them? Tess estimated how many cookies were on the full tray. She'd assumed he'd ask for a couple of dozen. But if he took the whole trayful—

"Is there a problem?" He rose slowly and came up to the counter.

"Problem?" Tess echoed hollowly. "No, of course not." Not if you discounted the fact that her profits for the day would amount to zero.

Concluding that at the rate she was going she might be better off just to close up the shop and save herself a few dollars, Tess quickly emptied the tray. "Ten dozen cookies is a lot to eat by yourself," she observed, feeling fairly certain he wasn't a family man. He didn't look like the domesticated type. "You must be awfully hungry." Realizing too late that she'd sounded just as nosy as she felt, Tess hammered a dozen staples into the tops of the bags as an excuse not to look at him.

Refusing to be ignored, he settled his elbows on the counter. "I guess I'm just not as reticent as some people. When I see something I want, I go for it." He reached over and tucked a loose strand of brown hair back behind her ear. "How about dinner tonight?"

Stunned by the casual invitation—and her instantaneous reaction to his touch—Tess stared at him in alarm. "I can't." She didn't dare. The last time she'd responded to a man this rapidly, this *physically*, was when she'd met Randall for the first time.

And if *that* wasn't enough warning, she reminded herself, there was always her shop to think of. Still struggling to make the bakery a success, she needed to pour all of her time and energy into it just to keep her chin above water.

"No?" He smiled faintly as she shook her head. "Maybe another time." He took the stapled bags from her hands and turned to leave. At the door, he turned back to her. "Don't go jumping any more people with canes, will you now, Tess? They can sometimes be lethal weapons in the hands of the elderly."

Knowing she'd probably deserved that, Tess wrinkled her nose and watched him limp slowly back to the Porsche. He was already climbing behind the wheel before the glimpse of something pale green on the counter nabbed her attention.

Chapter Two

Tess stared in confusion at the fifty-dollar bill he'd left behind, then glanced up as Fran Bellows, a faithful customer and the tireless mother of four rambunctious offspring, walked across the threshold with her twin toddlers racing ahead of her. The bell on the door tinkled lightly as the robust young woman closed it behind her.

"Hi, Tess," she said with a cheerful grin as Kevin and Kiley, her two youngest, flung themselves at Tess's jeaned knees.

"Hi, Fran." Laughing, Tess fought to keep her balance. She fondly ruffled the toddlers' soft blond locks before gathering the bouncing twins up into a hug. "Hello to you, too. What's up, pumpkins?"

"Tookie, Teth," they chorused, clearly recognizing a pushover when they spotted one.

Receiving an affirmative nod from their mother, Tess set the two youngsters back down and handed them each a granola cluster before turning back to Fran. "You're looking chipper today."

"Robby got an A on his last geometry test," Fran said, referring to her oldest son. "You're looking at a mother who's unashamedly wallowing in pride." She accepted a sample cookie and paid for two dozen more.

Smiling, Tess quickly filled Fran's order and passed over the aromatic bags. "Robby's a smart boy. Takes after his mother."

Pushing up the sleeves of her sweater, Tess tried not to think of why she no longer had any pecan chocolate-chip cookies left and went to work on another batch.

Fran, approaching to pick her order, caught sight of the fifty-dollar bill and picked it up. "My goodness. Where did *this* come from?"

Hoping her cheeks weren't still flaming in indignation, Tess nodded toward the man starting up the Porsche. "Him."

"Really?" Fran handed back the bill. "Who is he?"

"Trouble visited upon our town," Tess joked half seriously.

Fran nodded. "He looks it. What did he want?"

"I'm not sure." Tess watched the Porsche pull smoothly into traffic. "I think he's suffering from acute boredom."

"Don't tell my Frank I said this, but I think he's a-cute, period."

Tess thought so, too, and it worried her. Leanly attractive in a very virile sort of way, he was the kind of man who could make a woman throw caution and common sense to the wind without even trying. And who probably would.

Not knowing what else to do with it, Tess stuffed the fifty dollars under the cash-register drawer.

Fran put down her purse. "I swear he looked vaguely familiar. Do you suppose he's a famous rock musician or something?"

Harboring a similar feeling of recognition, Tess wrinkled her nose. "Infamous is probably more like it."

Fran sighed. "Infamous or not, if I wasn't already happily married, he could ring my chimes any time."

Fairly certain he'd probably rung more than a few female bells in his life, Tess finally remembered where she'd seen his face before: a picture of him standing in front of a sleek white racing car adorned the wall of the local Burger Queen. Wearing a metallic blue jumpsuit with the names of at least half a dozen different sponsors prominently displayed on his chest, arms and legs, he was among a bevy of race drivers who'd negotiated the nearby Watkins Glen racecourse at one time or another. Tess wondered if his profession and his leg injury had any relation to each other. For all she knew, a disgruntled woman *had* kicked him in the shins—

"Oh, no!" Fran caught her youngsters in the process of defoliating the philodendron decorating the store's front window. As their mother firmly guided the two children away, Tess walked over to the small cabinet she'd purchased at a garage sale with her customers' children in mind. She pulled out some brightly colored clay and other childproof paraphernalia and set the assortment on a low table.

Fran shot Tess an appreciative look as her offspring sat down to play, the shyer Kevin poking pudgy fingers into the clay while the more precocious Kiley whapped hers firmly with a tiny rolling pin.

"You have no idea how a simple thing like this makes life with kids so much easier. I wish the banks and the post office would get with it. But then, bank managers and the postal service probably don't love children the way you obviously do." She paused to nibble on a cookie. "I know it's none of my business, Tess, but if you're having trouble maybe I can help."

"Trouble?" Tess repeated blankly, wondering if the conscientious mother of four meant her current financial dilemma.

"I wouldn't blame you if you were getting worried," Fran added. "If I were a nice young woman like you, I would be, too."

"Worried?" Tess echoed.

"I can see I'm not putting this very well." Fran chewed her lower lip a moment before confessing, "We're not really that far apart in age, and I just thought if you were interested in meeting a nice young man who's keen on settling down and having a family, well, frankly, my brother-in-law Stanley is going to be in town for a few days."

Keeping to her vow to stay unattached and uninvolved at least until her business was on its feet again, Tess was forced to use every ounce of tact and diplomacy she possessed to get out of a date with Stanley Bellows the following weekend.

That accomplished, Tess honestly didn't know whether to laugh or cry when Dorothy Wilder floated into her store half an hour after Fran left.

Tess was inordinately fond of Dorothy, who had been her mother's dearest friend. Stepping in when it had become obvious that Tess couldn't handle the financial end of the shop alone, Dorothy had cajoled, persuaded, then all but insisted that Tess accept her thirty thousand dollars as "an investment." They'd been partners and friends ever since.

Tess genuinely looked forward to their weekly outings to the movies, even though the older woman had made no secret of the fact that she'd decided to remedy Tess's single status for her—namely with her only son, Bennett.

In fact Dorothy had persisted with the idea for nearly six months now, in spite of a total lack of encouragement from Tess.

Small-boned but far from frail, the petite older woman fluttered through the door like a pastel butterfly. "Tess, darling. Thank heavens you're alone. I have the most wonderful news."

It didn't take psychic ability to figure out that Dorothy's son probably figured into the announcement somehow. Readying herself for another bombardment of persuasive charm concerning the man, Tess smiled at her diminutive friend with genuine affection. "Hello, Dorothy. How are you?"

"Oh, fine, dear. Fine. So nice of you to ask." The sweet scent of lavender filled the air as she approached. Anxious to get on with things, Dorothy wasted no time getting to the point of her visit. "Do you remember my son, the one I've been telling you so much about?"

Tess remembered. After six months of listening to lengthy discourses on the man she'd secretly nicknamed Wilder the Wonderful, Tess had concluded that the male in question was either a saint, or his doting mother devised the best fiction in town.

Almost afraid to open her mouth lest something overly encouraging should pop out of it, Tess settled for a polite "Yes, Dorothy."

"Well." Dorothy's serenely unlined face lit with obvious pleasure. "He's finally decided to come visit. Isn't that wonderful?"

Repressing a smile, Tess agreed solemnly, "Wonderful. When will he arrive?" Tess figured that forewarned was forearmed.

"Rather soon, I should think. When he called last night he wasn't sure, but he's offered to pick up a few things for me at the farmers' market Friday while I'm at the dentist's office. He's such a thoughtful boy."

Nearly bursting with motherly pride, Dorothy further embroidered on the already well-decorated tapestry Tess privately referred to as The Many Attributes of Bennett Wilder.

"Well, I'm sure that's more than you probably want to hear about a man you've yet to meet," Dorothy finished with a charming smile, which in her prime had probably launched more than a few male libidos into orbit. "But you know how mothers are about their children.... Well, maybe you don't," she amended after a moment. "Neither does Bennett, to tell you the truth, but I'm sure you will when you two have your own family."

Even though Dorothy persisted with the idea that her son and Tess would make "the perfect couple," Tess found it impossible to take offense when the older woman was so clearly well-intentioned.

"By the way, dear—" Dorothy smoothed a parchment-thin hand over her skirt "—will you be at your usual booth at the farmers' market this week?"

Suspecting she might live to regret it, Tess smiled. "Yes, Dorothy."

"You will? Oh, that's wonderful." Dorothy positively beamed. "You and Bennett really should meet. You've so much in common." Her gray eyes twinkled. "Why don't I have him stop by and say hello since you'll both be there? I just know you'll get along."

Dorothy's enthusiasm was so contagious, Tess couldn't help smiling. Why not? If Bennett Wilder were even half the man his mother purported him to be, he was bound to be safe and sane, not to mention intelligent. A successful businessman, he might even be able to pass on a helpful tip or two. For all she knew, he might even turn out to be... wonderful.

The suspense was killing her. Manning her usual booth inside the pavilion used each Friday morning for the local farmers' market, Tess scanned the bustling commerce center. Filled with the echoing sounds of laughter and the enticing earthy aroma of fresh-from-the-garden vegetables, the partially enclosed building was bursting with activity.

So was Tess's nervous system.

Where *was* the man? she wondered in exasperation. For the last hour her eyes had rested hopefully on every male who'd even remotely fit her vision of Wilder the Wonderful, but so far he'd yet to materialize.

Looking futilely for signs of the paragon, Tess sighed again and pushed the sign that read Cookie Consortium into a more obvious spot.

"What's the matter?" asked a smooth male voice from behind her. "Accost another innocent soul and lose another ten dozen cookies?"

There was no way on earth she could mistake that smoky purr. Tess turned slowly around and found herself staring into an equally familiar pair of mischievous gray-green eyes.

She had a name to put with the face, now that his picture had been plastered all over last night's newspaper: Ben Young. It struck Tess as far too tame a moniker for a man who regularly risked his neck for a living.

Tess studied him in mild alarm. "What are you doing here?"

"Tsk. What manners." Cleanly shaven but looking no more respectable than he had the day before, Ben Young shoved the sleeves of his off-white linen blazer up on his forearms, revealing a generous sprinkling of dark hair and the hint of sinewy muscle. "Didn't your mother ever teach you anything?"

"My mother taught me a lot of things," Tess said, disturbed at how her pulse had started to sprint at the mere sight of him. "One of which was never to talk to strange men."

"I'm not strange. A little unconventional, maybe," he allowed. He settled a lean hip on the corner of her table and smiled engagingly at her. "I'm just a regular kind of guy. How's business, Tess?"

His faintly exotic after-shave reminded her that he was highly *irregular*. And so was his behavior. "Fine."

"How's the ankle?"

"Fine," Tess repeated. Her heart pounded as he reached across the table.

"Attack any handicapped people lately?" He picked up the heart-shaped locket resting on her white sweater and examined it.

Determined to remain cool, calm and rational no matter *what* he did or said to provoke her, Tess retreated, forcing him to drop it. "Not lately."

He winked. "I guess this means we live and learn from experience."

"Some of us do." Tess shot him a meaningful look. "Some of us don't."

"And some of us apparently don't have much in the way of experience to draw from." Clearly willing to add to hers, Ben made himself more comfortable and gave her white turtleneck sweater and black wool suit a thorough review. "I guess some of us don't have much in the way of a wardrobe to choose from, either," he teased. "Where the dickens did you dig up that outfit? The local nunnery?"

Tess realized he was simply trying to break the ice and prod her into talking, but she still found herself faintly irritated. She'd dressed for her meeting with Dorothy's son. Since she didn't really know him, she hadn't had the faintest idea what to wear, so she'd picked the only thing in her closet that had seemed suitable: the neatly tailored suit she'd bought when she was still in her "Dress for Success" stage back in New York.

Knowing she was going to get into trouble, Tess still couldn't stop herself from retorting, "I was desperate. All my purple satin capes are at the cleaner's." She surveyed his stone-washed black jeans and neon-green T-shirt. "What's *your* excuse?"

Appalled at herself, Tess halfway expected him to take offense and leave. Instead, his eyes twinkled. "I never make excuses. Waste of time and energy."

"Meaning you're in a hurry, lazy *and* incorrigible?" Tess surmised, recognizing it was going to take a lot more than small insults to send the man on his way. It was apparently going to take more than big ones, too.

He grinned at her. "No, meaning I'm honest. I say what I mean, and mean what I say. What's your personal philosophy of life, Tess?"

He said it as if he thought she probably hadn't managed to develop one. He obviously thought she was about as worldly as a four-month-old baby, she reflected wryly. And about as easy to bamboozle.

"I believe in DeSain's Golden Rule," Tess told him.

He looked amused again. "Which is?"

"Do unto others as they're doing unto you." Tess looked past his shoulder and smiled in genuine pleasure. "Hello, Mrs. Mitchell. The usual?"

"Yes, dear. Thank you," the other woman replied.

Ben rose from the table and watched in fascination as Tess waited on the elderly lady who, from her shabby cloth coat and worn shoes, clearly had little in the way of funds. It didn't surprise him in the least that Tess charged the woman less than half the going rate. He recognized from the look in Tess's eyes that it was all she could do not to bag up the cookies and send the elderly woman off with the money besides.

Tess seemed as free of artifice as her skin appeared to be devoid of makeup, Ben thought. He found it virtually impossible not to stare at her, even though he knew it flustered and annoyed her. He simply couldn't help it. He'd never really understood what a "peaches and cream" complexion was. Now he knew. Brown eyes bright with intelligence, with a soft, full mouth made for smiling—and kissing—she practically glowed with good health and good humor. And, much to his surprise, he was finding himself wildly, improbably, attracted to both.

He waited until she'd sold the woman a dozen carefully selected chocolate-chip cookies and had put away the cash before he spoke again.

"What's that for?" he asked, referring to the coffee can Tess had prominently displayed in front of the plastic containers of cookies.

Tess wished he would leave before she said anything else she was likely to regret. "For customers to put money in when I have to be away from my table."

She sighed in resignation as Ben settled himself more comfortably on her table and surveyed the other vendors' booths filled with macramé plant hangers, ceramic mugs and bowls, paper bags of popped corn fragrant with butter, and an assortment of fall fruit and vegetables.

"Aren't you afraid of theft, leaving money lying around like that?"

"I believe in people's inherent honesty," Tess replied truthfully.

He gave her conservative suit and high-necked sweater a languid inspection. "Do you also believe in truth in advertising?"

Suspecting he was going to make another personal remark about her wardrobe, Tess gave him a wary look. "Yes. I do."

"So, when it comes to you, what I see is what I get?" A smile pulled at the corners of his mouth as he watched her fight to remain silent.

"Most people get what they deserve," she finally allowed. If he continued to prod her, he was certainly likely to.

"In my experience, some do." His voice dropped to a purr. "Some don't. I don't recall being inside here before." He surveyed the cavernous interior of the high-ceiled stone market structure. Built during the last century, it had once been used as a livestock auction house. "Interesting building."

"Yes, it is," Tess agreed, eternally glad that instead of bulldozing it as planned, the city had finally decided to designate it as an "unofficial" historic landmark. Not without a little encouragement, of course.

But since she'd been sitting in on the city council meetings anyway, encouraging council members to "do the right thing" had seemed a better use of her time than knitting hats and mittens for Fran's twins, who already had at least a dozen sets each.

"They don't make buildings like this anymore," Tess added.

"They don't make *women* like you anymore. Can I ask you something?"

"You can ask," Tess replied, not quite sure whether she'd just been insulted or complimented.

"What was it about me yesterday that set you off?"

Surprised that a man as self-confident as he clearly was would care one way or the other, Tess confessed, "It wasn't you. I have something of a personal stake in that parking spot." Briefly she explained why.

"Eight months is a long time to attend city council meetings."

Tess sighed in wry agreement. "It seemed like eight years."

"You must have been very determined to get your way."

"I suppose I was," Tess admitted, never having really thought about it in quite that way before. She'd always considered herself principled, not stubborn.

"I can't imagine why the city council didn't go along with it within the first eight minutes." Ben studied her glossy brown hair, which she'd secured with a white ribbon at the nape of her neck. "Are people here that far behind the times?"

Every time she started to like him, he managed to say something that irritated her all over again. Offended by this latest generalization which she took to include her, Tess found herself rising unexpectedly to the council's defense. "For your information, they represent their constituents, who are conservative, by making decisions only after much deliberation."

"Must be something in the local drinking water," Ben murmured, "that makes everyone around here so afraid to climb out of their ruts."

Tess glowered at him. "I heard that."

"You were supposed to." He left her side briefly to assist one of the neighboring vendors in unloading a crate of vegetables from the back of a van. He returned with a cauliflower and a bundle of carrots under his arm. "Tell me. If I hadn't parked in the Handicapped zone, would you have come out to talk to me? Me being so obviously from out of town, as it were."

"No," Tess replied, sure she wouldn't have. She didn't normally strike up conversations with men she didn't know. She especially didn't initiate conversations with men who drove flashy red sports cars. And if she were at all sensible, Tess figured, she wouldn't be talking to him *now*, either. "Speaking of yesterday—" Tess noticed he wasn't moving as awkwardly as before "—what happened to your cast?"

"Came off this morning. I feel about ten pounds lighter," he confessed.

So did she. From the neck up. Briefly Tess wondered why her composure seemed to take a hike at the mere sight of him as she watched him leave to peruse the flower booth run by Ruth Wheeler. One dazzling smile from the man, Tess noted wryly, and the other woman looked ready to keel over.

Oddly comforted by the fact that she apparently wasn't the only female he flustered, Tess suddenly remembered the slip of paper in her pocket. She waited until he'd finished buying a bouquet of yellow chrysanthemums from the clearly bowled-over Ruth, then said, "There's something I've been meaning to ask you." She never got a chance to finish.

Ben had thrust the bouquet into her arms. "Here, these are for you."

Tess stared down at the colorful blooms. "What's this?" she asked. Could it possibly be some sort of peace offering? she wondered.

"I just remembered mums make me sneeze."

The casual comment deflated Tess like a pin jabbed into an overfilled balloon.

Exasperated at herself, she held up the note she'd received the day before. "What is this?"

"Looks like a thank-you note," he said helpfully.

It *was* a thank-you note. "I didn't donate ten dozen cookies to the day-care center," Tess pointed out.

"Did you really think I'd eat them all myself?" he teased.

"Yes." The fact that he'd apparently donated the cookies had shocked her nearly as much as his reappearance. "Why do they think I donated them?"

Leaning over, he repositioned the sign she'd so meticulously placed, shifting it slightly to the left. "They asked me where the cookies were from, so I told them. Can I help it if everyone around me jumps to conclusions?"

"People wouldn't keep jumping to conclusions," Tess told him, shoving the sign back where it had been originally, "if you didn't encourage them to. In any case, this money belongs to you, not me." From her coin purse she extracted the fifty-dollar bill he'd left behind the day before.

He didn't take it. "Why isn't that in the bank?" he scolded.

Not partial to criticism from people she barely knew, Tess retorted, "Because I didn't deposit it, that's why."

An admitted creature of habit, she always went grocery shopping on Monday nights, faithfully went to the movies with Dorothy on Tuesday nights, did her housecleaning on Wednesday nights, hit the laundromat on Thursday nights and did her banking and bill paying on Friday—all interspersed with running her shop. By Sunday night she usually fell into a heap of exhaustion.

"You don't make deposits every night after you close?"

Momentarily forgetting his recent philanthropy, Tess bristled at his open disapproval. "I don't usually make enough in one day to make it worth my while." Sometimes she barely made enough in a *week* to make it worth the effort, but that was her business, not his. "Are you going to take this back or not?"

"Not," he declared. "Consider it as penance for my sins."

"I suppose you have lots of sins to pay penance for," Tess surmised, torn between keeping the bill and insisting he take it back.

"A few more than you do, I dare say." He repositioned the sign for a second time.

Moving it right back again, Tess calmly read the message emblazoned across his chest. "You said you're unconventional. How?"

As if she didn't know. She couldn't think of anyone she knew who would dare to wear designer jackets with ten-dollar T-shirts that lamented, Denton Falls Isn't The End Of The World, But You Can See It From Here.

Ben picked up a cookie and dropped a quarter into her money can. The coin clinked noisily in the empty metal receptacle. "Well, I prefer white satin sheets on my bed, blue jumpsuits on myself and red silk undies on my ladies. I've always been a very patriotic guy." He bit into the cookie and chewed thoughtfully. "I don't suppose you're wearing red underwear, you being a small-town girl and all?"

As a matter of fact she was, though they were nylon, not silk.

"If I was, I wouldn't be likely to tell you," she responded dryly. "Would I?"

He lifted his broad shoulders. "I don't see why not. I'd show you mine if you asked."

Tess felt her cheeks going the same shade of crimson as her briefs. "Are you trying to come on to me?"

"Trying?" His black eyebrows arched slightly. "Lord, I guess I've been out of circulation too long. No, sprout. I wasn't trying. I thought I *was* coming on to you. Stop frowning like that." He polished off the first cookie and selected another before dropping a second quarter in the can. "Anyone watching us would think we weren't even friends."

"We aren't friends," Tess pointed out. "We aren't even what I'd call acquaintances. And the cookies cost thirty cents."

She waited for him to mention the fact that she'd just sold the same cookies for a dollar a dozen to Marjorie Mitchell. He didn't.

Digging into his jeans, Ben came up with two more nickels. "Happy?"

Actually, she was. Wondering why she couldn't work up any real animosity no matter what he did or said, Tess wrinkled her nose. "I'd be happier if someone would buy the other twenty dozen cookies."

"No sooner said than done." Ben whipped out a lustrous leather wallet and stuffed a crisp hundred-dollar bill into her money can.

"I don't mean you!" Embarrassed, Tess pried open the coffee can and attempted in vain to give the money back to him.

"I know you didn't." He ignored her outstretched hand. "I just decided suddenly that I couldn't live without twenty dozen chocolate-chip cookies."

"Actually it's only eighteen dozen. And half of them are oatmeal-raisin." Tess attempted to stuff the bill into his jacket pocket.

Ben caught her hand and pressed it to his chest. "I like to live dangerously."

So must she, Tess decided, considering she'd just touched him of her own volition. Her suddenly clammy hand was captured in his larger, drier one. Tess swallowed. "How dangerously?"

"Well." His slate-green eyes gleamed as he laced his fingers with hers. "On a scale from one to ten, I suppose I'm about a twelve and a half."

That's what she'd figured. The intoxicating aroma of his after-shave teased her senses. Appalled at the way her resistance was melting like ice in the tropics, Tess tried without success to retrieve her hand. "If you want the cookies, I'm going to need two hands. Let go."

He stroked her damp palm with his thumb. "What's the magic word?"

Tess couldn't remember any words, let alone magic ones. Her mind had gone the way of her knees: to mush. "Stop that."

He shook his head and slowly caressed her fingers. "Not even close. I'll give you a hint. It starts with *p*."

A queer hollowness seemed to invade what was left of her legs. Tess put her other hand on his chest for support and felt her mouth go dry as his body heat beckoned to her through his soft knit shirt. "Please stop it."

Ben surprised her by gently letting go. "That's three words, but it looks like it'll have to do if I want the cookies before sundown. Didn't they teach math in your school?" he scolded as she backed away.

"Math was never my best subject," Tess managed.

Neither, obviously, was sexual parrying.

Which ought not to surprise her, Tess conceded, considering that the only man she'd ever had a really serious relationship with had been Randall, who'd given every indication that he thought foreplay was something to do with the game of golf.

Wishing she weren't quite so unversed in the subtler aspects of male-female relationships, Tess began bagging the cookies. "What are you going to do with all these cookies, anyway?" she asked, trying to guide the conversation back onto safer ground—if there was such a thing around Ben Young, which she doubted.

"That's an awfully personal question," he teased.

"They're my babies." Tess grabbed a second bag and started filling it. "I'd like some assurance they're going to a good home."

"How do you feel about nursing homes?"

"Nice places to visit, but I wouldn't want to live there."

"From what I hear, I doubt the cookies will be around long."

Tess fluttered her lashes at him. "I suppose it's too much to hope the same thing about you?"

"Now, Tess. You're not getting hot and bothered on me, are you?"

"I'm cool as a cucumber," Tess lied, feeling anything but.

What was it about the man, she wondered, that made her feel flushed and flustered and furious all at the same time?

She continued to bag the cookies with a vengeance. When she turned around again, Ben was handing her a cup of coffee. "Here, you look like you could use a break."

Tess took the cup, careful their hands didn't meet. "Thanks."

Imitating their first conversation, Ben clipped, "You're welcome."

Unable to resist, Tess, remembering that conversation as clearly as he did, quipped, "For a minute there I thought you might dump it on me."

Ben blew into his steaming cup of coffee. "I considered it."

Tess gingerly sipped from hers. "What stopped you?"

His voice dropped to a teasing purr. "I have better ways to warm up women than bathing them in hot coffee."

This time everything from her nose to her toes tingled. Nearly as exasperated with his persistent teasing as she was with herself for responding, she went back to bagging cookies. "I thought you were just passing through town."

Ben grabbed a bag and started to help. "I thought I was, too."

"What happened?"

"I decided to stick around awhile."

Tess took a step sideways to put more distance between them. "Why?"

He closed the gap with a sidestep of his own. "Why not?"

Tess could think of all kinds of reasons. Rising panic on her part, for one. Incipient boredom on his, for another.

The man hardly belonged in a quiet, out-of-the-way place like Denton Falls. Even if she hadn't already figured that out just from talking to him, the article accompanying yesterday's newspaper headline proclaiming, The Rocket's Back In Town! would have convinced her. According to the caption under the picture of him holding an uncorked bottle of champagne in one hand and the teeny-tiny waist of a gorgeous blonde in the other, Ben "The Rocket" Young was a champion Grand Prix race driver with a well-known penchant for "fine clothes, fine wine, fast cars and faster women—not necessarily in that order."

"If you look real hard," Tess told him, "you could probably find a bottle or two of fine wine at one of the nearby wineries." For fast women, he'd have to settle for the bored housewives who frequented Danny's Bar down on

Main Street—not that she had any intention of telling him that.

"I suppose that stern look of disapproval means you saw last night's newspaper article."

"It was a little hard to miss." Tess stapled a bag and started on another. "You appear to be something of a local celebrity." She refused to call him a hero, which was what the paper had called him.

"In a town like this, it doesn't take much to stand out in a crowd." He took the stapler from her hand. "How much of it did you read?"

"Enough." Unfortunately Fran's visiting twins had trashed most of it with a combination of fingerpaint and applesauce before Tess had gotten the chance to finish it. She'd been dying of curiosity ever since.

"The incriminating part, I take it. If it matters, the article was a slight exaggeration."

"Which part? The bit about the expensive clothes?" Tess asked dryly. "Or the fast women?"

Ben reached for another bag. "The part about the fine wine. I prefer fine beer. You like putting me on the spot, don't you?"

As a matter of fact, she did. Probably as much as he liked giving her the business. "Does it bother you?" Tess placed the bags in a large box.

"Not particularly. I like competition. Always have. That's why I got into racing in the first place."

Tess frowned at him. "We're not competing."

"Aren't we, Tess?"

Tess studied his bland expression. "What are we competing over?"

"The last word, of course. Care to continue this discussion over dinner?" He looked unsurprised by her silent refusal. "No, I didn't think you would." Tess chafed as he rearranged the bags of cookies into four straight rows. "What's the matter? In a hurry to leave?"

"No, I'm in a hurry to have you leave," she retorted, frustrated because in his view she apparently didn't do anything right.

"Why?" He restapled a bag that had come undone.

Tess considered using the stapler on him. "I'm meeting someone."

"Male or female?"

"Male. Not that it's any of your business." Tess turned her back on him.

"What's he look like?"

"I haven't the faintest idea."

"This sounds like a promising relationship."

Tess turned and gave him a withering look.

Ben cheerfully ignored it. "This fellow you're going to meet. Is he intelligent?"

"Brilliant."

"Sensitive and caring?"

"Extremely so." Goaded, Tess expanded: "He volunteers for community service and never, ever criticizes the manners, wardrobe, personal philosophies or banking practices of women he doesn't know very well." Tess watched as he continued rearranging the cookies. "He doesn't criticize anyone else's neatness standards, either."

"Sounds like either a wimp or a pillar of the community," Ben mused.

"He's the epitome of manhood," Tess sniped. "The perfect male. Every woman's dream come true. Now, if you'll excuse me." She turned away again.

Ben studied Tess's stiffened spine, fascinated by the way her neck had pinked in indignation. It had been practically forever since he'd seen a woman turn that dainty shade of rose, and in spite of the fact that he knew he had her at an advantage, he couldn't seem to resist provoking her.

Where the hell had she been hiding all this time? Siberia? He figured she had to be in her mid to late twenties, and yet she appeared to be as easily flustered as a high-school girl. Unfortunately her wardrobe took away any impression of youth. He hadn't been kidding about the nunnery. Her clothes looked appropriate for someone thirty years her senior.

Ben stretched to relieve the throbbing ache in his right leg. He really shouldn't keep goading her the way he had been. He realized he was toeing a thin line between being exasperating and downright obnoxious. She looked as if she could cheerfully murder him after that last crack. But if she weren't annoyed at him, she'd probably either ignore him or pity him. He wasn't exactly enthused about either.

She was the first woman he'd met in nearly five months who didn't flutter and fawn all over him—or even worse, treat him like some sort of defective piece of merchandise. The fact that it had taken her at least four minutes to notice that his cast was gone had to be taken as a good sign.

He needed the encouragement.

This was his first foray back into the real world, and in spite of what she apparently thought of him, he wasn't so secure that rejection didn't smart. He certainly wasn't half as fearless as he'd let her believe. His accident had given him a very healthy view of mortality.

He looked before he leaped now—something he would have scorned eight months ago. A concussion, two smashed legs and a painful stay in the hospital had convinced him it was the wiser course.

Taking a chance on setting himself up for another tongue-lashing, Ben flicked an imaginary speck of dust from his jacket.

"This epitome of manhood you're meeting—" he kept his voice purposefully bland "—wouldn't happen to be any relation to Dotty Wilder, would he?"

Chapter Three

How did you—?" Tess turned slowly around. A queer feeling developed in the pit of her stomach at his benign expression and spread slowly to her limbs. "No." She shook her head in denial. "You can't possibly be..."

"Dorothy's son? I'm afraid so."

"But your name..." Tess began in consternation.

"She remarried after my dad died. I guess she never mentioned that." He gave Tess a maddening smile. "Mom's told me a lot about you."

"Your mom's told me a lot about you, too." Tess stared at him in disbelief. And not *one* word of it matched the man before her.

After listening to Dorothy, Tess had half expected the man to be larger than life: a cultured seven-foot male of Einsteinian intellect, with the looks of Robert Redford and the charm of Cary Grant.

Never in her wildest nightmares would she have associated the impeccably mannered, impeccably dressed Dorothy with a *race-car driver*. When Dorothy had said her son liked living in the fast lane, Tess had thought she'd meant he was a stockbroker!

In fact, Tess was certain Dorothy had referred to her off-spring as some sort of "investor," and she said so to Ben.

"Mom told you that?" He looked supremely unconcerned by the inaccuracy. "Well, I suppose I've invested a dollar or two in my time."

"In what?" Tess asked politely. "Cases of fine beer?"

"Now, Tess," he chided, looking far more entertained than injured. "Don't get nasty. After all, we hardly know each other."

Tess gave him a cool stare. "I think I know all I need to about you."

"'Think' being the operative word, of course," he mused. "Or is it lack of thought we're dealing with here? Women are so notoriously emotional."

Tess's ears burned in indignation. "Now wait just a minute—"

Ben blithely checked his Rolex. "You've already had a minute. Actually, you've had about two minutes so far, by my reckoning. Damned little time for you to be making judgments about someone you've only just met, don't you think? Are you always this prejudiced?"

The burning sensation spread to Tess's cheeks. "I haven't prejudged you."

"No? What are you going by, then? A crystal ball?"

"Something more concrete. A thorough assessment."

"Really?" Ben flashed a smile as sexy as it was totally maddening. "I thought those were looks of vast disapproval, not assessment. And what, pray tell, have you discovered from your in-depth appraisal of two minutes?"

"That you're not the least bit like your mother." Tess gave him a critical surveyal to let him know that the judgment was not in his favor.

"People tell me I'm more like my father." He winked. "You would've liked my dad, Tess. He was a real sensitive guy. The epitome of manhood."

Tess smiled sweetly. "I thought you just said he was like you."

"Actually, he was a lot like you, Tess. All bark, no bite. I, on the other hand, don't mind taking a nibble now and then when it's warranted." He looked pleased that her cheeks were flaming again. "I promised to pick up a few vegetables for my mother. Interested in squash, Tess?"

"No thank you," Tess replied firmly. She gathered up her mums and her empty containers and prepared to leave. She wasn't the least bit interested in establishing any kind of relationship with Ben Young, either, any more than he was truly interested in her. He just liked aggravating her. Not that she considered it, or him, a problem, since she had no intention of ever seeing him again....

As it turned out, she ran into him at the bank later that afternoon. Carefully keeping her distance and her self-control, Tess smiled wanly and wondered if she was the victim of some sort of warped Murphy's Law that demanded the more you wanted to avoid a person the sooner you saw them.

Convinced that Ben's doing his banking on the same day, at the same hour, at the same place had to be a bizarre coincidence, Tess tried to go on with her life as if nothing strange was happening. Never mind that she and Ben met out at the curb while she was taking out her trash on Sunday night. Just because Dorothy habitually took her refuse to the curb in the morning while Tess always readied hers the night before didn't necessarily mean their meeting was *planned*. Newly arrived in town, Ben couldn't possibly know her schedule. His mother could and did, of course. But even Dorothy, Tess assured herself, wouldn't possibly construe their meeting over household trash as anything remotely resembling a romantic encounter.

In any case, she could hardly fault the man for helping his mother with her household chores. She could, however, fault his manners, especially after she literally ran into him at the supermarket during her regular Monday-night shopping trip.

In search of the can of tomato puree she needed for spaghetti sauce, Tess rounded the end of an aisle and rammed her grocery cart squarely into the side of Ben's.

Looking highly amused, if somewhat surprised by her presence, he stood back from the display of bananas he'd been perusing and calmly appraised her all-brown sweater and slacks. Then he gave her that knock-'em-dead smile and drawled, "Hello, Tess. Given up the nunnery, have we? What are we masquerading as today? A baked potato?"

Tess knew perfectly well he was teasing. He had to be.

Anyone who wore Armani jackets and Gucci loafers would recognize her designer outfit for what it was: classically tailored and horrifically expensive. When she'd lived in New York, it had been the perfect thing for weekend getaways at Randall's Connecticut home—which was exactly why she'd bought it in the first place.

Giving Ben exactly the same look he was giving her, Tess surveyed his fashionably baggy black slacks, black and white jacket and yellow shirt that, for once, had no message on it. "I thought you always dressed like a billboard. What happened? Run out of T-shirts and social commentary?"

His tone was peaceable. "I decided I'd made enough social commentary for the time being." Looking infinitely relaxed, he surveyed the contents of her cart, which held, among other things, two cans of chicken noodle soup, and a can of water-packed tuna. "I didn't expect to see you here."

Tess considered his cart in turn, which, in contrast to hers, held cans of smoked oysters and other unfamiliar packages whose contents she could only guess at. "I didn't expect to see you here, either."

Though, knowing Dorothy as she did, she probably should have.

Certain that Ben had to have noticed the astounding frequency with which they kept appearing at the same places at the same time, Tess tried to think of a tactful way to bring up the subject.

"Ben?" she threw out tentatively as he hefted a pineapple.

"Mmm?"

Tess eyed some fuzzy brown kiwis, eventually deciding against purchasing them. "Have you noticed how we seem to be running into each other a lot lately?"

"As a matter of fact, I have." Turning to the vegetables, Ben stuffed a bundle of leeks into his grocery cart. "You aren't following me, are you?"

Tess stopped in the process of picking out a bunch of celery. "Me? Following *you*?" She felt her cheeks heating. "Of all the—"

"Stop sputtering," he scolded mildly. "I was joking. It's strange the way we keep popping up in the same places at the same times, isn't it?"

Strange was one word for it, Tess reflected. *Exasperating* was another that could be applied to the situation—and definitely to him.

Surveying her cart's contents, Ben reached over, picked up the bottle of laundry detergent she'd selected and read the label. "Is this the best soap to buy?" he asked, giving it far more interest than Tess thought it deserved.

"It does an adequate job for the price," she answered cautiously, waiting for the other shoe to drop.

Returning the bottle, Ben tucked a stray lock of brown hair back into her French braid. "Is that what you're looking for, Tess?" he purred in a soft voice that did terrible things to her resolve not to respond to him. "Adequate?"

Tess took a quick step out of reach. "At the moment all I'm looking for is peace and quiet."

"Think you're likely to get it?"

"Not with you around." And that was why she couldn't, *wouldn't* let Ben into her life. It wasn't that she didn't like him; she did. She hardly knew him and he was already the most interesting man she'd ever met. He was certainly the most entertaining. But he was also the most disturbing, and disturbance wasn't what Tess wanted. Peace was. Returning to Denton Falls after the one-two punch of her mother's unexpected death and the bitter break-up with Randall, it had taken her a long time to get her feet firmly back on the ground. She wasn't about to let Ben knock her off them again—no matter how fond she was of his mother.

Fairly certain from his look of bemusement that it wasn't Ben, but Dorothy, who was responsible for their repeated rendezvous, Tess decided it was high time to bring the subject out in the open.

"Look, Ben." She carefully placed two tomatoes in her cart. "I don't know how to say this, but I think your mother has some...er...rather original ideas where you and I are concerned."

Ben bagged two cucumbers. "You mean she's trying to hitch us up."

Tess frowned at his easy admission. "You *know*?"

"She practically insisted on me picking up a few things at the market tonight and all but drove me to the bank on Friday. My mom isn't the most subtle person in the world," he confided easily. "Hadn't you noticed?"

She had noticed. She'd also noticed that Ben didn't seem overly concerned about his parent's errant behavior. In fact, at the moment he seemed a lot more interested in Tess.

She swallowed dryly as he studied her face with flattering thoroughness. "Yes. Well..." She cleared her throat. "What are you going to do about it?" As she spoke, she grabbed a head of iceberg lettuce.

"Do about it?" Ben reached for the same head of lettuce at the same time. Tess quickly abandoned the mountain of iceberg in favor of romaine.

"How are you going to convince her to stop?" she clarified.

"Convince her to stop?" Ben gave up his surveyal of her long enough to move his cart out of the way so that a young mother with three youngsters in tow could get to the ears of corn.

Tess waited until she had his attention again. "I feel like I'm talking to a parrot in a pet shop. Do you realize you're repeating everything I say?"

"Everything?" He threw a bunch of green onions into his cart.

Tess's brown eyes narrowed in suspicion. "It's a ploy some people use to manipulate conversations and avoid facing up to situations."

Ben picked out a pound of mushrooms. "Is that what you think I'm doing?"

"I haven't the faintest idea what you're doing," Tess countered.

"I was trying to do a little creative shopping until you distracted me. Is that all you put in your salads? Lettuce and tomatoes?"

Suspecting he was going to start getting personal again, Tess gave him a cool look. "I happen to like lettuce and tomatoes."

Ben eyed the contents of her grocery cart and sighed. "Where's your sense of adventure, Tess? What about bean sprouts? What about alfalfa sprouts and artichokes?" He ignored her protest and dropped them in her cart. "What about sun chokes?"

Tess watched as a bag of brownish roots joined the other items she didn't want, and couldn't afford. "I'm allergic to artichokes and bean sprouts," she said, removing them again. "They give me a terrible rash. I'm also inflamed by mushrooms, green onions and presumptuous people who criticize my eating habits when their own personal habits are highly suspect."

"You think my personal habits are suspect?" He seemed to find the notion intriguing. "What is it, exactly, you think I do?"

"I'm still waiting to hear what you're *going* to do," Tess said.

"Encourage you to eat a bigger variety of fruits and vegetables?"

"I meant about your mother!"

He shrugged. "Maybe I don't worry about things as much as you do."

From his expression, Tess doubted he worried about anything, ever.

"You really ought to be a little more imaginative, Tess." He surveyed her braided hair and clucked reprovingly. "Life's too short to be so careful."

"I plan on living a long time," Tess responded. "But if you go around criticizing other people the way you keep on criticizing me, I can see why you'd worry about your longevity."

His gray-green eyes gleamed. "I'm not being critical," he protested mildly. "I'm just trying to show you there's more to life than lettuce and tomatoes."

"I know," Tess agreed. "There's frustration, exasperation—"

"Not to mention love and marriage," he added, clearly enjoying himself.

Tess let out a sigh. He obviously wasn't going to be any help at all. Which meant, Tess concluded, that she was going to have to talk to Dorothy herself, before things—and Ben—got truly out of hand.

The opportunity arrived the next evening when she and Dorothy attended bargain night at the local movie theater together.

Dispensing with the tailored black and brown outfits Ben had panned in favor of a red sweater and jeans, Tess knocked on Dorothy's door at ten to seven. Tess surreptitiously studied her companion as they climbed into Tess's station wagon. Looking closer to fifty than seventy in a soft pink sweater and skirt, Dorothy was clearly curious about Tess's meetings with her beloved son. But at least she waited until they'd parked the car and entered the theater, Tess reflected with amusement, before she brought up the subject.

"Well, dear." Dorothy offered Tess some of her unbuttered popcorn as they sat in a middle row and waited for the movie to begin. "What did you think? Bennett's special, isn't he?"

"Yes, Dorothy," Tess said truthfully, "he is. Definitely one of a kind."

Dorothy smiled in acknowledgement. "I knew you'd be impressed. He told me he's never met a girl quite like you before."

Tess ate the popcorn. "I've never met anyone quite like him, either," she admitted.

It was probably the only thing she and Ben had reciprocal opinions on. If Ben Young thought there weren't many women like her in existence anymore, Tess reflected, there were definitely not too many men like Ben Young walking around, either. Fortunately.

"You might have mentioned that he raced cars for a living," Tess added with mild accusation.

Dorothy's lips quirked in faint apology. "I was afraid you might think he was reckless."

Dorothy was right.

"You must have made quite an impression on him," Dorothy continued cheerfully.

Tess looked at Dorothy a moment. "Why do you say that?"

"Because Ben told me you make the best cookies he's ever eaten," she confided, apparently taking that comment to mean a lot more than Tess was certain he'd intended.

It hadn't been until after she'd left him at the farmers' market that Tess had remembered the dry remark he'd made about her cookies being "just like Mom used to make." Considering she was using *his* mother's recipe, it wasn't all that surprising. They were exactly like his mother's—something he'd known, Tess suspected, remembering his fleeting look of recognition when he'd first discovered her name.

"You must be awfully pleased he's come to visit for a while," Tess ventured, halfway hoping that "a while" was actually "not for long," so that she wouldn't have to worry about disappointing Dorothy.

"I am." Dorothy's face lit up. "It's been a long time since he came back home. Too long, really. He calls all the time, of course. But that's never quite the same as being able to give someone a great big hug, is it?"

"No," Tess agreed. "I suppose it's not. If he's staying with you," she said casually, fishing for the length of Ben's visit, "is there anything you need in the way of extra blankets or anything? I have some I could loan you for a few days." Tess tried to imagine Ben sharing Dorothy's tiny bungalow even for a short time and found it impossible to visualize. Cozy but small, the one-bedroom home was just right for a widow, but would be cramped if pressed to accommodate overnight guests.

"Oh, he's not staying with me." Dorothy gave a soft laugh. "Heavens, Bennett's much too independent to be living with his mother even for a short while. In any case, he's decided to stay a bit longer than he'd originally planned. He's living in a place at the edge of town."

He must have been only visiting when she'd run into him putting out the garbage, Tess realized. No wonder she rarely saw his car parked in Dorothy's driveway. But she was going

to have to tell Dorothy the truth, no matter how much it hurt
to do so.

Dorothy's smile was suddenly very much like her son's.
"I know I'm being terribly nosy, but did you two arrange to
see each other again?"

Tess drank from her diet soda, stalling for time. "Not
exactly." She tried to bolster her courage as she said,
"Dorothy, I hate to tell you this, but we really don't get
along all that well."

"You don't?" Dorothy turned toward her.

Tess shook her head, her unbound brown locks brushing
against her shoulders. "No. We don't." She paused,
choosing her words with care. "Actually, Dorothy, this is
sort of a good-news, bad-news story."

"Oh, dear." Dorothy's softly lined face saddened per-
ceptibly. "I suppose you should tell me the good news first."

"All right. The good news is that he's obviously a very
attractive man." Too attractive, Tess thought, for his own
good—and hers.

"Well, that wasn't too bad." Dorothy smiled bravely.
"What's the bad news, dear?"

"The bad news is that we don't seem to have all that much
in common."

"Really?" This time Dorothy sounded more thoughtful
than disappointed. "How odd. I was so sure..." Her gentle
voice drifted off.

"In fact," Tess forged on before she changed her mind,
"we sort of had a spat the other day at the market." Tess
wondered if trading clothes critiques qualified as a spat, and
decided it probably did. "He's not overly fond of my
wardrobe," she ventured. "He says I dress like a potato. I
told him he looked like a billboard."

"I suspect he fully deserved it, too. Don't pay any attention to him, darling." Dorothy shook her head. "He's teasing you. He's really a very conservative dresser himself,
normally. It's just, at the moment, he seems determined to
stir up the natives, so to speak."

"He's being wildly successful," Tess said dryly.

"My, he must have given you the business. I should have warned you. You're not angry with me, dear, for wanting you to meet, are you?"

"No, Dorothy," Tess replied honestly. "I'm not angry at you." Though she was still a tiny bit peeved at Ben for the unsolicited remarks about her wardrobe. "But I think it might be best if you wouldn't make any further attempts at bringing us together. You won't, will you?"

Dorothy smiled and offered Tess more popcorn. "Don't worry, dear. You know me."

Yes, she did, Tess reflected. That's why she was asking.

Any woman who could keep her unswerving attention on one particular topic for as long as Dorothy had this one had to be given credit for persistence—and single-mindedness.

"I just don't want you to be disappointed," Tess said, trying to soften the blow a bit. The very last thing she wanted was to hurt Dorothy. "I know how you'd hoped we'd hit it off."

"Well, I have to admit I'm surprised you two didn't at least become friends. You seem so perfect for each other."

"Believe me, Dorothy," Tess urged as gently and tactfully as she could. "If we wanted to get together, we would."

"But you don't?"

"I don't." Tess figured that since Ben was a big boy, he could speak for himself.

Dorothy suddenly sighed. "Oh, my. This situation is getting awkward."

"It's not that bad," Tess assured her.

"Well, maybe not yet," Dorothy agreed. "But you see, it's not over."

"It isn't?" Tess frowned in confusion.

"No. You see, I've been waiting to tell you when the time was right, and I assumed that after you saw each other at the supermarket...." Dorothy's voice drifted off in obvious consternation.

Outwardly calm but inwardly alarmed, Tess asked, "Tell me what?"

"That wasn't actually my money that I gave you as an investment in the shop. Really, it's so unfortunate you and

Bennett aren't getting along, because, well, you see, I'm not actually your business partner." Dorothy patted Tess gently on the forearm just as the lights dimmed in preparation for the film. "Bennett is."

Chapter Four

She wasn't going to panic—yet. Tess tapped her fingers thoughtfully as she waited for Cheryl Gates and Judith Richards to join her at Fosby's Café. Fosby's was a small, inexpensive eating establishment that offered the best breakfast in town. Comfortably cozy with polished oak tables and gleaming brass fixtures, it brought in locals as well as out-of-towners attracted by the world-famous glass factory located at the edge of town. The tour buses stopped just outside the café's front door.

Tess stirred cream into her coffee and wondered half seriously if she could bribe the tour-bus driver to stop in front of her shop, as well. She could use the business. Maybe while she was at it, she could try bribing Ben Young to go back to wherever he'd come from and stay there.

"Hi, Tess." A soft voice broke into Tess's thoughts. "Sorry we're late." Cheryl, a shy brunette, sat down with a sigh.

"Couldn't find a bloody parking spot," added Judith, the brashest and fairest-haired of the three women.

Secretaries at the glass factory, best of friends and trusted confidantes, Cheryl and Judith were ever helpful in matters of business and the heart, which is why Tess had called and asked them to meet her for an early breakfast.

"I've missed you two," Tess said—though she was glad they hadn't been in town the past week to witness her exasperation. "How was Vermont?"

"We saw lots of cows and maple trees, which is what you should expect when you insist on vacationing in the hinterlands." Judith aimed this remark at Cheryl, a Vermont native.

"Don't listen to her." Unoffended, Cheryl dug into her purse for her glasses. "We had a wonderful time, once it stopped raining."

"It rained nine days out of ten," Judith added for Tess's information.

"It rained off and on again here, too," Tess said sympathetically as the waitress set out water glasses. "So you didn't miss anything by leaving."

"Take it from one who's lived here long enough to know," Judith deadpanned. "A person could leave Denton Falls for decades and not miss anything."

"I know. That's why I moved back," Tess quipped. "It's so stable."

"I knew there was a reason I stayed here. Now I have a name for it. Stability." Judith rested her elbows on the red tablecloth and gave Tess a long look. "Was it my imagination, or did you sound slightly harassed when you called? Your business woes aren't keeping you up at night again, are they?"

"My business isn't keeping me up at night," Tess assured her friend. Ben Young being her partner was. "Do I look harassed?"

"If you want the truth." Judith tipped her head to one side. "I've never seen you quite so pink in the cheeks."

Exasperation and frustration, Tess acknowledged, had a way of putting color in your face. Tess picked up her coffee cup and sipped. "Well, it's nice to know I look healthy."

"I didn't say you looked healthy. I said you looked pink." Judith studied her with discomforting interest. "I realize this is probably a ridiculous question, considering you nearly broke your neck rescuing one of Cheryl's cats last week, but did you do any other crazy things while we were away?''

"No," Tess admitted. "But I'm considering doing something crazy now that you're back."

"Like what?" both women immediately wanted to know.

Tess hesitated. "Like asking for your help. I was hoping you two could help me figure out how to avoid a man."

"Any specific man?" Judith asked. "Or were you hoping to hide from the male species in general?"

"It's a specific man." Tess put down her cup. "My business partner."

Both Judith and Cheryl were stunned into silence. Judith was the first to recover. "I thought Dorothy Wilder was your partner."

"I thought she was, too." Tess nabbed a date muffin from the basket on the table. "This is sort of a new development."

"And one," Judith guessed, "I gather you're not too crazy about. What do you want us to do?"

"I want you to help me figure out how to keep him out of the shop."

Judith pursed her lips. "Why? Is he pushy and unreasonable?"

"I don't know yet if he's unreasonable," Tess admitted. "But he's definitely pushy." And exasperating. And hard to resist.

"Is that the problem?" Cheryl asked, puzzled. "You don't get along?"

"The problem," said Tess, "is I don't want an active partner. I liked the arrangement I had with Dorothy. I don't need or want anyone messing with the way I run the shop." Especially not someone she was likely to become emotionally entangled with. Someone who could sweep her off her feet, then sweep out of town before she knew what had hit her.

"In Tess code," Judith said to Cheryl, "I think that means she's afraid she's going to get romantically involved with him." She turned back to Tess. "Is he taking an active role in the shop, then?"

"I don't know yet. I only found out he was my partner last night."

Cheryl continued digging through her purse. "Then don't you think you're sort of jumping the gun? Maybe he'll just leave well enough alone."

Tess grimaced. "I don't think so. He likes stirring things up."

"This is getting more interesting all the time." Judith picked up her glass of freshly-squeezed orange juice. "How does he stir things up?"

Tess felt her face grow hot. "He wears ridiculously flashy clothes and makes critical observations of a very personal nature when none are requested. Every time I see him," she added, "he gets me going."

Judith shrugged. "Maybe you're taking his remarks too personally."

"If someone compared you to nuns and baked potatoes," Tess retorted, buttering her muffin, "you'd take it personally, too."

"Brash, isn't he?" Judith observed in amusement, having coaxed the details from Tess. "I suppose he's big, blond and brawny, as well?"

"No, he's tall, dark and exasperating."

Judith leaned back and grinned. "Goodness, he has gotten your dander up, hasn't he? Is he smart?"

"Yes, he's smart. Not that that has anything to do with anything."

"Tess, dear—" Judith reached over and patted her hand "—it has a lot to do with everything. If you're going to be bothered, it might as well be by someone attractive and intelligent. Lord knows, there are enough men running around who don't qualify as either."

"I hate to interrupt." Cheryl pushed back her halo of dark curls and stared myopically at the table nestled in a corner alcove. "But what in the world is going on over there?"

All three women focused their attention across the gold-carpeted room to where a small crowd had gathered.

"I haven't the foggiest idea," Tess said after a moment.

"I can't find my blasted glasses," Cheryl complained. "What's that they're holding in their hands?"

"Looks like napkins," Judith said.

Cheryl's dark eyebrows winged upward. "Why on earth would anyone hold napkins and hover around a table like that?"

"Maybe someone got coffee spilled in their lap?" Tess ventured.

"Am I crazy," asked Judith, "or are they also waving pens?"

Napkins and pens, Tess realized with a sudden sinking feeling, sounded like an impromptu autograph session. She peered over her menu.

There was only one person that she knew of in Denton Falls who might be famous, or infamous, enough to elicit that kind of attention.

Ben Young.

The last person he'd expected to see at the café was Tess.

Picking up his coffee cup, Ben settled back onto the oak chair after the four fans had finally left. He let out a sigh of exasperation. He and Tess showing up at the supermarket on the same night at the same time was bad enough, considering he'd had a long talk with his mother just the night before. But this was ridiculous. He didn't blame Tess for looking at him as if he were some sort of horrifying apparition. He was beginning to *feel* like a skeleton popping out of the woodwork in a badly made horror flick.

Ben shot a look of reproval at his bland-faced mother who, when he'd offered to take her out to breakfast, had insisted Fosby's was the only worthwhile restaurant left in town. "Okay," he said, trying to instill at least a modicum of censure into his voice. "How did you know she was going to be here this morning?"

Waving at Tess and receiving a wan smile in return, Dorothy Wilder gazed at her son in total innocence. "Who's that, dear?"

"You know who," Ben scolded. He sipped the cold coffee, grimaced and set it down again. "Stop trying to look senile. You're sharper than a razor blade and we both know it." He shoved up the sleeves of his yellow blazer. "I thought you said you weren't going to do this sort of thing anymore?''

Dorothy brushed imaginary lint from her lavender sweater. "What sort of thing is that, Bennett?"

Ben prayed for patience. "Matchmaking. Insisting on maneuvering Tess and me into ludicrous situations. Conniving to put us in the same place at the same time."

"Oh, that." Dorothy attempted to look apologetic. "Well, I didn't really have anything devious in mind this morning," she said as Ben shot her a wryly skeptical smile. "When you asked me where we could have a nice breakfast—"

"You just happened to think of Fosby's, which just happens to be where Tess has breakfast every morning," Ben said dryly, shaking his head.

"Actually, she's not here every morning." Dorothy smoothed her skirt. "Tess usually heads straight for the shop. It's just when she's upset that she eats out. So she can talk things over with her friends—"

"Hold it," Ben interrupted, sensing trouble ahead. "How do you know she's upset?"

"Well—" Dorothy smiled cautiously "—because of something I said to her last night at the movies. Did you know Tess treats me to the movies every Tuesday night?" she asked brightly. "Such a lovely child . . ."

"I think you might have mentioned it ten or fifteen times." Ben gave his mother a stern look as she attempted to change the subject. "What did you say to Tess that upset her?"

"Yes. Well. I told her that I wasn't her business partner."

Ben steeled himself. "Why did you tell her that?"

"Because it's the truth, of course," Dorothy chided. "You remember the money you gave me last February, don't you, Bennett?"

Ben nodded.

"Well, Tess was in terrible financial straits, taking over the shop right after her mother died so suddenly, and after that unfortunate business in New York, too. So I gave some of it to her. Quite a lot of it, actually."

"Which means?" Ben tried extrapolating, but his mind refused to work.

"Which means, since it was your money and not mine, I don't have any financial interest in her shop at all. Ergo, I'm not her business partner. You are." Dorothy ate a small bite of scrambled egg. "Your coffee looks cold. Would you like some more, dear?"

What he'd like, Ben decided, as the scope of Dorothy's actions started to sink in, was to throttle his own mother.

He couldn't believe the way his errant parent was single-handedly managing to take a potentially promising relationship and turn it into a three-ring circus. Well, maybe not single-handedly, Ben conceded, signaling the overworked waitress for a coffee refill. He could take his share of the blame, as well.

He still couldn't believe he'd been so taken aback at the supermarket that he'd actually compared Tess to a spud. *Way to go, Rocket.* At this rate he'd easily qualify for jerk of the year.

The funny part was that he honestly had no idea why he kept putting his foot in his mouth every time they met. He wasn't usually so inept around women, but for some reason he acted like an adolescent stuck in the midst of puberty around her. Maybe it was catching. He and Tess were both acting like sixteen-year-olds. She blushed; he blurted. Each time he saw her, strange things happened to his self control *and* his vocabulary.

Ben sent Tess an apologetic smile, then forced himself not to stare in her direction. Maybe if he tried concentrating on his toast and eggs instead of the smile lines forming commas around Tess's mouth, he could keep his distance and manage not to offend her this time.

Half hidden behind her menu, Tess felt her neck burn as Ben gave her a big, innocent smile and then calmly went back to his breakfast. There was a small, potent silence at her table as Tess studied the menu with utmost attention.

"Did he just smile at who I think he smiled at?" Judith demanded.

"I don't know." Tess pretended to look the menu over. "Who do you think he smiled at?"

"You," Judith said bluntly.

Tess tried to focus on the menu. "Maybe he was smiling at you."

"Are you kidding?" Judith snorted. "No one's smiled at me like that since I was twenty."

Cheryl squinted across the room. "Do you know him, Tess?"

Tess hesitated. "Not exactly."

"What do you mean, 'not exactly'?" Judith prodded.

"I mean I don't exactly know him. I just sort of know of him."

Judith studied Tess with thoughtful interest. "He wouldn't happen to be the same man you want us to help you avoid, would he?"

"Your new partner," Cheryl clarified.

Tess cleared her throat in embarrassment. "Well..."

Cheryl and Judith exchanged a knowing look that made Tess extremely uneasy.

"Things are suddenly beginning to make sense here," Judith decided as she flipped out her napkin and spread it on her lap. "He wouldn't also happen to be the man you insulted out on the sidewalk in front of your shop, would he?"

Tess felt her neck flame as she realized that Judith had been back in town less than twenty-four hours and she'd already heard all about Tess's verbal assault on Ben. Which probably meant the whole town knew.

"You insulted him?" Cheryl turned to Tess. "Why on earth...?"

Judith lowered her voice to a stage whisper. "I heard that he parked in the Handicapped zone in front of her store."

"Oh, well. That explains it, then." Both women knew all about Tess's rabidity when it came to that particular parking spot.

"All I did was question his right to park there," Tess protested, realizing that this would be a wonderful moment for her to simply shut up. "It wasn't my fault things got out of hand. He was impertinent."

"He's been known to be a lot more than impertinent," added Judith. "Don't you realize who he is?"

"Trouble," Tess replied decisively.

"I'll bite," said Cheryl. "Who is he?"

Judith sighed in exasperation. "Only the best-known race driver from this part of the country. A local celebrity, as it were." Judith shook her head at Cheryl. "I can understand Tess not recognizing him. She was already in New York when his career took off, and she isn't exactly what I'd call a sports fanatic. But you've lived here for nearly six years now. I can't believe you don't know who he is. His face and name must have been plastered all over the newspaper a zillion times."

"You know I can't see anything without my glasses," Cheryl said in self-defense. "I wouldn't recognize my own mother from this distance without my specs." She turned to Tess for help. "What's his name?"

"Ben." Tess averted her eyes from Judith, who was perusing her with disconcerting interest.

"Benjamin's a nice name," Cheryl offered. "Sensible. Dependable."

Tess, having once been under a similar delusion, couldn't help pointing out, "His name isn't Benjamin. It's Bennett. And he's anything but sensible."

Judith batted her lashes. "I thought you said you barely knew him."

"His mother managed to inject his full name into the conversation one day," Tess confessed. That, and Ben's birth date, January 3, his favorite color, baby blue, and his shoe size, 11 D. The only thing she'd neglected to mention so far, Tess reflected, was his Social Security number and his IQ. But given time, Tess was certain Dorothy would eventually get around to those, too.

"Would I be wrong in assuming his mother has something to do with him being your business partner?" Judith asked.

Tess wrinkled her nose. "This is her way of playing matchmaker. She thinks we make the perfect couple."

Cheryl sipped her tea. "Who's his mother?"

Tess sighed. "Dorothy Wilder."

"That nice little old lady with the mauve hair who's sitting next to him," Judith supplied. "I know her. She's the one who loaned Tess the money to get the cookie shop going again."

"I didn't realize she had a son who was a race-car driver," said Cheryl, adding, "Bennett is an unusual name."

"He's an unusual man," Tess assured her. And his mother was a little unusual, as well. Tess wished she could work up at least some irritation at Dorothy, but she knew Dorothy meant well. It was Ben's intentions that continued to elude her.

"Bennett Wilder." Cheryl repeated the name thoughtfully. "It's funny, but that name doesn't ring a bell with me at all."

"His name isn't Wilder," Tess explained. "It's Young. His mom remarried."

"He was a class or two ahead of me in high school," Judith said, attempting to jog Cheryl's memory. "I've mentioned him before. He was the one who was voted most likely to succeed—with women. Three years in a row."

"Why?" Cheryl asked, curious.

"Put on your glasses," Judith suggested, "and you'll know why."

Finally locating her glasses, Cheryl slipped on her oversized lenses. "Goodness. I see what you mean. Attractive, isn't he? In a basic, male sort of way. Is he married, engaged or otherwise attached to a female member of the species?" she asked, clearly finding him fascinating.

Resigned to the single-track minds of her friends, Tess set down her menu. "The way Dorothy's trying to marry him off, I certainly hope not."

Judith gave Tess a speculative look. "I don't know about you, but I'd say the man's definitely marriage material."

"You two think every man between the ages of seventeen and seventy is marriageable. You ought to go into business for yourselves."

"Don't laugh," Judith warned, brushing croissant crumbs off her lap. "Someday we may do just that."

"I'd like to be my own boss someday," Cheryl put in.

Tess picked up her menu again. "Are you two ready to order?"

"First things first. I want to hear more about this partner of yours." Judith pulled Tess's menu down to look her in the eye. "His mom must have talked about him, him being famous and all."

"Dorothy might have mentioned him ten or twenty times a day," Tess allowed dryly.

"So, how long is he going to be in town?" Judith asked. "And what's he going to do while he's here?"

"If I knew that," Tess answered, avoiding looking in Ben's direction, "I wouldn't be in such a panic to avoid him, would I?"

"Oh, I don't know. Seems to me the man could put a woman into a panic just by breathing." Judith turned in Tess's direction. "He's looking at you again."

"I know," Tess confirmed. And it was doing strange things to her body temperature.

Cheryl's solemn brown gaze followed Ben as he firmly guided his mother toward the door. "Am I imagining it, or is he limping slightly?"

Judith plucked another croissant from the basket in the center of the table. "I understand he's still recovering from a serious accident. Nearly got himself killed. He was always something of a pistol, as I remember."

Tess felt her chest constrict and realized that the thought of Ben Young suffering through a disastrous crash upset her far more than it should, considering she barely knew the man.

Cheryl pursed her lips. "He looks awfully pale, don't you think?"

Tess allowed herself a quick peek. As a matter of fact, he did look pale. Beneath the faint traces of a tan, his leanly sculpted face had an unhealthy pallor that no number of mischievous smiles could disguise.

Tess tried, without success, to feel absolutely no sympathy at all. "Are you two going to help me or not?"

"Help you what?" Cheryl asked, still distracted.

"Help me figure out how to avoid him," Tess answered patiently.

Judith shrugged. "Why don't you just throw caution to the wind and let fate take its course? You're not going to get any younger, you know."

"If I let men like Ben Young into my life," Tess declared, "I'm not likely to get any older, either. He's trouble on the move."

"You make him sound like a viral menace," Judith remarked in amusement. "You have to at least give him credit for having a sense of humor."

Tess shook her head. "No, I don't."

"Well, Dorothy's inventiveness at getting you two together is pretty amusing. Imagine, making you and her son partners—and you didn't even realize it."

"Stop snickering," Tess scolded. "You're looking at a desperate woman."

Who was likely to get even more desperate if Ben decided to take an interest in the shop, as well as in her. "He didn't get to be a professional race-car driver," Tess reasoned, "by being a choirboy."

"That doesn't mean he doesn't understand the English language," said Judith. "If the situation bothers you, talk to him. Tell him how you feel."

Tess sighed. "I already did. He thinks Dorthy's matchmaking attempts are entertaining."

Judith lifted a shoulder. "So talk to Dorothy."

Tess sighed again. "I have."

"What did you tell her?" asked Cheryl.

"That he was attractive, but we don't seem to have much in common."

Judith rolled her eyes. "No wonder she didn't give up. With hedgehopping like that, she probably thought you were giving her the go-ahead. You need to be more forceful. Talk to her again."

"And say what? Gee, Dorothy, I'm really very fond of you, but I never want to see your son darken my door? I don't think I could stand seeing her disappointed. She's done nothing but talk about the man for months."

"Well, don't panic. Cheryl and I will think on it. We're bound to come up with something." Judith raised a ques-

ioning eyebrow. "You're sure this isn't a case of you both
protesting too much?"

"Positive," Tess answered firmly. She didn't care how
charming he was—and he was charming, in an exasperating sort of way. If she ever got involved with a man again,
she'd choose someone sane and sensible. A man who drove
hot rods for a living was hardly what she had in mind.

For all she knew, she might not be what he had in mind,
either.

Tess considered that. Maybe she was making a mountain
out of a molehill. After all, he hadn't even stopped by the
shop since that first day. Which probably meant that he had
as little interest in cookie making as he did in cookie mak-
ers.

Heading for her shop after breakfast, Tess worked on that
theme and continued to think about it for the remainder of
the day. By six o'clock that evening, she'd almost convinced herself she would probably never even see Ben Young
again—until she found him waiting for her outside her shop
at closing time.

Chapter Five

Tess spotted Ben standing beside the petunia planter in front of her shop as she was preparing to lock up. Her mind shrouded in fog—the result of an exhausting day following a sleepless night spent worrying about her growing involvement with a man she didn't really know and had no real reason to trust—Tess stood beside her mother's prized antique oak coat tree in indecision as she debated what to do. Her choices seemed limited.

Exasperating or not, Ben had every right to enter the shop, considering that he owned more of it than she did. Deciding she might as well face him now while she was on familiar turf, if for no other reason than to clarify her position, Tess walked to the door and opened it a scant four inches.

"I'm busy cleaning up," she told him with firm conviction. "So if you want to come in you're going to have to promise to behave yourself."

Ben immediately stuck his right foot just inside the threshold so she couldn't slam the door shut again. "Now, Tessy," he chided, "is that any way to greet your partner? Whatever happened to 'Hello, Ben. How are you'?"

Knowing she shouldn't even consider letting him in under these circumstances, Tess studied his foot at length before letting the door swing open. "Hello, Ben," she said flatly. "How are you?"

"Relieved." Ben slipped through the doorway before she could change her mind again. "For a minute there, I thought you might bop me one."

"I'm still considering it." Tess decided to play it safe and took refuge behind the counter. "I suppose you've come to check on your investment."

Leaning on his cane, Ben walked across the polished tile floor. "Actually, I've come to apologize for giving you a hard time the other day."

"I see." Tess put away a stack of stainless-steel bowls. "Does this mean you're not going to give me a hard time in the future?"

Ben's eyes danced. "I didn't say that." Impossibly attractive in snug jeans and a bomber-style jacket, he slowly surveyed Tess's moss-green slacks and matching sweater.

Tess recognized the look. Deciding that offense was the best defense, she gave him a level stare. "Compare me to a nun or a vegetable again," she swore, punctuating the air with a large spoon for emphasis, "and I may do something physical this time."

"Is that a promise? No, don't throw it." He put his hands up in self-defense. "I was kidding. I like your outfit. It's very tasteful. Expensive as hell, too."

That's because it was another leftover from her extravagant days in New York. Tess gave him a suspicious look. "I didn't think you noticed my clothes' cost, only their color."

"Honey, I notice everything—on a racecourse, and off it." He unzipped his jacket. "Would I be right in assuming you wear outfits like that for a reason other than their spectacular dullness?"

Tess considered him, wondering if he was as astute as she suspected. "If you must know, they remind me not to get too big for my britches."

Ben's flatteringly direct gaze warmed her like a hot summer breeze. "I like the way you fit in your britches."

She liked the way he fit in his, too. Quashing the thought, Tess opened a drawer and put the spoon away.

Discarding the cane, Ben shoved his hands in his pockets. "I gather from my mom that you were shocked to discover that you and I are partners."

"'Shocked' is one way of putting it." Tess closed the drawer again. "It never occurred to me Dorothy wasn't investing her own money."

"You don't like surprises?"

"I love surprises. I'm just not crazy about being strung along." Tess continued to clean as they talked. "Was keeping me in the dark your idea?"

"No. Not that I wouldn't love to keep you in the dark, of course...."

Tess decided to ignore that. "You could have told me when we first met," she accused mildly.

Walking to the toy cabinet in the corner, Ben sat on his heels in order to survey its contents. "Believe it or not, I didn't find out myself until this morning."

"How could you not know?" Tess scrubbed the stove.

Ben stood. "When I sent the money to my mom, I asked her to keep half and invest the rest in something local with promise. She never listens to me." He turned and Tess saw he was smiling. "She put part of it into your shop and used the rest to buy the old Weston place at the edge of town."

Tess wasn't sure if that meant he was sorry his mother had invested in the cookie shop, or if he was just trying to explain how it had happened.

"I didn't realize you owned the Weston place." Tess tried to contain her disappointment. For six months she'd been trying to talk a local philanthropist into buying it and turning it into much-needed senior citizens' apartments; and now, it seemed, it was too late.

"My mom thought I could fix it up and live in it if I should ever decide to come back home and settle down," Ben explained, clearly amused.

Tess was surprised at how much the possibility of Ben staying in Denton Falls unsettled her. "Are you planning on fixing it up?" she asked.

"Actually, I've already started. It's too valuable a piece of property to let sit empty the way it has for the last couple of years."

Tess wondered whether that meant he had decided to stay in Denton Falls, or if he was renovating the old cobblestone mansion simply to increase its value when he sold it. Afraid to ask, she watched Ben peruse his surroundings with the air of a man who wasn't sure what his mother had gotten him into. Fearing what Dorothy had gotten her into, as well, Tess flushed when he suddenly turned around and caught her watching him.

"You don't mind if I look around, do you?"

Tess wiped down the counter with a damp cloth. "It hardly seems as if I have a right to object, considering at least half the shop is yours."

As soon as it was out, Tess recognized it sounded a lot less nonchalant than she'd intended, but she couldn't help it. The shop was one of the few things she had left to remind her of her mother, and now she suspected she was losing that, too.

Ben came over to the counter. "You don't like the idea of me being your partner a hell of a lot, do you?"

Reared to be polite, Tess started to deny it, then decided there was no sense beating around the bush. "No."

"Why?"

"Because it's occurred to me that a man who makes a living competing for first place isn't likely to accept a partner on an equal footing."

Ben appeared unoffended. "If you feel so strongly about it, why don't you buy me out? I won't fight it. I'll even give you fair market price."

Tess rinsed out the cloth and hung it over the faucet to dry. "I would if I could, but the bank is already holding the mortgage on my house. They won't give me an additional loan. That's how I ended up accepting money from Dorothy in the first place."

"Speaking of that, exactly how much did my mom give you, anyway?"

Tess raised her eyebrows in surprise. "Don't you know?"

"Would I ask if I did?"

"Thirty thousand dollars."

"You must have had one hell of a financial hole to dig yourself out of," Ben commented mildly.

"I did. Actually," Tess amended, "I still do. I haven't been able to make the last two payments on the shop." She thought she'd better tell him, since, as her partner, the shop's debts as well as the assets were legally his, too.

"I realize this is probably an indelicate question, but why not?"

"Because the shop's income isn't equaling the 'outgo.' That's why not."

"How long have you been running it?"

"You mean, how long have I been running it into the ground?" Tess surmised dryly: "About eight months now."

Ben walked behind the counter. "I understand you inherited the shop from your mother."

Tess eyed him warily. "Yes."

"It must have been a blow to you when she died so unexpectedly."

Tess stared at him. "How did you know my mother died unexpectedly?"

"She was my mother's best friend," Ben reminded her. "I heard about her often. A very lovely woman, your mother. You look a lot like her."

Unsettled by the turn the conversation had taken, but nonetheless flattered, Tess studied him a moment. "Did you know my mother?"

"Not well." Ben opened and closed drawers, scanning the neatly arranged contents as he want along. "I met her once or twice. My trips home have always been what you might call infrequent."

"I don't remember ever meeting you before last week," Tess confessed.

"That's not surprising. I left home when you were probably in pigtails. By the time I got around to coming back, you were already in New York. Working in an accounting office?" He turned to her in question.

"An investment firm," Tess corrected, knowing perfectly well she was being pumped for information. "I worked as a secretary for Bates, Baskin, Harbro and Mc-Nary.''

"Impressive.'' Ben squatted down to check one of the lower cupboards. "Are you always this uptight?'' he asked as Tess hovered.

"I'm not uptight. I'm understandably wary. I know what you're thinking,'' Tess added as he closed the cabinet and rose.

Ben leaned back against the counter. "What's that, sprout?''

"You're wondering how I could have run up such an enormous debt even though I was probably making a perfectly good salary.''

"You're right.'' Ben flicked back her braid. "So how did you?''

"I made a bad investment, then followed it up by taking over my mother's business, which was already in debt and showed no immediate signs of recovery. I suppose now you're wondering how you can dump me as *your* partner.'' Tess grabbed her jacket and walked to the rear of the store.

"Actually, I was wondering if I could walk you out to your car.''

"I'm not leaving yet,'' Tess called over her shoulder. "I need to move these into the storeroom before I go.'' She pointed to where her supplier had dumped the hundred-pound sacks of flour just inside the back door.

"No problem.'' Ben slipped off his jacket, revealing a torso-hugging blue sweater, and hung it on a peg beside the doorway.

"I was only telling you what I needed to do,'' Tess said as he moved to the sacks and hefted one over his shoulder. "I wasn't asking for your help.''

"I know you weren't.'' Ben carried the first sack into the storeroom and emerged a few seconds later for the next. "But we're partners now, remember?''

Grabbing a sack by one end, Tess dragged it across the tiled floor. "What does that mean?''

"It means we share the work as well as the profits. There now,'' he said as he shoved the last bag into place and dusted off his hands. "Now, if we just get this thing out of the way, we'll be finished."

Tess wasn't sure what "this thing" was until she turned around and found him moving the tub of molasses propping open the door.

Tess held out a cautioning hand. "Wait! Don't touch that—"

Released from its prop, the heavy door thunked shut before she could finish. Tess groaned and sat down on the neatly stacked sacks of flour.

Ben raised his eyebrows. "Something wrong?"

"As a matter of fact," Tess said, "yes. You just locked us in."

"Are you sure?" Tess simply gave him a long look as Ben grabbed the ancient doorknob. "This thing looks old as the hills," he remarked when it rattled but didn't turn.

"It is as old as the hills," Tess told him. "And it has a nasty habit of not working right. That's why I keep the door propped open. The first week I was here I locked myself in and your mom had to rescue me. I suppose now you're going to tell me your mother didn't mention it."

"My mother doesn't tell me everything. Anyway, why would I want to lock us in a storeroom together?"

"You seem to think we should get to know each other better. Maybe this is your way of doing that."

Ben shook his head at her open suspicion. "That would require an excessive amount of deviousness."

"Yes." Tess continued to look at him. "It would. What are you doing?"

Ben was digging into his jacket pocket. "I think we might as well go ahead and celebrate as long as we're stuck in here together, don't you?"

Tess looked at the tiny bottle that had materialized in his hand. "What are we celebrating?"

Ben shook his head at her. "Our partnership, of course."

Tess eyed the squat little bottle. "What are we celebrating with?"

"It's called Petite Liqueur. Shall I open it?"

"I'm not sure. It looks potent."

Ben held up the bottle for inspection. "Look at it. This things holds two glasses at most. That's one for each of us. How drunk can you get on one glass of anything?"

"You're talking to a woman who gets tipsy on butter rum Life Savers."

"No, I'm talking to a woman who's afraid to enjoy herself."

Tess lifted her chin in indignation. "I'm not afraid to drink it." She was afraid of what she'd do after she did.

"Good." Ben liberated two plastic wineglasses from his other jacket pocket. "Because the doctor says I shouldn't drink to excess and this is too good to toss out." He whipped the foil cap off the bottle and uncorked it. "You *do* want me to get better so that I can go back to racing, don't you, Tess?"

"There's an interesting thought." Tess took the glass he held out to her and decided it was also an idea worth exploring in more depth.

Ben clicked his plastic glass against hers. "To success," he toasted.

"And swift recoveries," Tess murmured, taking a sip of the liqueur. Her eyes opened wide as the sparkling liquid slid down her throat. She looked suspiciously into her glass and watched the bubbles rising to the surface. "What's in this stuff?"

"Champagne and brandy," Ben said easily.

Tess picked up the empty bottle and read the label. "It says it's thirty-six percent proof."

"Does it?"

Tess's gaze instantly narrowed. "You're trying to get me drunk."

"No, I'm trying to get you to relax. Stop looking at me like I'm Jekyll and Hyde," Ben scolded as she continued to eye him with trepidation. "Just because we're stuck in here for a few hours together doesn't mean you're in dire danger of being molested. I do have a little self-control, you know."

"Stuck in here until tomorrow morning," Tess corrected. "Unless your mother knows we're here. I don't know about you, but no one's going to miss me until I don't open the shop tomorrow morning."

Ben whistled the opening theme from *Dragnet* through his teeth.

Tess frowned in reproval. "Something tells me you're not taking this very seriously."

"How seriously do you want me to take it? Our meetings are beginning to resemble the Keystone Kops. Speaking of comedies, would you mind setting that down? I'm not going to attack you." Looking infinitely at ease, Ben sat on a crate of raisins and stretched his legs out.

Still clutching the bottle as if it were a weapon, Tess flushed in embarrassment as she placed it on a shelf. "I don't think I'm exactly irresistible."

"No," Ben agreed. "If anything, you go to the other extreme. You don't think you're attractive at all. But you are. Very attractive."

Tess, suddenly finding it hard to breathe, glanced around the tiny storeroom. "Is there enough oxygen in here, do you think? It seems stuffy."

"I can't think of anyone I'd rather suffocate with."

Tess said dryly, "How romantic."

Ben smiled back. "I'm a romantic at heart."

No, he wasn't, Tess reflected. He was a *Young* at heart—which wasn't exactly reassuring, considering that the incorrigible Dorothy had parented him.

"If you're trying to convince me that being locked up in here with you is nothing to be concerned about," Tess informed him, taking another sip from her glass, "you're going about it the wrong way."

"At the moment I'm trying to get you to unwind." Ben watched her pace nervously back and forth. "Why don't you just sit down and relax?"

"How can I relax? I'm entombed with a sex maniac."

"Try closing your eyes and thinking pleasant thoughts," Ben suggested.

"If you think I'm closing my eyes around you, you're deluding yourself."

"What do you think is going to happen if you do?"

"The imagination," Tess replied, "runs wild."

"Yours does, at any rate." Ben sighed. "You need to get your mind on something else. Why don't I teach you a new dance step I learned in Paris?"

"Touch me and I scream," Tess promised.

"This may be the answer. Maybe if you scream, help will arrive."

"This building is made of brick. And the pub next door plays its jukebox at top volume. No one would hear." Which pretty well neutralized her threat, Tess realized, but Ben was hardly menacing, just maddening.

"All right. We're back to distraction. Let's play a game. How about show and tell? You show, and I'll tell you what I think. No?" He took in her silent refusal. "Well, I suppose there are other ways to pass the time. Can you name the Seven Dwarfs?"

Tess tried to decide if the door could be removed. "Can I what?"

"Name the Seven Dwarfs," Ben repeated.

Tess shot him an exasperated look. "I don't know. Can you?"

"Of course." Ben ticked them off on his fingers. "There's Mopey, Dopey, Dreamy, Schemey—"

"That's you," Tess decided, sipping her liqueur. "Schemey."

"There's also Grouchy, Dumpy, Touchy..." Ben stopped and smiled. "That's you. How many is that?"

"Seven in all. One correct," Tess said dryly. "I'd stop if I were you."

"I was trying to forget the fact that all the cookies are in the other room."

"Hungry?" Tess sympathized.

"Famished. I forgot to eat lunch."

So had she. Tess searched her slacks pocket and dug out a chocolate bar. "Here. You can have half of this." She snapped it in two pieces.

"Is that actually candy? Ms. DeSain, you shock me out of my shoes."

"Just so long as your shoes are the only thing you come out of while we're in here together," warned Tess, "we'll get along just fine."

Actually, Tess realized five minutes later as they tore open a box of dates and shared those, too, they seemed to get along remarkably well, considering they had nothing in common. Then again, Ben probably got along with everyone who was female. Studying him as he chewed, Tess asked, "Does your mom do this kind of thing very often?"

"What's that, sprout?"

"Foist women on you when you come home to visit."

Ben popped a date into his mouth and chewed thoughtfully. "As a matter of fact she's never done this sort of thing before. I can't imagine what's gotten into her."

"Maybe she's beginning to think you'll never settle down on your own."

"Or maybe she's afraid I won't recognize the right woman when I see her."

"I," stated Tess firmly, "am not the right woman for you."

Ben's gaze dueled with hers. "Who is the right woman for me, Tess?"

"Someone with infinite patience and no need for permanence."

Ben ate another date. "I think you just described Mother Teresa. How about you? Dating anyone in particular at the moment?"

Tess stalled, wondering if she should lie. "You aren't really interested."

"Have I got anything better to do than listen to you discuss your love life?"

"As a matter of fact, yes." Tess tried the doorknob again, just in case. "You could help me figure out how we can get out of here."

"Why don't I give you a French lesson instead?"

Tess eyed him with suspicion, wondering if he had in mind what she had in mind. She'd always had a ridiculous fascination for the French language, even though she'd never been able to learn it. Actually, her interest extended to anything French. She adored French movies, French music, French painting, French architecture. She especially loved French food.

Tess sat down and asked casually, "Do you really speak it?"

"What's that, love?"

"French."

In response Ben rattled off a fluent, melodious phrase in the romantic language of Charles Aznavour and Yves Montand. "How's that?"

Tess tried not to look affected as her stomach seemed to quiver in response. She cleared her throat. "That's very good. What does it mean?"

"Hurry and bag the trash. I think the garbage collector has arrived."

Tess, knowing he was pulling her leg again, shook her head at him. "Do you speak anything besides French?"

"Spanish and some Italian." He gave her a swift demonstration of both.

Fairly sure from his bland expression that he'd said something she'd rather not be privy to, Tess asked, "Was it difficult learning them?"

"Not really. I remember most things I hear. Especially when they're spoken by females. You'd be surprised how many European women are willing to teach American males the ins and outs of their culture. Well, maybe you wouldn't." He reconsidered his remark. "You'd probably be shocked."

Fairly sure he'd said that just to annoy her, Tess noted dryly, "I'm sure your knowledge of languages must come in handy during your travels."

"It's gotten me in, and out, of trouble a time or two." Ben pushed up the sleeves of his sweater, revealing strong forearms. "You disapprove of my profession, don't you, Tess? In fact, you disapprove of me in general."

"Do you care whether I disapprove or not?"

"Everyone wants approval," he answered, "at least some of the time."

"People who want approval," Tess said, "don't wear colors that clash."

Ben, who was presently wearing a lavender shirt under his blue sweater, shrugged. "This town could use a little shot of nonconformity."

"Is that what you are, a nonconformist? I thought maybe you were color-blind."

Ben clearly loved the fact that he'd gotten her going again. "You think I should wear brown and navy blue like you?"

"What? And cheat the locals of their major topic of conversation?"

"I've always had a knack for making waves," Ben confessed. "That's why I left town in the first place. I figured that what was a major storm here would cause barely a ripple elsewhere."

He didn't cause ripples, Tess thought. He instigated typhoons. "When did you leave Denton Falls, anyway?"

"When I was seventeen."

"Awfully young age to be on your own."

"Not when you're ready to tackle the world the way I was." Ben stretched his arms. "I figured I might as well move on since I was making life miserable at home for everyone around me. After my dad died, my mom remarried and I, being a teenager and full of myself at the time, made life hell on earth for my mom, my stepdad, whom I saw as an interloper, and everyone else around me. My stepdad finally gave me an ultimatum: Shape up or ship out."

"And you decided to ship out." Tess tried to imagine Ben on his own at seventeen. "What did you do?"

"I was physically mature for my age, so I lied about my birth date and signed on with a touring racing team as a gofer. And the rest," he said wryly, "is history." Ben folded his hands across his trim midriff. "What about you? I suppose your life was like *Leave it to Beaver.*"

"I was a disgustingly normal child," Tess agreed dryly. "Even when my folks divorced when I was sixteen, I remained ridiculously well adjusted."

"Didn't you ever want to stir things up and shake a few leaves off the trees when you were a kid?"

"Shaking trees was never my thing. I'll bet you were a handful, though. Especially as a teenager."

"I was hell on wheels," Ben agreed. "Always a rebel. Always wanting things to be different than they really were.

To tell you the truth, I was a royal pain in the derriere. Speaking of derrieres, you've got dust on yours."

Eyeing him, Tess dusted off her bottom. "Leave it to you to notice."

"I'll tell you what else I've noticed about you."

Tess willed herself not to respond to the soft huskiness in his voice. "Pray tell, what's that?" Her eyes rounded as he moved closer.

"I've noticed that whenever you and I get within a foot of each other you get all pink-cheeked and crabby."

"I do not get pink-cheeked and crabby!" Tess denied, her face hot.

Ben gave her a maddening smile. "I rest my case."

"I wouldn't get crabby," she told him as he stretched out beside her, "if you wouldn't keep getting so personal."

Ben nudged her foot with his. "I could get a whole lot *more* personal . . ."

Tess stepped back. Her ears perked. "Did you hear that?"

Ben listened a moment. "Sounds like rain."

Tess felt as deflated as a burst balloon. "Oh."

Ben flexed his arm muscles. "Were you hoping for a dramatic rescue?"

Tess looked away. "Actually, I was hoping you'd make at least a token effort and help me figure out how we're going to get out of here."

"There's a window behind you," Ben said. "It might be a way out."

More likely it was a way to become stuck. Tess estimated the dusty, cobweb-ridden slit was maybe eight inches high and ten inches across. "That's not a window. That's a miniwindow. And it has bars over it."

Ben considered it. "Could probably be kicked out with a little effort."

Dubious, Tess said, "How about a lot of effort and two elephants?"

Ben noted mildly, "I guess this means you're not interested in getting out of here, after all?"

Tess gave him a hard stare in response. "How do we get up there?"

"We don't. I do. Help me move some more boxes over, will you?"

Tess frowned as he shifted a box closer. "You can't climb up there. You'll hurt your leg. Let me think about this a minute."

"No."

"No?"

"You think too much," said Ben.

"You think too little," Tess retorted. "I'll do it."

Ignoring him, Tess balanced herself precariously on a stack of boxes and attempted to open the window. But it was stuck. Neither the screen nor the bars, which turned out to be embedded in concrete, would budge. "Lord," Tess panted, "these things were built solid."

Ben's hands clamped on to her ankles as Tess slammed her palm against the bars. "I wouldn't do that if I were you."

"Yes, you would." Tess glanced down at him. "What's the matter? Aren't you pleased I'm finally being a daredevil at last?"

Ben held on to her. "I'm not sure you're cut out for daredevil stuff. You're scaring the pants off me."

"I'd better not be." Tess pulled on the bars, trying to loosen them. "Anyway, now you know how it feels to be on the other end of the stick. Your mother probably worries herself silly when you race." And so would any woman foolish enough to get involved with him, she reminded herself.

"Does this mean you're not coming down?"

"I feel a whole lot safer up here than—Oh!" The box Tess was standing on suddenly caved in under her weight. Tess threw out her arms as it toppled over, expecting to land in a heap on the floor, but Ben caught her as she started to tumble. Standing on his toes, Tess looked into the green depths of his eyes and found it impossible to breathe.

He touched her cheek. "You're quite a woman, Tess."

"Quite a woman," Tess repeated, appalled by the awareness prickling across her skin at his touch. "Is that one of those vague terms like 'unique' that can mean anything?" She could handle this, she told herself. Easily.

"I suppose it is." Ben's steady gaze settled on her mouth. "I'm not the most articulate man. I tend to communicate with my body."

His body was certainly communicating with hers. Tess swallowed. He was too close, too attractive, *too reckless*. "Speaking of bodies... How is your leg? I know a terrific doctor if you're interested—"

"I've seen enough doctors in the past six months to stock a hospital." His knee brushed against hers. "What I'm interested in at the moment is—"

"Getting out of here." Tess all but jumped backward. "Me, too."

"That's not what I was going to say," he chided. "It was music."

Tess watched in confusion as Ben brought out a microcassette recorder from within the folds of his jacket. "Does this come under the Boy Scout motto of Be Prepared?" she asked finally.

Removing the tape, Ben flipped over the tiny cassette and reinserted it. "I suppose it does. It's been a lifesaver more times than I can count. It's also become something of a habit."

"From when you were in the hospital?" Tess guessed.

Ben nodded once.

There was a small silence. "How long were you in?"

Ben put on the earphones. "Too long."

Recognizing he was reluctant to discuss his accident any further, Tess sat down on a large box and stretched out her legs as Ben sat back and closed his eyes. She watched him for five minutes before complaining. "The least you could do is share."

Ben opened his eyes. "I didn't think you'd accept the offer."

"Why not?"

"Because it means sharing the earphones."

Which meant her all but sitting on his lap. Or him sitting on hers. "Can't you take the earphones out and just turn up the volume?"

"It doesn't play that way."

Suspicious, Tess sat with her hip just touching his. The warmth of his muscled thigh almost sent her scrambling. "What are you listening to? Whitesnake?" She stopped in surprise as a melodious instrumental piece flowed into the earphones. "I like that. What is it?"

"Andreas Vollenweider. He plays an electric harp. Surprised?"

Tess wrinkled her nose. "Frankly, yes. I figured you'd go for heavy metal."

"The only place I like heavy metal," said Ben, "is in a car chassis when the back end passes me going two hundred miles per hour."

They listened in companionable silence to the instrumental piece—until Tess accidentally pulled the earphones out and realized that the cassette deck played perfectly well without them.

Ben marveled, "Well, what do you know about that?"

Tess slid away. "My Lord, but you're a sneaky man. First you try to seduce me with liquor, then you lure me onto your lap with music—"

Ben was unrepentant. "How do you feel about flowers?"

Remembering his supposed allergy, Tess deadpanned, "I love mums."

Ben grinned and bopped her gently on the nose. "Ah, Tess, you're so refreshingly honest. So free of artifice."

"You mean gullible and naive," Tess declared, trying to regain control of herself. "And easy to bamboozle."

"Sophistication isn't always as terrific as it's cracked up to be. There's a lot to be said for clean slates."

"Is that what I am? A clean slate? I thought you thought I was a hick."

"I like small-town girls," Ben said peaceably.

And they liked him, herself included. Afraid to explore that thought, Tess pressed her lips together.

Ben noticed her silence and shut off the cassette player. "You look tired."

"I was up at five this morning," Tess admitted.

Ben studied the door. "A shame the key's lost."

Tess shifted restlessly on the sack of flour. "It's not."

Ben's tone was one of hopeful interest. "Not a shame?"

"No," Tess corrected. "Not lost."

Ben just looked at her. "The key's not lost?"

"No. The lock's always sticking. I've been meaning to get it fixed. Until I do, I keep the key stuck in the other side of the door so it's not in the way—" Tess stopped as Ben started to laugh. "Why is that funny?"

"No reason at all." Ben dug into his pocket and pulled out a jackknife.

Tess felt her nape prickle in sudden alarm. "Now what are you doing?"

"What I would've done sooner if I'd asked a few more pertinent questions. Do you have a piece of paper?"

Tess located a stack of old newspapers. Sliding one under the door, Ben took his knife and inserted it into the keyhole. The thud of metal hitting the floor was audible. Carefully, Ben pulled the paper back under the door, picked up the key and inserted it into the door. He jiggled it a moment. "Voilà!" He smiled as the door swung open.

Tess raised both eyebrows. "Where did you learn that?"

"From television, where else?" He put his hand on her shoulder and guided her toward the back door. "Let's lock up. You look exhausted."

She was exhausted, Tess realized. Too exhausted to put up much of a defense if Ben should start getting personal again.

As if he knew how to be anything else. Barely out of the storeroom, Tess felt Ben's left hand resting on her lower spine. "What are you doing?"

"Looking for the doorknob, of course."

Standing in the dark with him now that she'd switched off the interior lights, Tess observed wryly, "On my back?"

"Actually," he amended, "I'm thinking about where the outside light switch might be. No sense fumbling around in the dark."

"I thought that was exactly what you were doing." Already concerned about his injured leg, Tess ended up stubbing her toe as she spoke. "Maybe you should stay put while I get the lights," she suggested.

"I'm not the one running into doorjambs. Stop worrying about me. I'm not helpless, Tess."

"I know that. It's just, well..."

"You don't want me to get hurt." Ben nodded in understanding. "I'm touched, Tess. I really am."

And this would be a wonderful moment for him to stop touching her, Ben realized as he consciously removed his hand from her back—before he ended up getting them both into hotter water.

Chapter Six

Ben waited as Tess locked up the shop, then he escorted her out to her station wagon, which was parked in a small lot at the rear. Bringing out her keys, Tess looked in vain for the red Porsche. "Where's your car?"

Ben slipped his jacket on. "At my Mom's. The doctor says I should get more exercise, so I walked downtown. You sure you're sober enough to drive?"

"I'm fine," Tess answered, knowing her light-headedness had nothing to do with the small amount of alcohol she'd imbibed. Realizing Ben was probably as tired as she was, she debated whether or not she dared offer him a lift as she inserted the key into her car's ignition and turned it. Nothing happened. Thinking she'd flooded the engine, Tess tried again. Still nothing happened.

Ben whistled as she tried to start it for a third time. "Need help?"

Tess glanced at him as she got out of the car. "I'm not sure. It worked fine this morning." She walked around to the front of the station wagon. Fully experienced when it came to pumping gas and checking her car's oil, Tess readily acknowledged she wasn't exactly a mechanical genius.

Still, she optimistically opened the hood and peered into the complicated maze of machinery.

Ben leaned indolently against the car and studied the star-studded night sky. "Figure out what the problem is yet?"

"Not yet," Tess admitted. She could probably look at the motor for a decade and still not figure out what was wrong with it. "Would you care to have a look?"

"Are you asking me to?"

Tess flung her braid over her shoulder. "I thought I just did."

Smiling at her exasperation, Ben moved to the front of her car. "You don't like needing anyone or anything, do you, Tess?"

"I like running my own life," Tess responded. Her five years in New York had taught her that she got into far less trouble when she didn't depend on anyone but herself.

"That's what I figured." Ben positioned the prop to her car's hood. He took his time looking over the oily tangle of engine parts.

"Well?" Tess prodded when he didn't speak. "Do you have any ideas?"

Ben adjusted something inside the motor. "I've always got ideas when you're around, sprout."

Tess ignored that. "I meant do you have any idea what's wrong with it?" She opened the back of the Volvo and rummaged for a rag.

"Sure. The distributor cap's missing."

Figuring a man who drove cars for a living would know, Tess asked, "Can they just fall off on their own?"

Wiping his fingers on the rag Tess handed him, Ben thought about the car part in question, which he'd personally removed earlier that evening. "It's not impossible." Not likely, he added to himself, but not impossible.

Tess bit her lip. "The car won't work without one, will it?"

"No, sprout. It's sort of an essential item."

Tess gave him a long look. "Why do I get the strange feeling you have something to do with this?"

Ben raised innocent eyebrows. "I don't know. Why do you?"

"You look suspiciously satisfied with yourself."

"I guess I'm just the type that always looks guilty."

"Where there's smoke," Tess decided, buttoning up her jacket, "there's fire." And if she didn't watch herself, she was likely to get burned.

"You don't think I sabotaged your car just so I could be alone with you, do you?" Ben managed to look shocked.

"Are you saying you didn't sabotage my car?" Tess countered.

"Would you believe me if I denied it?"

"I don't know," said Tess. "You haven't denied it yet. You know, I think I'm beginning to see similarities between you and your mother, after all. You're both apparently incorrigible." Tess folded her arms across her chest and frowned in reprimand. "Isn't this sort of thing illegal?"

Ben closed the car hood. "What's that, love?"

"Tampering with someone else's car."

Shrugging, Ben zipped up his jacket. "Probably depends on the intent."

Tess knew what the intent was: to get her alone so he could give her the business. She sighed in exasperation. "I wish you'd figure out some other way to entertain yourself. I can't do without my car. I make deliveries with it."

"I'll fix it first thing tomorrow, if that makes you feel any better."

It didn't. "What's to keep you from sabotaging it further?"

"My sense of honor? My high moral standards? My total lack of knowledge of Volvo engines?"

Tess felt her lips curving upward. "Very funny." Her eyes widened as he moved closer and touched her lightly on the nose.

"You know why you're irritated at me, don't you, Tess?"

"Because you're irritating?" Tess guessed.

"Because you're afraid," Ben chided.

Tess shook her head. "I'm not afraid of you."

"I know you're not. You're afraid of yourself and what you might do."

"This is fascinating. What am I afraid I'm going to do? Strangle you?"

"No, you're afraid you're going to start liking me. And for some reason that scares the hell out of you."

He was right. It did. Falling for him was just asking to be hurt.

"Come on." Ben laced his longer fingers with hers. "Stop frowning like that. It's not that far. I'll walk you home."

"Oh, no you don't." Appalled at the way her whole body went hot and prickly at his touch, Tess quickly disengaged her hand again and shoved both fists into her jacket pockets where he couldn't get to them.

"No walking you home?" His breath puffed white in the chilly air.

"No holding of hands," Tess said firmly. "Might give people the wrong idea."

Ben bopped her on the nose. "And just what wrong idea might that be?"

Tess quickly backed up. "Us being more than casual acquaintances."

"I don't think that would be a wrong idea." Ben trapped her against the side of her car. "I figure that's a pretty damned good idea."

Having run out of places to go, Tess stood her ground. She swallowed as Ben rested his hands on either side of her. "I don't think—"

"Of course you don't, sprout." Ben stood so close, Tess could feel the warmth of his body. "You're a woman. You feel."

She felt, all right, Tess decided as a warm wave of awareness washed over her. Totally female. And totally out of control.

Ben leaned closer. Acknowledging she'd better go while the going was still possible, Tess quickly ducked under his right arm and started across the parking lot.

Letting out a loud sigh of disappointment, Ben caught up with her. "Hold on, sprout. This isn't a race. Or are you running away from me?"

She was running away from him. Trying to look cool, calm and unruffled, Tess glanced in his direction. "Why do you keep calling me sprout? Do I still remind you of some sort of vegetable? Celery, perhaps? Or lettuce?"

Ben halted her progress by standing in her path. He brushed her brown braid over her shoulder. "I call you that because despite your time in New York, you're like a little plant just beginning to poke your head up to see what the world is like. I'd like to expose you to new things."

Tess could just imagine what kinds of things he'd like to expose her to: him. "Touch me again without my express permission," she warned mildly, skirting around him, "and you're hamburger."

He gave her a lazy smile. "Come on, sprout. Couldn't I at least be chopped sirloin?"

"My name," Tess reminded him, "isn't sprout."

"No? So, what do people call you? Testy Tessy?"

Knowing perfectly well that he was teasing, Tess gave him a cool look. "My father is the only one who calls me Tessy. People who don't know me very well—and that includes you, by the way—call me *Ms.* DeSain."

"I'll bet they say it with respect, too. Where is your dad, anyway?"

Deciding it was probably as innocuous a topic as was likely to come along, Tess found herself saying, "Florida. He retired there a few years ago."

"What did he do before retiring? Bake cookies?"

"No, he was a corporate jet pilot."

"That's good news. At least your caution wasn't inherited from both sides." Ben smiled at her quelling look. "Did he remarry?"

"Yes." Tess continued to eye him repressively. "About two years ago."

"You see your dad often?"

"Not as often as I'd like." Not that he didn't call. Every other week or so he checked in to see how she, and the shop, were doing. Tess didn't want him to worry, so she did what any self-respecting, self-supporting daughter would do: she lied.

"You get along with your stepmother all right, do you?"

Tess considered telling him to mind his own business, then remembered that in a way, she *was* his business. "I've never met her."

"You didn't attend their wedding?"

Tess felt a wave of heat infuse her cheeks. "No."

"Why not?"

"Because I didn't want to intrude on them, that's why not."

"Your dad, he wouldn't happen to be of French descent, would he?"

Tess felt as if she'd been handcuffed to a carousel gone dizzily out of control. "What's that got to do with anything?"

"Nothing, except..." Ben let his voice trail off.

Positive she shouldn't pursue it, Tess prompted, "Except what?"

"I know this is going to sound paranoid, but if the name DeSain is French, whatever you do, don't mention it to my mom, will you?"

"Why the dickens not?"

"Her maiden name is Gillette."

Tess refrained from rolling her eyes in exasperation. "So?"

"So, she might see us having French blood in common as encouraging."

"Trust me on this one," Tess deadpanned. "We have absolutely nothing in common."

"I wouldn't say absolutely nothing," Ben objected. "We're both in need of a bit of rest and relaxation."

Neither of which, Tess swiftly realized, she was going to get.

Telling himself to cool off, Ben watched her stride ahead. Recalling her injury as his own leg began to throb, he asked, "How's your ankle?"

Tess glanced over her shoulder. "It's fine now. Thank you."

"How did you hurt it, anyway?"

"You've already asked me that." Tess slowed her pace to his.

"I guess your answer slipped my mind." It was an improvement over saying he hadn't believed her, Ben figured. Which meant, maybe, that he was developing some tact with her, after all.

Tess buttoned her collar under her chin. "I fell out of a tree."

Determined to make it to his mother's house if it crippled him, Ben concentrated on putting one foot in front of the other. He'd gone and forgotten his blasted cane in the shop, and he was damned if he was going back for it. If he left her now, he knew Tess would take off like a bullet. And he had no intention of letting her out of his sight after he'd all but dismantled her car to get her alone. "How did you fall out of a tree?"

"Rescuing a friend's kitten," Tess confessed.

"It never occurred to you to call the fire department?"

"It occurred to me."

Ben crossed the street three feet short of the crosswalk. "Then why didn't you?"

Tess looked both ways before following. "Because this particular kitten is inordinately silly, and I didn't dare leave it even for a minute, that's why. It needed me."

It popped out before Ben could stop himself. "If I said I needed you, would you take care of me, Tessy?"

Tess swung around, but a convertible filled with laughing teenagers jetted by before she could lay him waste. As the sound of their blaring radio faded into the dark night, Ben swerved to the left suddenly, apparently intending to take a shortcut through the park.

Tess hesitated at the edge of the wet grass. "Are you sure you know where you're going?" she called after him.

"Of course I'm sure." He shoved his fists into the pockets of his jacket. "This town hasn't changed one iota since I was boy. Unfortunately."

Tess flushed. She kept forgetting he'd grown up in Denton Falls; he was so different from any of the other locals.

Ben turned around at her hesitation and walked backward so he could talk to her. "Are you coming or not?"

Tess debated which was more dangerous—walking alone at night, or walking alone with Ben at night. Deciding that she could handle him if she kept her distance, Tess started after him, unconsciously humming the catchy Phil Collins tune that had been blaring from the car radio.

"The last thing I expected you to like," Ben teased as she caught up.

"What did you think I listened to? Lawrence Welk?"

He grinned at her indignation. "Not quite. I just assumed a well-bred woman like yourself would go for something less commercial. Something highbrow and filled with social significance, like opera. Do you like opera?"

"Not particularly. You're very smooth, aren't you?"

Ben's elbow brushed against her. "All the better to woo you."

"I don't want to be wooed by you." She didn't want to be touched by him, either. It did terrible things to her composure. Tess put a foot and a half between them. "Please pass that on to your mom," she added, "before she decides to torch my house in the hope that I'll move in with you."

Ben's mouth curved. "You don't think Mom's going to give up on us, do you? Even after conniving to make us partners."

Tess sighed. "I'm an optimist, but I'm not that much of an optimist."

"No, you're just an old-fashioned girl."

"You mean a fuddy-duddy," Tess decided. "A veritable stick-in-the-mud."

"No, I mean you're a classic." Ben shook his head. "Fuddy-duddy. Where the hell do you get words like that?"

"From books. Where else?"

"You say that like you don't think I ever cracked one open. What's the matter, Tess? You don't see me as a scholar?"

"I see you as a man not inclined to experience anything secondhand. A man inclined to test limits. Speaking of testing limits..." Tess gave him a pointed look as he hooked an arm around her shoulders. "When are you going back to racing?"

They'd reached the park playground. Letting go of her, Ben sat on a swing. "You aren't anxious to get rid of me already, are you, Tess?"

She gave him a long look. "I'm not?"

"I only just arrived in town a few days ago," Ben pointed out.

Which had been plenty of time for him to stir things up—especially her.

"What are you planning on doing here, anyway?" Tess asked.

"Would you believe me if I told you I hoped to improve my mind?"

Tess dusted off the empty swing next to him and sat down. "No."

"You don't think I need to improve my mind?" he teased.

"I didn't say that." Tess swung a moment, then asked, "Are you?"

Ben surreptitiously took the weight off his injured leg. "Actually, yes. I'm hoping to earn my diploma. Or, at least, the equivalent of one."

Tess stopped in midswing. "Are you saying that you never graduated from *high school*?"

He noted her ill-disguised shock and mocked, "What's the matter, sprout? Do you think school is the only place you learn anything?"

"No, of course not." Tess bit her lip in consternation, knowing she hadn't sounded overly convinced.

"Just the things that matter, right?"

"I didn't say that. Stop putting words in my mouth."

Ben grabbed the chain on her swing and pulled her closer. "I can tell you what I'd like to do with your mouth."

Determined to stay put, Tess swallowed dryly. "What?"

His voice was a smoky purr. "Kiss it till the cows come home."

Tess felt her heart skip. "I don't own any cows and neither do you—although there does seem to be a lot of fertilizer being spread around here lately—"

She'd almost forgotten how entrancing his laugh could be. Low and rich and sexy—Before she knew what he was up to, he dipped his head and kissed her swiftly, thoroughly on the mouth. With every cell in her body tingling, Tess stared at him, too stunned to move. "What was that for?"

"For being you." Reaching up, Ben slowly traced her left eyebrow with his thumb. "I've never met anyone quite like you before, Tess."

Tess licked her lips. "I've never met anyone like you before, either."

Ben smiled faintly as he ran a finger down the bridge of her nose, then traced her upper lip. "Is that good or bad, do you suppose?"

Suddenly forgetting how to breathe, Tess had to fight for air before she could speak. "I haven't decided yet."

"Sounds as if you need help making up your mind." His voice was soft, persuasive. "Why don't we work on it? Could be interesting."

Tess was certain it would be a lot more than interesting; it would be downright dangerous. Some inexplicable chemistry flowed between them, and Tess didn't find it particularly reassuring. She'd taken enough science in school to recognize that some perfectly innocuous chemicals blew roofs off buildings when combined.

Knowing she was neck deep in trouble and sinking fast, Tess hurriedly slid out of the swing. Looking far more composed than she thought he had any right to under the circumstances, Ben watched calmly as Tess straightened her jacket and tried to pull it—and herself—together.

"I take it that quick retreat means no. Stop backing up," he scolded, as she moved away. "Opposites are supposed to attract."

So they were. But they didn't necessarily remain together. Sometimes opposites ended up repelling each other in spectacular fashion. Fearing what might happen if she tempted fate, Tess started walking again, letting Ben catch up. "Why didn't you graduate from high school?"

"You're awfully nosy," he said in mock complaint. "Considering we don't know each other all that well."

"You're the one who keeps making personal remarks," Tess pointed out. "Besides, I think I have a right to know everything there is to know about you, don't you? Considering the way your mother is determined to join us in matrimony."

Ben sighed in agreement. "There is that."

"So, what happened? Did you drop out of school to race cars?"

"Actually, I was kicked out."

"What for? Riding a motorcycle down the hallways?"

"No." Ben tweaked her nose playfully. "Wearing a miniskirt to school."

Alarmed at how she kept reacting to him, Tess cleared her throat. "A miniskirt," she repeated. There might be a lot of things she didn't know about him, but there was one thing she did know: Ben Young, whatever else he might be, was indisputably all male. "Some fad at the time?"

"No, I was protesting the dress code."

"You resented the fact guys couldn't wear miniskirts?"

"Not quite. I resented the fact that girls could." At her raised eyebrow, Ben explained, "The principal wouldn't let us wear shorts on hot days, while the girls wore skirts shorter than any Bermudas could ever be. He wouldn't even discuss the dress code, so I decided to take issue with it."

"Wearing a skirt was a little drastic, don't you think?"

"I was trying to make a statement that couldn't be ignored. Let me tell you, it wasn't easy finding a miniskirt that would fit. I finally ended up swiping one from my buddy's sister and modifying it. Looked pretty good in it, too, if I do say so myself. Should have shaved my legs, though."

Tess shook her head at him. "You're crazy."

"So says a woman who climbs trees to save kittens and gave up a hot career in the city to bake cookies for a living. As long as we're getting personal, why did you give up your job in New York to come back here?"

Reluctant to discuss her New York debacle, during which she'd lost not only a fair amount of self-esteem but a sizable amount of cash as well, Tess quipped, "Would you believe I was trying to expand my horizons?"

"Keep working in a bakery," Ben chided, "and what you're likely to expand is your waistline."

Having noticed just that morning that she'd managed to gain two pounds in the past week, Tess was in no mood to be needled on that particular subject. "I see. In addition to all my other faults, which you seem only too happy to enumerate, you think I'm overweight."

"I don't think you're overweight. Just incredibly oversensitive." Ben caught her by the hand. "Who was he, Tess?"

Tess didn't have to feign obtuseness. "Who was who?"

"The man you're mad as hell at. The man who obviously hurt you. The one who's made you so cautious."

Tess debated lying, then decided it would serve no useful purpose. "His name was Rand McNary. I used to work for him."

"Am I like him? Is that why you keep comparing me to him?"

"No. You're nothing like him." Randall had been slick, shrewd and forever scheming; but where Ben could apparently be equally manipulative, it was in a maddening sort of way, not a self-serving one.

"He disillusioned you." It was a statement, not a question.

Tess raised an eyebrow. "Why do you say that?"

"The way you react to me. For a woman willing to shimmy up trees and climb through windows, you're notably cautious when it comes to me."

Tess tried for lightness. "So much for the feminine mystique. I didn't realize I was so transparent."

"You're not transparent. I'm just good at putting two and two together and coming up with five." Lifting her hand in his, Ben studied her neatly manicured fingers a moment. "This McNary character wouldn't happen to have anything to do with your bad investment, would he, sprout?"

Knowing that Ben wouldn't be satisfied until he got an answer, Tess admitted, "Actually, Rand had a lot to do with it. He was the one who persuaded me to borrow money to invest in the stock market."

Ben nodded in acknowledgement. "And you ended up losing a bundle and now you're angry at him for pushing you into it."

"No, I'm angry at Rand because when he realized the stock was sliding, he pulled out, but he never quite got around to advising me to do the same." And now she had a terrible time trusting her judgment when it came to men— especially when it was one she might be getting involved with.

"Were you involved with him?"

Afraid he'd read her mind, Tess took her time before answering. "Yes. Unfortunately."

"I gather you don't like to talk about him."

"Just thinking about him always makes me want to throw things," Tess confessed.

"I'll remember that if the subject should ever come up in the future."

Tess didn't want the subject to come up in the future. She didn't want it to continue in the present, either. Searching desperately for something else to talk about, she noted that Ben's limp had become more pronounced the farther they walked, and she latched on to that. "How long ago was your accident?"

Ben's look told her he knew exactly what she was doing, and why. "About six months ago. I crashed at the Miami Grand Prix back in March."

Tess remembered not long after she'd arrived in town how Dorothy had suddenly left with a rather vague explanation about her son "needing her."

Disturbed that Ben was still obviously in pain after so much time had passed, Tess slowed her pace even more. "Was it bad?"

"I suppose about as bad as an accident can be where you still live to talk about it."

Tess repressed an involuntary shiver. "It must have been awful."

"Pretty awful," he agreed, seemingly far less affected by the easy admission than she was. "Not something you'd want to experience twice, at any rate."

Wondering if he ought to be walking so far, Tess tried to think of some sensitive way of broaching the subject. "Does your leg still hurt?"

Ben knew exactly what was on her mind and had absolutely no intention of becoming an object of pity. He swept her into his arms and bent her backward so she had one foot off the ground. "Only when I dance." His gray-green gaze caressed her face, lingering on her mouth. "You know what your trouble is, don't you, Tess?"

No longer breathing, Tess stared up at him. "Your mother and you? Not necessarily in that order?"

"You're in dire need of fun and frivolity." With his hands spanning her slim waist, he pulled her up until they were facing each other. They stood so close together that Tess could feel the hard muscles of his thighs pressing against hers.

"Right now," Tess managed, "I'm in dire need of air. Let go." Weak-kneed as the heat of his body melded with hers, Tess waited in vain for him to release her. She saw the mischief gleaming in his eyes.

"I think I've just been put in my place." He rubbed his nose slowly against hers. "Why don't you come to my place, too? After all, now that we're partners, we ought to be getting better acquainted, don't you think?"

Tess swallowed. "I don't think, remember? I'm a woman. I feel."

"You feel damned nice, if you ask me."

So did he. He felt wonderful. His hands were strong but gentle. And his voice was as warm and inviting as summer rain when he whispered, "I'd like to get to know you better, Tess."

Dizzy and light-headed, Tess needed a moment to realize they'd already reached her house. It took another moment for her to realize Ben was going to kiss her.

"Ben, I—" Tess was still protesting when his lips touched hers. Easing her hips against his, he silenced her with a hungry, openmouthed kiss that was as leisurely as it was exquisitely thorough. Rocked by an unexpected wave of desire, Tess swayed against him as his tongue found hers. The taste of him was as exotic, and as erotic, as his cologne.

With her pulse throbbing, Tess put her hands to his chest, intending to push away. Instead she found her fingers curling into the soft knit of his sweater.

"Tess." Her whispered name was an invitation, an appeal, for even more intimacy. Opening her mouth to the gently insistent pressure of his, Tess had already put her arms around his neck and was clinging to him like a woman drowning, when she realized they were all but making love squarely in the middle of a public thoroughfare. Shocked down to her toes, she hurriedly backed away from him, nearly tripping in her haste. "No."

"Tess .`.." This time his voice was filled with reproach.

Though he made no move to come after her, Tess turned and leaped up the steps to her door. It took her three tries to unlock it.

"Aren't you going to invite me in for a cup of coffee?" His soft reprimand caught her with one foot already over the threshold.

Composing herself with an effort, Tess turned. "I'm sorry. I can't." She didn't dare. "I need to get up early tomorrow."

"Are you always this sensible?" Ben scolded as she turned away again.

With her hand on the door, Tess hesitated, then turned to face him once more. "I'm afraid so. Genetic disposition. I take after my mother."

Ben stood on the step below, so that his eyes were on the same level as hers. "So do I," he said softly.

Tess slowly shook her head, determined to resist the pull of attraction binding them together. "You're nothing like my mother." He was like her father, however: just as charming, just as reckless...."

Ben's slight smile had her focusing involuntarily on his mouth. "I meant I'm like my mother."

No, he wasn't. Though both mother and son did appear to be inordinately strong-willed, Tess thought, Dorothy was pale and frail and delicate and unequivocally well-intentioned; while the darkly attractive Ben, in spite of his injuries, appeared perfectly capable of getting them both into trouble without any qualms at all.

Chapter Seven

He was inside the shop the next morning, waiting for her.

"You're up early," Tess commented, entering and closing the unlocked door. She was going to stay calm, she promised herself. And sensible.

In the process of fixing the storeroom's tricky lock, Ben looked up and smiled at her. "He who hesitates," he intoned, "is lost."

And she who insisted on playing with matches, Tess reminded herself as she felt an instinctive tug of awareness, was going to get burned. Knowing she possessed a truly deplorable habit of getting herself in trouble with remarkable ease—especially where Ben was concerned—Tess put on a teakettle and began preparing for her day.

"I fixed your car," Ben said after a moment. "I thought you might be needing it today."

Tess, having enjoyed walking to work in the early morning much more than she'd expected, paused to look at him. "Thank you."

"You're welcome, sprout."

"Did I forget to lock the shop door last night?" Tess asked, pulling out mixing bowls and spoons. "Is that how you got in?"

"You didn't forget. I talked my mom out of her key."

"Why?"

Ben picked up the screwdriver he'd apparently brought. "I was afraid you might not let me in this morning after the way I behaved last night."

Actually, Tess conceded, she might not have let him in because of how *she*'d behaved last night. When she'd locked her door, it had been as much to keep her in as him out. She'd never met a man so hard to resist.

Seemingly content to be the model of decorum for the moment, Ben finished with the lock and gathered up his tools. He sat down at the table.

"Nice day," he commented as she made no move to join him in further conversation. "A bit warmer than yesterday, don't you think?"

Tess whipped together a mixture of sugar, flour, eggs and spices, with quick efficiency. "I'm sure you didn't stop by to discuss the weather."

"No," Ben agreed, accepting the cup of instant coffee she offered him. "I thought it was time I made myself useful around here. After all, if we're going to be working together—"

"We aren't going to be working together," Tess interrupted. She pushed her bangs back in exasperation. "Look, I'm sure you're a very nice man . . ." Actually she wasn't at all sure of that, but she was trying to be diplomatic here. "But I don't need a partner."

"You've had a partner for almost eight months now," Ben pointed out. "My mother."

"That," Tess said firmly, "was different."

"How is it different?"

"Your mother was always a silent partner." And it was beginning to look as if Ben might well turn out to be the hands-on sort. Literally.

Ben tipped his head to one side. "Does this mean you don't want me to tell you what's wrong with the business?"

Tess knew she shouldn't respond. She knew the wise thing would be just to ignore him, but she couldn't.

"There's nothing wrong with my shop."

"Nothing a fresh perspective couldn't cure," he agreed mildly.

Tess wasn't sure about the "perspective" part, but the "fresh" aspect he certainly had down pat. "You'll pardon me if I beg to disagree with you."

"Love, I'd be surprised if you didn't disagree with me. Just so I don't go stepping on your toes any more than necessary, did you promise your mother you'd never change anything?"

"No," Tess said truthfully, surprised he'd bothered to ask.

"You don't have sentimental reasons for keeping the shop in a financial hole, then?"

Setting down the spoon, Tess shot him a withering look. "No."

"Good." Ben smiled back. "That ought to make the process easier. You don't mind if I just sit and watch awhile, do you? I'd like to see what a normal day is like for you."

"Nothing's normal when you're around," Tess assured him, having no idea how true that statement was until her first customer of the day strolled in ten minutes later.

Ben rose and introduced himself as Fran Bellows entered. "Hi. I'm Ben Young."

"Yes, I know." Looking somewhat surprised by his presence, Fran flushed as she took his extended hand. "I'm Fran Bellows."

After Ben had given them a semblance of privacy by discreetly moving into the storeroom with Tess's inventory book in hand, Fran approached the counter. "Hi, Tess."

"Hello, Fran." Wondering if she'd overslept without realizing it, Tess glanced up at the cookie-shaped wall clock that Cheryl and Judith had given her as a grand opening present. It was still fifteen minutes before she normally opened the shop. "The first batch of cookies isn't quite ready yet," she said, giving Fran a wry smile as the latter stared after Ben.

"I came to satisfy my curiosity," Fran admitted, keeping her voice low. "I heard you and he were an item, but I didn't believe it."

"We're not an item." Tess checked the errant stove to make sure it was still baking and not burning. "We're partners. Business partners," she clarified before Fran could misinterpret the remark.

Fran blinked at her. "You're joking."

"I wish I were. It's Dorothy's idea of livening up my life. Ben is her son." Tess filled her friend in on the details, figuring she might as well get used to the idea of explaining the situation. Fran might be her first curious customer for the day, but it was likely she wouldn't be the last.

Fran looked genuinely concerned. "I know how much the shop means to you. Are you going to mind not having it all to yourself?"

"I don't know how I feel about it yet," Tess confessed, bagging two dozen fresh-from-the oven cookies and handing them over to Fran.

One hour and twenty customers later, Tess still didn't know how she felt about it, or about the fact that her patrons seemed to have increased markedly in number all of a sudden.

At least half, Tess noticed, seemed far more interested in meeting Ben first, and buying cookies second. Emerging from the storeroom, Ben seemed to take the inevitable requests for his autograph in stride. He even took the initiative and started prebagging cookies by the dozen, signing the bags as he went along.

"Using one's celebrity to sell things," he confided to Tess as he applied his name to another bag with a flourish, "is an old ploy."

And clearly a very successful one. Astounded not only by the rapidity with which news of Ben's involvement in the shop had whipped around town, but also by the increase in business it had generated, Tess baked batch after batch of cookies, struggling to keep up with the demand.

All her worrying about the man, she thought wryly, had apparently been for nought. For the next two hours, she and Ben barely had time to look at, let alone speak to, each other. He certainly had no opportunity to lure her into temptation or point out her business's problems.

Still, it was only a matter of time, Tess supposed, before he asked to look over her financial records. Deciding it might be better to hit him with it when he was still in a generous mood, Tess waited until they had a brief respite. Then, passing a plate of cookies his way, she pulled the ledger out of the drawer and offered it to him. "Would you care to look this over?"

"I thought you'd never ask." Helping himself to a cookie, Ben perched on the edge of a table to peruse the spiral-bound book.

After a series of deep frowns and a couple of soft grunts, Tess could hardly stand it. "I wish you'd stop that and just say what it is you want to say."

Marking a spot with his finger, Ben looked up. "I'm not sure what to say. When we were at the farmers' market and you said math wasn't your best subject, I thought you were kidding."

Tess gave him a repressive look. "I was kidding."

But she was no accountant. Tess was honest enough to admit that. The baking part she could handle. Despite her lack of formal training, she had a natural flair for it. It was the business end of the shop that baffled her. It was because she was afraid to make gross mistakes—not because she felt it would go contrary to her mother's wishes—that she'd done little to alter what her mother had established in the way of business and accounting practices. These were clearly destined for change.

Ben walked around the small shop with his fists in his slacks pockets. Recognizing just from his expression that his mind was working overtime, Tess shoved a fresh sheet of cookies into the hot oven.

"All right." She put her potholders down and turned to look at him. "What plot are you hatching inside that devious mind of yours?"

Ben continued to look back and forth between the stove set against the back wall and the counter that ran down the right side of the room. "Do I look as if I'm hatching something?"

"As a matter of fact, yes. You're all but clucking in discontent. Why do you keep looking at the counter like that?"

"I was thinking about moving it over there, so it's the first thing people see when they walk into the shop."

Tess measured out flour and oatmeal for yet another batch of dough. "If you move it there, the afternoon sun will hit it."

Ben lifted his shoulders. "So?"

"So it'll melt all the chocolate chips in the pecan chocolate-chip cookies you like so much." In the past hour alone, he'd devoured nearly a dozen of them.

Ben considered her remark. To Tess's frustration, he didn't argue so that she could try to talk him out of it; he came up with a new plan instead. "You're right," he agreed after a moment. "We should install an awning over the front window. It would add to the shop's character and keep the sun out, as well."

"If you move the counter there, it will also be in front of Pele," Tess pointed out, cracking eggs into a bowl.

"That," said Ben, "was the general idea. As fond as you are of the stove, not everyone wants to be greeted by it when they walk in. I've been watching. The thing seems to scare most people to death. Me included."

Sometimes it still scared Tess, too. Overfiring out of control, Pele had nearly burned the place down twice in the past two months alone.

"I never said I was fond of Pele," Tess said. "It's a very temperamental stove and sometimes hardly worth the trouble. But that's beside the point. There's another good reason not to move the counter in front of it."

"What's that, sprout?"

Ignoring the indulgence laced through his voice, Tess walked over in front of the black mountain of a stove and beckoned for Ben to follow. "Come here a moment, would you please?"

Clearly amused, Ben stood where she pointed. "What are we doing?"

"Participating in a small experiment. Where would the counter go? Here?" They stood six feet in front of the stove, facing each other.

Ben assessed the distance. "That looks about right."

Tess nodded. If he insisted on moving the counter there, that meant whoever stood behind it would also be standing directly in front of Pele. Having no intention of being turned into a brisket, Tess asked sweetly, "Do you have health insurance, Ben?"

"Am I going to need it?"

"Well—" Tess thoughtfully scratched her nose "—we hope not, don't we? Now, if you'll just stand right there." Tess backed up and surveyed him from a distance of a yard or two. "That's good. Feel free to face Pele or turn your back on her, as you please."

"Or rotate like a rotisserie?" Ben asked, already beginning to perspire from the stove's radiating heat.

"You're getting the idea." Tess nodded in mocking approval.

"I think what I'm getting is the heat. Literally." Ben wiped a damp black curl off his forehead with the back of his hand. "How long do you want me to stay here?"

"Well, between making cookies and selling them, I'm generally behind the counter for anywhere from eight to twelve hours a day."

"You want me to stay here twelve hours?" Ben looked wounded.

"I didn't say that," Tess chided. "I said that was what I'd have to do—"

"If I insist on being thickheaded," Ben finished for her. Looking more amused than offended, he tipped his dark head to one side and surveyed her. "You know, I'm beginning to think you're a lot less innocent than you look."

Tess smiled beatifically at him. "If you can't stand the heat..."

"Get out of the kitchen," Ben concluded. "I'll remember that."

For a whole hour after that, Tess thought she'd won the battle, but she discovered soon enough that she'd only survived the first skirmish. Ben waited until there was another short break in the stream of customers walking through the front door. Then, clearly not giving up on the topic, he suggested they get a new stove, then move the counter in front of it.

"Buy a new stove?" Tess repeated. "What would happen to Pele?"

"It would go to that great stove heaven in the sky." Ben signed a new stack of white bags as Tess fought to keep the glass case stocked.

"You mean junk it?" Tess couldn't quite hide her dismay.

"That was the general idea. I thought you said you weren't fond of it."

"I'm not. It's just that a new one would be so...so modern." So expensive. "It wouldn't have any personality," Tess declared.

"Stoves don't need personality," Ben countered reasonably. "They need even temperatures. There's no point in you making fabulous cookies, then having the stove turn them into charcoal briquettes."

"You're just trying to flatter me, so I'll let you do what you want."

"I'll tell you what I want."

At the sudden huskiness in his voice, Tess turned to find him standing close behind her. Inhaling the unsettling fragrance of his cologne, Tess swallowed, half expecting to have a physical battle on her hands, as well as a verbal one. "What's that?" she managed.

"I'd like you to stop jumping every time I get within a foot of you."

"I don't," Tess denied, knowing she did; she couldn't help it.

"Yes, you do." He reached out and brushed a smudge of flour off her cheek. "You act like a nervous cat parked under a rocking chair."

"I'll start taking Valium tomorrow," Tess promised, tongue in cheek.

"I don't want you to start taking Valium," Ben scolded. "I'd like you to try and relax. I'd also like to install an exhaust fan."

He never said, or did, what she expected. Not sure she'd heard right, considering his knees were no more than a millimeter away from hers, Tess repeated blankly, "An exhaust fan?"

Ben tucked a loose strand of hair behind her ear. "Over the front door, so it vents out into the street."

Disturbed by his closeness, Tess fought down an urge to climb onto the counter to put more distance between them. "Whatever for?"

"You obviously haven't ever been to Sturbridge Village," he chided gently. "Have you?"

Tess tried, unsuccessfully, to make a connection between the restored collection of colonial shops, buildings and houses found in Massachusetts, and exhaust fans. "What does Sturbridge Village possibly have to do with what we're talking about?" she wanted to know.

"Everything. In Sturbridge, they have a wonderful cookie shop that vents all the delectable baking aromas right out into the adjoining square where everyone will smell them. Consequently, people wander into the shop. Net result? More sales."

"Our sales have already increased." Just by virtue of his being there. Tess wasn't sure whether it pleased her or exasperated her more.

"That's because people are curious about me. We still have a long way to go before we're on firm financial ground."

Wishing her feet were on firmer ground, Tess took a steadying breath. "Why am I getting this terrible feeling you're not through yet?"

Ben smiled back. "Because I'm not. I want to advertise."

"I can't afford to advertise," Tess responded automatically.

"We can't afford *not* to advertise." He tugged lightly on her braid. "You have to spend money to make money."

"You have to have money to spend money," Tess argued back.

"I'm glad you brought that up. No offense, but you made a critical mistake when you borrowed money to get the shop out of hock. Instead of thirty thousand dollars to clean up your debts, you should've borrowed twenty thousand more.''

"Then I'd be fifty thousand dollars in debt," Tess reasoned.

"No," Ben countered mildly. "Then you'd be in business."

Tess discovered it was impossible to look down your nose in indignation at someone who was half a foot taller than you were. She settled on an aloof stare. "Is that your subtle way of saying that I lack business savvy?"

"No. It's my clumsy way of asking you to let me be a part of the business. I need to keep active, Tess. I'm not used to sitting around twiddling my thumbs. Look at it this way." His wicked smile sent heat swirling through her veins. "If I'm busy, I'm less likely to give you trouble."

Tess decided to store that information for future reference. It also wouldn't hurt to utilize it in the present. Thinking he was through, that there couldn't possibly be anything else he could pounce on that day, she turned around and caught Ben eyeing the white plastered walls with disfavor.

Easily recognizing The Look by now, she automatically tensed. "Now what?"

Ben raised innocent brows. "I was thinking we should do something with the walls, is all. Maybe spruce them up with some paint. Add a little color to the place."

"I think that's a wonderful idea," said Tess. Relieved that he was still apparently interested in surface rather than structural changes, Tess was perfectly willing to let him choose the kind and color of paint when he asked her opinion.

That was before she discovered he had every intention of hiring a struggling local artist to paint a wall mural of nineteenth-century Denton Falls.

"You never said anything about murals," Tess accused when she found out after returning from the farmers' market on Friday morning. "You let me think you meant a new coat of enamel."

"If I'd told you what I had in mind," Ben reasoned, smiling in satisfaction as the apparently hearing-impaired artist blithely continued to sketch in charcoal on the pristine white wall, "you would've told me we couldn't afford it."

He was right. She probably would have—even though it was beginning to look as if the increased sales were taking that argument away from her.

"I'm sure I'm probably just naive and inexperienced," Tess agreed as she hung up her jacket, "but I don't see how a mural is going to improve sales. In fact, it'll probably disrupt business."

Ben waved a dismissive hand. "It's only a temporary inconvenience. Anyway, the mural is a creative response to adversity."

Tess tied on her apron and vowed never to leave him alone in the shop again. "A what?"

"A creative response to adversity," he repeated patiently. "You have a product you want to sell, but customers trickle in. Why? Because they're not fully aware of what you have to offer: great cookies at a fair price."

"I still don't see how the mural fits into this."

"The key to promotion is to get the most for your money. The mural serves two purposes: it spruces up the place and it'll give us lots of free publicity—I've invited a reporter to come view it in progress, by the way. Later, we can follow it up with daily promotions. When are the slowest times for business?"

Dizzy again, Tess replied, "Monday mornings and Saturday afternoons."

"So we either close during those times, or we run specials to bring more customers in. It also wouldn't hurt to cut out the deadwood if you have any poor sellers. But not the pecan chocolate-chips," he clarified with a smile. "Those are irresistible. Speaking of irresistible..."

Tess waited for him to make a pass at her. Instead, he picked up a binder and began flipping through it. "It's not enough just to increase sales. We need goals and controls." As Tess considered her increased heartbeat and total lack of control, he pulled out a sheaf of papers and handed them to her. "You might want to look these over tonight. Then tomorrow we can start talking about cash-flow dynamics and marketing analysis. We need to go over profit management, marketing management, debt management, current assets, quick assets, fixed assets, intangible assets, current liabilities, net worth, cash-flow projections..."

"Stop! I concede that you know more about this than I do." Tess studied him in genuine amazement. "Where on earth did you pick all this stuff up? Not on a racecourse." And not in school.

"I've been reading up on small businesses. And you thought I never cracked open a book," he teased, clearly showing himself to be more complex than she'd realized.

After that, Tess got nervous every time Ben got too quiet. For good reason. After ruminating for another hour, he waited until they were alone, then announced, "The new mural is a step in the right direction, but we need a stronger marketing angle—a theme that people will recognize and respond to emotionally."

"I'm a baker," Tess responded dryly, "not a musician."

Ben ignored that. "How would you feel about using more in the way of old-fashioned recipes? Emphasize the use of wholesome ingredients?"

Relaxing, Tess admitted, "I'd like that." She already used unbleached flour—even though it was more expensive—because it was healthier.

Ben nodded. "Then there's the name—"

"I'm not changing my name for you or anyone else," Tess informed him.

"Not yours," Ben chided. "The shop's. Did your mom come up with the name Cookie Consortium?"

"No," Tess confessed. "I did. It didn't really have one before. Why?"

"It gives the wrong message. Sounds too corporate. Would you object to something homier?"

Tess transferred cookies from the hot metal pan to a cooling rack and braced herself. "What did you have in mind?"

Ben snatched a warm chocolate-chip cookie and bit into it. "Something like Ye Olde Cookie Shoppe. Then we could use the 'Just Like Grandmother Used to Bake' angle in our promotions."

Tess instantly liked the suggestion. "My Lord—" she feigned amazement "—do you think we dare go that wild and crazy?"

Ben's fingers curled gently around her wrist as she gave in to a sassy grin. "I'd like to see you get all wild and crazy."

It might not show, Tess admitted, but her heart was doing wild and crazy things already. "I know what you're up to," she told him.

His fingers laced with hers, Ben guided her hand behind her back and pulled her into the curve of his right arm. "What's that?"

Tess told herself to remain calm. "You're trying to distract me so I won't keep track of the number of cookies you're eating."

Ben palmed the cookie in question and smiled innocently. "What's your definition of distraction?"

He was. "What you're doing. That was twenty-three, by the way, which just lowered our profit margin by maybe one or two percent."

"And you said you were bad at math," Ben murmured, pulling her closer. "Have I told you how much I appreciate your keen business savvy?"

Taking a deep breath, Tess gently disengaged her hand from his and turned back to the counter. "From the way you've been going at it, I didn't think you thought I had savvy of any kind."

"Not true." Ben stood close behind her.

"Now, what are you doing?" Tess asked as he peered over her shoulder.

"Observing." He rested his rougher cheek next to hers, sending awareness of him swirling through her veins.

Tess took another steadying breath. "Observing what?"

"You. And what you're doing."

"I'm baking cookies," Tess pointed out helpfully.

"So I see. Have you tried using a mixer instead of doing it all by hand?" Ben's mouth was barely an inch away from hers.

Forcing herself not to turn and meet it, Tess managed to croak, "No."

"Why not?"

"I like doing it this way."

"How can you be sure you wouldn't like something if you've never tried it?"

Knowing they were no longer talking about baking, Tess replied, "I've never drowned. And I know I wouldn't like that."

"Have you ever been to Paris in the spring?" Ben coaxed.

"No."

"How about London?"

"No."

Ben's lips were pressed against her ear. "Ever been kissed until you forgot what continent you were on?"

Tess swallowed. "No."

Ben brushed his lips against her earlobe. "Decide anything yet?"

Tess had to take a deep breath before she could speak. "About what?"

"About whether or not you think you'd like it."

Tess stared down at the bowl of cookie dough, unable to remember whether or not she'd added baking soda. "I never make hasty judgments."

"Yes, you do." His hands on her waist, Ben turned her around.

Facing him, Tess felt dizzy as her gaze met his. "About what?"

"Me, for one thing." Ben's mouth brushed hers. "You think I'm trouble."

Her body weak with wanting, Tess managed to step away before her next customer walked in. She didn't think Ben was trouble; she *knew* he was. The kind that began, Tess realized in dismay, with a capital *T*.

Determined to come up with some way to keep him at a distance before she fell totally under his spell, Tess was still without a plan when Judith stopped by the shop, just after closing.

"You look frazzled," Judith said, entering and closing the door behind her.

"Never mind frazzled." Tess pushed her hair off her forehead. "Do I look sane?"

"Just barely." Judith flopped onto a chair. "What's the problem?"

"The problem," replied Tess, bringing her friend a cup of coffee, "is Ben Young." And how she reacted to him. "You just missed him, by the way."

"I take that to mean he decided to take an interest in the shop, after all," Judith surmised. "Is he the one who put that sparkle in your eye?"

"That's not sparkle," Tess contradicted. "That's murder."

"Looks more like exasperation to me." Judith grinned over her coffee cup. "What's the matter? Doesn't he know how to behave himself?"

"That's hard to say," Tess acknowledged, cleaning off the counter. "I'm not sure I've seen him behave yet. He's a very tactile person."

"Busy hands are happy hands," Judith murmured.

Tess sighed. "I think they're more like roamin' hands."

Judith shrugged. "Roamin' hands are looking for something to fill them. Put him to work. Goodness knows, you could use help around here."

"I've considered that approach," Tess confessed. "But if I keep him busy, he won't rest. If he doesn't rest, he won't mend. And if he doesn't mend, he won't leave and go back to racing."

"You're not in a hurry to get rid of him because you're falling for him, are you?"

Tess raised her chin. "Certainly not."

"You mean you are falling for him and don't want to. Don't bother to deny it," Judith advised, as Tess opened her mouth to do just that. "It's all over your face every time you start talking about him. The only reason you're not acting on it is because you're still hurt from what happened between you and Randall McNary."

"Randall," Tess stated firmly, "has absolutely nothing to do with this."

"Randall," Judith corrected, "has everything to do with this, and you know it. Look, I know you were burned once," she scolded, "but believe me, avoiding men isn't going to guarantee your heart won't be broken again—"

"Avoiding this one might," Tess disagreed. "He says he's just passing through town. I'd like to hurry him up before I do something stupid."

Judith nodded. "Like fall in love with him. I understand what you're talking about. I can't see him sticking around Denton Falls anymore than I can see you traipsing around the world after him. Maybe we could buy him out. Cheryl's been talking about us going into business for ourselves."

Tess told her how much it would probably take to do so.

"Then again," Judith replied, swiftly reconsidering, "maybe we'd better think of something else." As she spoke, Judith tugged off the silver fox jacket she'd recently bought at a thrift store because it "matched her hair." She flung it over the back of her chair, sending a blizzard of fur floating into the air.

Tess waited for the snowstorm to abate before commenting. "I think we've just discovered why that thing was such a bargain. What kind of pelt did you say it was again? Kangaroo?"

Judith brushed off her sweater. "It's genuine silver fox, and you know it. You're just jealous because I saw it first."

"It didn't match my hair." Tess tucked a brown tress behind her ear.

"It would if you'd lighten yours a little like I keep telling you you should. Anyway, you could have bought the beaver coat. That matched."

"That wasn't beaver," Tess assured her friend. "It was musk-ox or mountain goat. No doubt about it."

Judith shook her head in amused reproval. "I still think you ought to go blonder. Dark colors are aging."

So were friends who were frustrated beauticians, Tess reflected. And so were ridiculously attractive men who insisted on flirting.

Cheryl, having stopped next door to check on the latest litter of kittens in the pet-store window, entered the shop and joined the two women. "Lord, those little rascals are cute. If I had more room..."

"Adopt one more kitten," warned Judith, her housemate, "and I'm throwing it, and you, out into the street."

Cheryl gave Judith an injured look. "There's no need to get so excited. I was only admiring them. What's up?"

"Tess is desperate." Judith sipped her coffee.

Cheryl looked from Tess to Judith. "Why?"

"She's falling for Ben Young and thinks she shouldn't," answered Judith. She turned to Tess. "How about a vacation? You could use one."

Tess shook her head. "I don't dare go away. He's already come up with at least fifty things he'd like to change, and all I did was leave him at the shop while I went to the farmers' market. Who knows what he'd do if I actually left town?"

"Are his suggestions bad, then?" Cheryl asked in a consoling voice.

"No." Tess sighed in despair. "They're good ones. If I implemented all of them, I'm certain the shop's profits would go up at least one hundred percent. Every time I turn around he's got another terrific plan." And every time he did, she found it harder and harder to remember why she shouldn't get personally involved with him. "I don't know what to do," Tess admitted.

"Well, don't do anything perspicacious," Cheryl advised.

Tess gave her Cheryl a blank look. "Perspi... What?"

"Perspicacious," Cheryl repeated.

Judith rolled her eyes at Cheryl. "*Perspicacious* means discerning and judicious, which is what Tess is to a fault. I think the word you're looking for is *precipitous*."

Cheryl waved a dismissive hand. "Whatever."

"Don't mind her," Judith advised Tess. "She's been reading the dictionary again."

"There's nothing wrong with trying to improve one's mind," Cheryl said in self-defense.

"I'd recommend it to anyone," Judith agreed dryly. "Especially the last two men you dated."

Cheryl tsked at Judith. "Keep on the subject, would you? It's obvious Tess needs us. You're being positively pococurante."

Judith shook her blond head. "I can't wait until you get out of the p's and start in with the q's."

"Go ahead. Be snide." Cheryl pretended to be miffed. "I'll bet you don't even know what it means."

"Little curator?" Judith guessed.

"It means indifferent," Cheryl informed her. "What *are* you doing?"

In the process of making a list, Tess looked up. "Trying to figure out where Ben's interests and talents lie. I was thinking maybe I could interest him in something besides my shop."

"Sounds positively propitious." Cheryl turned to Judith and smirked. "That means 'presenting favorable circumstances'."

"Your remarks," Judith cooed back, "are becoming pastiche. That," she added, "means superfluous."

"Would you two please stop?" Tess laughed, attempting to arbitrate. "The last time you got going like this, I literally had to jump between you."

"We like to see you keep physically fit," Judith confided.

And Ben, Tess recognized, liked to see her flushed and flustered. He'd only been in the shop two days, and already the man was driving her to distraction.

Driving.

Distraction.

Tess smiled suddenly as the idea occurred to her. That was it: she needed some way to distract him; something to get his mind off her and the shop. If it involved driving, so much the better, since Ben was clearly enamored of cars....

Chapter Eight

Let me get this straight," Ben said the next morning. "You want me to deliver these boxes of cookies to this address. Right?"

"That's right." Tess nodded in agreement. She'd spent most of the last evening trying to come up with an address that didn't exist but sounded as if it did—an address that would have Ben spending half the day looking for it. Already feeling guilty over the deception, Tess automatically tensed as he frowned. "Is there a problem?"

"As a matter of fact, yes. I don't know where this address is."

"I'll draw you a map," Tess offered. Hoping she hadn't overdone it, trying to get him as far away as possible for as long as possible, Tess proceeded to sketch him a map, making it as inaccurate as she dared.

Ben wrinkled his forehead as he leaned over and studied the drawing in progress. "I hate to say this, but that's not helping a hell of a lot."

"You'll do just fine," Tess assured him, stuffing the map in his hand.

Ben continued to hover. "How about you? You sure you can hold down the fort without me? With all the increased business—"

"I'll be fine." Walking him out to the curb, Tess resisted the urge to open his car door for him and push him inside to hurry him along. "My friend Cheryl offered to help out today," she added, having foreseen this problem. "She likes to pop in on weekends and try out her culinary skills. She's what you might call a closet baker." Tess spied the dark-haired Cheryl coming down the street. "In fact, here she is now."

Tess wished Judith could have come to her aid, as well, just in case she needed added reinforcements, but the latter had already committed herself to a Girl Scout camping trip.

"Hi, Tess. Hope I'm not late." Cheryl smiled shyly as she walked up to them. "I gather you must be Ben. I'm Cheryl Gates."

Smiling back, Ben extended his hand. "Tess tells me you're helping out in the shop today."

"I love to bake," Cheryl confessed. "I'd be here all week long if I could."

Nervously tapping her foot, Tess tried to be patient as Ben and Cheryl exchanged pleasantries. Wishing he'd leave before her plan fell apart before her eyes, Tess decided to take advantage of a small pause. Clearing her throat, she glanced pointedly at her watch. "I don't want to be rude, but I really think you ought to be going now—"

Ben turned and focused his very direct gaze on her. "You're not in a big hurry, are you, Tess?"

Tess's eyes opened wide at the purred query. "No, of course not, but—"

Ben smiled, showing off his straight, white teeth. "Good."

For a reason she couldn't quite put a finger on, Tess felt a frisson of alarm shimmy up her spine when Ben looked at Cheryl and said, "I'd like to have a word with Tess for a moment. Would you mind keeping an eye on things while we talk?" Tess watched in dismay as Cheryl deserted her to wait on a customer. Her skin prickled as Ben smiled at her knowingly. "You're not trying to get me out of the way for some reason, are you, Tess?"

Standing on the curb, Tess gave him a wide-eyed look of innocence. "Who? Me?"

"Yes, you." He shook his head in amusement at her and added, "It wouldn't surprise me if you were. I've been toying with a similar idea myself."

Tess surveyed him with hopeful caution. "You have?"

"Sure, except in reverse. You're the one who needs to get away from the shop. Not me. Admit it: you're overworked and overtired, and my being here hasn't helped. In fact it's made it worse."

"Lots of people are overworked," Tess countered, nearly breaking her jaw as she stifled a yawn from having stayed up late the night before.

"But not all of them have friends who are willing and able to take over," Ben reasoned. He shoved a hand through his dark hair. "Look, why don't you come with me? We could make the delivery together, have a little fun afterward. There's a fair over in Foley this afternoon. There'll be food, music and entertainment. It's just what the doctor ordered. And you know it."

It surprised Tess how appealing the suggestion was, considering that her plan had been to get him away from her. "I couldn't leave Cheryl alone—"

"Sure, you could. No one's indispensable, Tess. I'm sure she'd manage just fine. You've already baked enough cookies this morning to last for hours. But if you're worried, why don't you ask my mom to help?"

A soft, familiar voice came from directly behind Tess. "Help with what, Bennett dear?"

Tess slowly turned to find Dorothy smiling expectantly at the two of them. "Dorothy, I don't—" Before she could finish, Ben beat her to it.

"Tess is afraid to leave the shop in Cheryl's hands, even though she admits she needs a break. She was wondering if you'd mind helping out."

Again Tess opened her mouth to protest, but this time it was Dorothy who didn't give her a chance to speak. "Mind?" Dorothy gave them both a smile of pure delight.

"Why, I'd love to. I've been staying away the last few days," she confessed, "so you two could sort your situation out. I can't tell you how much I missed it. Is that Cheryl there already? I'll just go in and talk to her. I know she'll be as pleased as I am to finally have a chance to do this on our own." Dorothy whisked away in a swirl of pale blue material before Tess could stop her.

"This is ridiculous," Tess protested as she stared after her. "I can't leave the shop like this."

"Yes, you can." Ben stood in her way so she couldn't go after Dorothy. "You're not afraid to go with me," he asked solemnly as she tried in vain to skirt around him, "are you, Tess?"

"Of course, I'm not afraid." She was panicking. The last thing she wanted to do was to climb into his car with him. Who knew what would happen? Especially when she had to confess that the address she'd just given him was a total fabrication.

"Is this the same woman who nearly attacked the city council when they footsied around trying to decide if the town needed Handicapped parking spots?" Ben chided at her hesitation.

"That was different," Tess told him. "I know all the city-council members." And what they would do. And not do.

"You know me." Ben gave her a reassuring smile.

No, she didn't. Not really. Though, the way things were going, if she got into his car with him, that would undoubtedly change.

"I'm not leaving without you," he told her, opening the passenger door, "so you might as well get in."

Tess eyed the gleaming red car with a mixture of admiration and trepidation. "The delivery could be canceled," Tess told him truthfully.

"Do you really want to hurt my mom and Cheryl by showing them you have no confidence in their abilities?" he countered.

"No," Tess admitted, knowing both women had long been willing and able to manage most aspects of running the shop.

"Then I don't see that you have much choice, do you?"

Not as long as he and his mother continued to work in conjunction. Certain that Dorothy's sudden appearance was no coincidence, Tess eyed him in exasperation. "Has anyone told you you're a very frustrating man?"

"Sure. You." Ben contemplated her gray skirt and matching sweater before concluding, "You're not just the most cautious woman I've ever seen, you're the oldest young person I've ever met."

"Insulting me won't get me into your car," Tess told him, bristling at the criticism.

"No? What will? You're beginning to remind me of a teacher I had once," he decided with a shake of his head. "The prim Miss Pimm."

Tess put her hands on her hips. "What's that supposed to mean?"

Ben leaned against the car and folded his arms across his fire-engine red sweater. "It means you don't know how to have fun."

Tess sniffed. "I do so know how to enjoy myself."

Ben raised a disbelieving eyebrow. "Oh, really?"

Tess lifted her chin. "Yes, really."

"When's the last time you did something for the pure joy of it?"

Tess thought a moment. "I went to the movies this week with Dorothy."

"Lord." Ben put a hand to his heart. "And here I thought small towns were dull," he teased. "It's a wonder you survived the excitement."

Tess gave him a dark look. "I like going to the movies with your mother. Just because I'm not an adrenaline junkie like you—"

"Now, Tess," he chided. "Don't get nasty. It's not my fault you're afraid of anything that even resembles an adventure—including me."

"You're not an adventure," Tess decided, still trying to walk around him. "You are a seemingly unavoidable obstacle that won't go away."

"Speaking of seemingly unavoidable obstacles—" Ben continued to block her escape "—you're not the type who runs into stationary objects like trees, fire hydrants and that sort of thing, are you, Tess?''

Tess narrowed her eyes at him. ''No.''

He walked around the car and held the driver's door open for her. ''Then there's no reason for you not to get in and drive, is there?''

Tess could think of all sorts of good reasons for her not to get in and drive the Porsche. So he could goad her all he wanted. There was no way he was going to get her into that overpowered car with him, she vowed.

But he did.

Coaxing and cajoling, he finally persuaded her to just ''try it on for size.'' Knowing he'd never be satisfied until she did, Tess slid cautiously onto the buttery leather seat and placed her hands on the steering wheel.

''You're showing all the enthusiasm of a woman walking the plank,'' Ben scolded as he climbed into the passenger seat beside her. ''What do you expect it to do? Bite you?''

''No,'' Tess responded, ''I'm afraid that's what you're going to do.''

''I never bite before noon,'' he assured her, buckling himself in.

Tess knew, even without looking at her watch, that it was somewhere in the vicinity of 10:43 a.m. Taking a calming breath, she studied the control panel, which looked complicated enough to fly the space shuttle. The car smelled of expensive cowhide and chocolate-chip cookies.

Ben shook his dark head at her. ''There's no need to be so nervous.''

''Yes, there is.'' Tess hesitated, then confessed, ''I lied about the delivery. I made it and the address up because, because—'' Her mind stalled as she tried to think up a convincing lie.

''Because you didn't think we should be alone in the shop together,'' Ben finished for her. ''You can stop flagellating yourself,'' he added as he stretched out his jeaned legs. ''I figured that out about half an hour ago.''

Tess felt her face warm. ''I suppose you're psychic?''

''I don't need to be psychic. You're a worse liar than my mom. Your nose turns bright pink every time you even think of telling a fib. I don't suppose you're interested in learning anything about tire patching and RPMs?'' he surmised as she grumped at him.

"I don't patch tires," Tess told him. "I leave that to the service station."

Ben looked as if he were going to say something, then decided not to. He scratched his nose. "How about braking techniques?"

"I stop for animals, people and stop signs. What else do I need to know?"

"Can you turn a one-eighty?"

Deliberately obtuse, Tess raised her eyebrows. "What's a one-eighty?"

"I guess not. And this is the woman who dislikes being called naive. Why don't you stop giving me the business and start up the car?" Ben suggested. "You know you're dying to drive it. You just don't think you should."

Fervently wishing she wasn't quite so transparent to him, Tess gave in and put in the clutch. Slowly she turned on the ignition, then, easing the car into first gear, she was still marveling at the powerful purr of the engine when she managed to touch her foot to the gas pedal.

The car leaped ten feet forward in less than a twentieth of a second. Startled, Tess stomped on the brakes, which were also finely tuned. The action nearly sent her and Ben through the windshield.

Half afraid to move again, lest something else unexpected should happen, Tess waited for Ben to say something withering. Instead he just commented mildly, "I forgot to tell you, it's a very responsive car."

And she was clearly a very responsive woman—at least where he was concerned, she thought, disgustedly. Because all he had to do was to put his hand over hers to help her guide the car into reverse, and her heart went all fluttery.

"Do you still want me to drive?" she asked after grinding the gears four times in a row. "Or would you prefer me in the back seat?" Tess flushed as she heard how the words sounded out loud. "Forget I said that. Show me something I don't already know." Hearing how *that* sounded, she added hastily, "About driving."

And so he did. Ben imparted an amazing amount of information in a minimal amount of time, teaching her how to brake before a turn, then accelerate out of it for more control, showing her how to turn toward a skid, not away from it, to bring the car back into line. Ben was far more patient than she'd expected him to be. He even managed not to burst a blood vessel when she refused to go over forty, though the car did everything but wrestle itself out of her hands in impatience.

Not sure whether that meant he was being saintly or had merely given up on her driving talents, Tess suddenly realized that her surroundings were no longer overly familiar. "Where are we?" she asked, instantly suspicious. Ben had taken over the steering wheel ten minutes earlier, supposedly to show her a shorter way home.

"Grape festival." Ben guided the Porsche down the main street of nearby Foley.

Tess read the banner strung across the street proclaiming Foley Has Grape Expectations. "Okay, I'll bite. What are we doing here?"

Ben parked the car and climbed out. "We're here to have fun." While she digested that, he opened her door and motioned for her to join him. "You, dear lady, are in dire need of fun."

"Is this another personal criticism?" Tess wanted to know.

"Nope. Just a statement of known fact. Come on, let's see what's going on." Ben grabbed her calmly by the hand.

"I really should be getting back," Tess began in protest. "It's really not fair to Cheryl and Dorothy to leave them alone—"

Ben stopped suddenly and turned on her. "When is the last time you did something for yourself?"

Taken aback by his bluntness, Tess faltered. "Well..."

Ben's mouth twisted in satisfaction. "See? You can't remember, can you? When's the last time you bought something for yourself?"

Tess, firmly decisive, responded, "Yesterday."

"What was it? A silk teddy? Your favorite perfume?"

Tess hesitated, then admitted, "If you must know, I bought myself a new spatula."

Ben clutched his chest. "Such extravagance!" he teased.

"I needed a new spatula!" Tess protested, laughing at his droll expression.

"What you need," he corrected, "is to forget work for a while and just enjoy yourself. Ever had Italian sausage with peppers and onions?"

"No," Tess admitted, hating to prove him right: that she never went anywhere or did anything.

"How about grape pie?" Ben asked. "Ever sampled that?"

"Yes," Tess was pleased to inform him. "Granted, it was only once, but—"

"Ever had it outside in the crisp autumn air?"

Tess looked at him a moment. "No," she confessed.

"A delicacy not to be missed," Ben informed her gravely. With his fingers laced between hers, Ben pulled her in the direction of a phone booth tacked onto the side of one of the few permanent buildings. "I'll get the food. Why don't you call the shop to make sure everything's okay so you can stop worrying?"

Resigned to being as mysterious as clear glass to him, Tess decided to take advantage of the opportunity while she had it. As Ben walked to the pie booth, she dialed the number of her shop.

Dorothy answered the phone on the second ring. "Tess, darling. It's so nice to hear from you. How was the drive?"

"Even more informative than I'd hoped," Tess said wryly. "Ben insisted on giving me a quick driving lesson. I now know how to make one hundred and eighty degree turns and stop on a dime. I don't suppose you knew anything about Ben spiriting me out of town?"

"Ben's taken you out of town?" Dorothy sounded more pleased than surprised. "How sneaky of him. I hope he's showing you a good time."

"Dorothy, he's giving me the business. And so, I suspect, are you."

Dorothy didn't sound the least bit repentant. "I know I've been pushy again, but you needed a day off, dear. Ben and

I agreed this was as good a way as any to make sure you got one. Were you planning on coming back this afternoon?''

"I'm not sure," Tess said. "That's why I'm calling. I thought if you needed me back—"

"Everything is just fine," Dorothy assured her. "There's absolutely no need for you to come rushing back. Where are you, by the way?"

"Foley," Tess admitted. "They're having a fair, and Ben insisted on coming. He thinks I need to learn to relax."

"Well, I wouldn't argue with him, dear. He can be terribly persistent once he gets something into his head."

So, Tess decided wryly, could his mother. Hanging up the phone in bemusement, she turned at Ben's approach. He passed over a paper plate laden with an enormous piece of pie.

"Everything under control?" he asked as they settled on a nearby bench.

"Apparently." Tess smiled wryly as she forked up a biteful of Concord grape pie, thick with fruity sweetness. "Your mother assures me there's absolutely no need for me to hurry back."

"Good." They were interrupted by a pair of girls seeking his autograph. "You know," he remarked to Tess after he'd signed his name to two T-shirts and they were alone again, "except for my mother, you're the only person in town who doesn't seem to want anything from me."

"Everyone else must have more sense than I do," Tess decided.

"Then again," Ben said, rising and taking her hand, "maybe you have more foresight."

Tess doubted that. Women with foresight didn't even consider spending whole days with men like Ben Young. They made their escapes as soon as it was feasibly possible.

Determined to show Ben that she could indeed enjoy herself, Tess laughed and shook her head as he showed every intention of examining every booth at the fair. Rolling her eyes as he insisted on buying her a pair of earrings in the shape of chocolate-chip cookies, Tess removed her more sedate pearls.

"You know I really don't need these," she protested mildly, putting the new earrings on and modeling them for him.

"That's why we're buying them." Ben latched on to her wrist again. "You need to buy something totally useless, now and then. Keeps you young at heart."

Tromping every inch of the fair, Tess was almost convinced she and Ben had seen and done everything worth doing until Ben insisted on hauling her inside the Las Vegas Casino tent.

"I know what you're doing," she accused mildly as Ben introduced her to the intricacies of gambling and she came within one number of winning the latest bingo round.

"What's that?" Even though all the proceeds went to charity, that fact hadn't dampened the excitement of the latest winner, whose whoop nearly drowned Ben out.

"You're trying to corrupt me," she declared.

"You could do with a little corrupting. Hell, you could do with a lot of corrupting." Whisking her out of the crowded tent, he pulled her close and whispered into her ear. "You know what you need, don't you?"

"A bigger set of muscles?" Tess asked breathlessly, loaded down with a basket filled with myriad stuffed animals she and Ben had won by pitching plastic hoops at ridiculously small targets—and hitting them.

"You need to kick up your heels more often." He laced his fingers with hers again. "Speaking of kicking up one's heels..."

Bemused, Tess found herself being led toward a large wooden vat surrounded by a hooting crowd. "Now what are you doing?"

Ben smiled and kept on walking. "Same intention, different location. I'm going to corrupt you, of course."

He led her through the raucous crowd. Then, without warning, he caught her around the waist and lifted her out of her shoes. Too surprised to do more than drop her basket and hang on to his shoulders for balance, Tess tried futilely to wriggle out of his arms as he carried her toward the vat with the clear intent of getting her to stomp wine grapes with him.

"Don't be so fastidious," Ben scolded as he set her down just long enough to remove his own shoes and socks.

"It's not fastidious not to want to step on something other people are going to ingest," Tess protested as he rolled up the legs of his jeans. "It's sensible."

"Nobody drinks this stuff," Ben assured her as he pulled her to the vat. "It's tossed out after the contest."

Tess ignored the claps of encouragement from the surrounding crowd. "You're just saying that so I'll come in with you."

"Are you coming in of your own free will, or not?"

A thrill of excitement spiraled through her at the softly purred words. Tess lifted her chin in challenge. "Give me one good reason why I should."

"This is a celebrity stomp, and I've specifically been invited."

"That explains why *you* should stomp grapes. I'm not a celebrity." Tess dug in her heels.

Rising to the challenge, Ben placed his palm in the small of her back and urged her ahead another foot. "I need a partner."

Tess tried to no avail to hold back. "That's still not what I'd call a good reason."

"Then how's this one? It's for charity."

"What charity?" Tess hedged, having as much fun resisting as he was convincing.

Ben's smile became even more maddening. "The new Denton Falls day-care center. You wouldn't let them down, now would you, Tessy?"

No, she wouldn't. The newly opened day-care facility, jointly shared and supported by the residents of Foley and Denton Falls, was her pet charity—something Ben obviously knew and had no compunction about using against her.

Ignoring the gleam in his eye, Tess put one foot into the cool, sticky mass of grapes and immediately pulled it back out again as they oozed through her bare toes. "I don't think I have the necessary talent for this." She gave Ben a hopeful look. "Couldn't I just make a donation?"

Ben stepped forward, pulling her with him until she had both feet in the vat. "All that's required to stomp is one partner with a raging desire to smash grapes and another partner with a knack for keeping his or her knees out of the way."

What she had, Tess reflected as Ben joined her, was a raging desire to keep her whole body out of his way before she did something she was going to regret. Knowing it was useless, Tess tried to keep as much distance between them as the three-foot-wide vat would allow. But a wildly enthusiastic stomper in spite of his injured leg, Ben was everywhere, seemingly all at the same time. "Keep your head up," he scolded, circling around her. "I can't see what I'm doing."

"I'll tell you what you're doing." Tess dodged his knee. "Stomping on my toes and making a mess of my skirt." Each time he splashed it, she clutched it higher and higher up her legs, to the obvious appreciation of Ben and the hooting crowd—which, she suspected, was exactly why Ben was splashing. She told him so.

"I can't help myself. You have grape calves, grape knees, grape thighs..." His murmured words sent a flush of color up her cheeks.

"If we don't come up with a better plan for stomping," Tess told him, "one or both of us is going to have some 'grape' big bruises."

It took them a few seconds to figure out that they did less damage to each other if Ben rested his hands on her waist, while she placed hers on his shoulders. Then they coordinated their stomping, doing it with such timing that the crowd let out appreciative cheers and whistles.

Tess immediately lost her rhythm.

"You'd better keep stomping," Ben told her. "People are looking."

So they were. Worse, some of them were taking pictures. Tess had unwelcome visions of her grape-spattered legs decorating someone's photo album—until Ben asked casually, "Do you read the newspaper?"

"Why?" Tess closed her eyes and steadfastly smashed a particularly large bunch of purple globes.

"Because I think you and I are going to show up on the front page of tomorrow's edition." Ben sighed. "It's the price of infamy, I'm afraid."

"I'm not infamous," Tess protested. She wasn't even famous.

Ben gave her a cheeky grin. "You will be tomorrow."

She was also going to be purple tomorrow. Their three minutes up, she and Ben were escorted from the vat to a bucket of warm soapy water. "Why couldn't they have chosen those little green grapes?" Tess mused, realizing that nothing short of sandblasting was going to remove the stain on her feet and ankles.

"Because they make lousy wine." Ben handed her a clean dry towel. "Actually those looked like de Chaunac, which make lousy wine, too. But what the heck. You look cute with purple toes."

"I look ridiculous and you know it."

"Would you prefer to have a purple nose?" Ben rolled the legs of his jeans down. "Think of it this way. You won't need to wear socks for a week as long as you wear coordinating lavender outfits."

"You're the one with the weird wardrobe," Tess responded, thoroughly enjoying herself, "not me."

"Not anymore." Ben grinned as he flicked her new earrings.

Staying to give a good-natured hoot or two until the celebrity portion of the contest had finished, Tess and Ben discovered that though they hadn't come in first, they were the recipients of the second prize: bright purple sweatshirts that proclaimed Foley And I Had Grape Expectations, and complimentary dinners at a nearby restaurant.

"The only reason we didn't win first place," Ben complained mildly, pocketing the dinner tickets, "is because Joe Findlay's feet are bigger than mine. He wears at least a 13EEE. All disk jockeys are born with clodhoppers," he told Tess with authority.

"Next time wear snowshoes," Tess quipped. "And drag in a faster partner. I think my career in stomping has just ended."

So had her thinking processes, she decided, if the crazy attraction she was beginning to feel for Ben was any indication.

"Admit it—" Ben yanked his sweatshirt over his head, oblivious to how the purple shade clashed with the red of his sweater "—you're glad I dragged you in with me."

Slipping her own sweatshirt on, Tess pulled a grape seed out of her hair. "You're right. I had a 'grape' time."

Ben clasped her hand in his and firmly led her down the grassy path to the next booth. "Where are we going now?" Tess asked in bemusement.

"To taste some wine and aspire to be wine snobs."

Tess turned swiftly from bemused to alarmed. "Wine made *here.*"

Ben shook his dark head at her in reproval. "It's from some local wineries. What's the matter? Afraid it was handmade by amateurs?"

"No," Tess conceded. "I was afraid it was foot-made by amateurs."

Ben tapped her lightly on the nose. "I told you they throw that out."

"I know what you told me. I figured you were just trying to talk me into something."

"I'm still trying to talk you into something. The wine-snob contest."

"I suppose you're going to come up with some bizarre reason why I should aspire to be a wine snob?" Tess queried, fairly sure she was going to do it anyway.

"I don't have to. It's for charity, Tess. Proceeds going to the local nursing home."

Every time she hesitated, he informed her it was for charity. He clearly thought he could talk her into anything using that approach, Tess reflected wryly. And he was right.

As they approached the largish booth with the purple-and-white striped awning, Tess felt distinctly nervous at the way Ben was smiling at her.

"What'll it be, folks?" The hearty booming voice of the man behind the counter carried halfway across the county. "Red or white?"

"White," Tess said at precisely the same moment Ben said "Red." Which only went to show, Tess reflected, that they never agreed on anything.

The huge man smiled amiably. "How about if I give you some of each and after you try 'em you can pour 'em together and call it rosé if you like?"

"That sounds reasonable." Ben handed Tess a glass of white wine.

"You wouldn't recognize 'reasonable' if it came up and bopped you on the head." Tess took the glass and set it on the counter again. "You taste. I'll watch."

Ben immediately put the glass back into her hand. "This activity requires a partner."

"How can tasting wine possibly require a partner?"

"We've got to try the wines together or we won't be able to feed off each other's comments. Being a wine snob takes imagination."

And her imagination was working overtime again, visualizing her and Ben doing all sorts of crazy things like this in the future, and wondering what life would be like having him around on a permanent basis.

As Tess tried unsuccessfully to put a muzzle on the thought, Ben tasted the first wine, pondered it, then pronounced with imperious dignity, "Brimming with insouciance, with a touch of the intellectual."

Tess looked from her wine to him. "That's ridiculous."

"It's supposed to be ridiculous. Come on—" he coaxed her glass to her lips "—give it a try. How does this wine strike you?"

"It's nice," Tess conceded after taking a small sip.

"Nice?" Ben snorted. *"Nice?"*

"It has a very nice color," Tess added, enjoying teasing him for a change.

Ben rolled his eyes.

Knowing she was entertaining him, Tess offered up a few more innocuous remarks. After a moment it struck her that while her comments were general, Ben's were starting to sound suspiciously personal.

"Innocent, yet sensual," he rhapsodized, giving her far more attention than the wine. "This one has great legs."

"Great *what*?"

"Great legs. The streaks down the side of the glass," Ben clarified, looking impossibly innocent.

Tess eyed him. "Are we still talking about wine?"

Ben's gaze was guileless. "What else would we be talking about?"

With him, Tess decided, you never knew.

He picked up another glass and took a small sip. "Now, this one is youngish, with just enough aging, but a bit on the tart side. Your turn, Tessy."

"It has a few flaws," Tess deadpanned. "But it might be redeemable in a few years—with proper handling."

Ben's amused look let her know she'd picked up the ball and bounced it back nicely. "How about this other one?"

"Charming," she concluded, "but a bit rough around the edges." And so, she decided, was Ben.

Ben nodded in satisfaction. "And the next?"

Tess thoughtfully judged the next wine. "A bit lacking in manners," she claimed, "but it might have potential."

"Now let's try the red." He looked directly at her. "Well-rounded," he purred, "with a great nose and body. What do you think, Tess?"

She thought she was in deep trouble—again. Because no matter how many times she told herself Ben was all wrong for her, it still felt so right to be with him. "I think we're getting awfully anthropomorphic, don't you?"

"It's common to give inanimate things human qualities. Especially wine." His eyes danced with mischief as Tess eyed him in open disbelief. "What's the matter, Tess? Did you think all race drivers were only familiar with words of one and two syllables?"

"Yes."

Ben planted a quick kiss on her forehead. "That's what I like about you. You're so honest. Nary a deceptive bone in your body."

"Speaking of bones—" Tess smiled in apology "—mine don't seem to want to support me any longer. I think I'd better sit down before I fall down."

Ben nodded solemnly. "I have that knock-'em-dead effect on women. I suppose this means you're not quite ready for the helicopter ride."

"Helicopter ride?" Tess had seen it take off and land every ten minutes, but it had never once occurred to her to ride it. "I'm keeping my feet firmly on the ground," she decided. At least, she was trying to.

Ben was gently curious. "Afraid of heights?"

"Yes." But she was more afraid of what was happening between her and Ben. "How'd you guess?"

"You turned a very interesting shade of green when I brought it up."

"How flattering."

Ben tweaked her ear. "Would you mind if I went up?"

"Of course not." She could use the time to repeat over and over to herself why becoming involved with him was such a very bad idea.

"Will you be okay till I get back?"

"I've managed to keep myself out of trouble for the past twenty-plus years," Tess said. "I think I can handle it."

"That's your problem—" Ben ruffled her hair "—keeping yourself out of trouble. It's beginning to worry me."

She was beginning to worry herself, because all he had to do was touch her in the most casual way and she started to hyperventilate.

Ensconced on a bench, Tess recited a litany of reasons why she should avoid him in the future as he climbed into the helicopter and buckled himself in. By the time Ben had finished his ride, she'd almost succeeded in convincing herself.

"What have you done now?" she asked as he returned.

"I thought you might be in need of another snack." Having stopped by yet another booth before joining her, Ben grinned as he handed over one of the potato-filled paper trays. The undersize spuds had been cooked unpeeled, sliced in half and smothered in melted butter.

"Salt potatoes," Tess acknowledged with a shake of her head. The man was obviously determined to sample every known local delicacy.

"You can't get these everywhere," he explained, shaking pepper over his potatoes, then Tess's. "You have to take advantage of things when they come to you." Tess was just starting to wonder if there was a philosophical message buried somewhere in that when he added, "I don't want to rush you, but there's less than an hour before the show."

Forking up the delicious, buttery chunks of salted potatoes still in their skins, Tess watched Ben dive into his with unabashed appetite. "What show?" she asked after a moment.

"Didn't I tell you? I agreed to do an exhibition at four o'clock."

At the too-casual way he said it, Tess came to full attention. "What will you exhibit?"

"My driving skills, naturally. I do have some, you know, Tess."

Tess felt her cheeks burn at his amused look. "I know that. But don't you think it's a little early for this sort of thing?"

"Four in the afternoon isn't all that early."

"You know what I mean." Tess felt slightly frustrated at his feigned obtuseness. "Your cast was removed such a short time ago."

"Actually, it was the last of many casts. I've been out of the hospital for weeks now."

"Oh, well," Tess relented, "that's different, then."

He fluttered his thick lashes at her. "Was that sarcasm?"

Tess knew what he was doing, but she was in no mood to be cajoled.

"What if you spin out? What if the track isn't properly prepared? This is a very small fair. What if they don't have an ambulance standing by just in case?" Tess went through her entire list of "What ifs" while Ben finished his salt potatoes and calmly started on hers.

He waited until she'd stopped to catch her breath, then commented mildly, "You worry an awful lot, don't you?"

As a matter of fact, she did.

"Someone has to show some concern over your physical health. You certainly don't."

"I'll be okay, Tess. I don't take unnecessary chances anymore."

Tess considered him with rampant disbelief. "Really."

Ben smiled back. "Stop worrying so much. I'm not planning on doing much of anything. A few one-eighties, a controlled skid or two. Pretty much what a high-school kid would do, only a little more showy for the crowd."

Tess's stomach clenched at the word. Exactly what, she wondered, did Ben mean by "showy"? She found out within the hour.

Having been guided by a fair official to a reserved seat in the front row of the stands overlooking the small oval track normally used for dirt-track racing, Tess watched in horror as Ben guided an overpowered black car through its maneuvers.

He handled the vehicle with the finesse of an animal trainer enjoining his charges to jump through hoops of fire. Recognizing, even admiring the skill he possessed, but appalled by the chances he took, Tess managed to work her way "backstage" just in time to see him take off his helmet and comb back his sweat-dampened hair with his fingers.

His dark eyes flashed with excitement. "So, what did you think?"

"I admired your skill," she said truthfully, trying to skirt the question.

Ben knew her too well. "But you were worried sick about me."

"Why do you say that?"

Ben lifted her hands, palms up, and silently examined the fingernail marks scoring her skin. "I was a little worried about you," she admitted. Her cheeks felt hot, but the rest of her body felt cold and clammy.

Ben put his arm around her shoulders. "I was in total control. Honest."

Tess wished she could say the same thing for herself.

She felt totally out of control again; torn between wanting to bury her face in his chest out of pure relief, and having a desire to clobber him for scaring her. He had been in control, Tess knew that; hadn't really been in much, if any danger. Even if he had been, it was nothing to do with her since she didn't really care for him . . .

All right, Tess conceded. She did care for him—a lot more than she knew was wise. He made her feel young and attractive and fun to be with, and it had been too long since she'd felt that way. But that didn't necessarily mean she couldn't control her feelings for him.

It took close to an hour before the crowd of admirers, photographers and reporters forming a circle around Ben dispersed. Finally extricating himself from the last of the fans, he came over to her. Still in his metallic blue jumpsuit, he looked as sleek and dangerous as the car he had driven.

"Sorry that took so long." He held his blue and white helmet tucked under his left arm as casually as most people would carry a newspaper. "I haven't been around here in a while."

"It's all right," replied Tess. "I didn't mind waiting." It had given her lots more time to remind herself why she shouldn't be spending any more time with him.

"So—" he checked his watch "—are you ready for dinner?"

"No." Tess shook her head. It was time to reinstitute some control.

"What about our free dinner?" Ben pulled the tickets from inside his jumpsuit and pretended to read. "Says here we have to use them in the next four hours or they're canceled."

"You're lying. Let me see those." Tess reached out for them.

Ben held them away and grinned at her. "Don't you trust me?"

"You must be joking."

"I'm starved. Aren't you?"

Actually she was—as peculiar as that seemed, considering all she'd ingested that day.

"You have to eat anyway. Might as well be a free meal with me."

"I love your reasoning," Tess said dryly.

The truth was, she was beginning to love everything about him. And that, Tess vowed to herself, was why she wasn't going to have dinner with him.

Chapter Nine

Lost?" Tess repeated in disbelief half an hour later. "What do you mean, you're lost?" He was supposed to take her home.

"Lost," Ben explained helpfully. "As in I don't know where we are. I think maybe I took a wrong turn."

"A wrong turn?" Tess repeated incredulously. "How about fifteen wrong turns?" He'd gone around in circles so much that she didn't have any idea where they were, either. She eyed him with open suspicion. "I thought you said you knew a shortcut."

"I thought I did. Maybe they changed the roads since I was a kid. Look in the glove compartment and see if there's a map, will you?"

Tess rummaged through the assorted papers and found one. Pulling to the side of the road, Ben turned on the overhead light. They peered at it together. "What map is this?" Tess finally asked.

"Utah," Ben eventually concluded, though the ragged-edged thing was nearly impossible to read.

Tess sat back and was about to say something about professional drivers who didn't have enough sense to carry the appropriate maps with them, when Ben pointed. "Wait a minute. Isn't that a light ahead?"

Tess strained to see. "I don't see anything."

Ben started the car and drove slowly forward. "I'm sure I see one."

After a moment it was clear that there was, indeed, a light ahead, though Tess was so totally disoriented she had no idea what it could be. It wasn't until Ben drove into the parking lot that she realized it was the restaurant for which they'd won free dinners.

"Well, I'll be damned." Ben sounded amazed. "What do you know about that? Fate takes a hand once again."

"You," Tess pronounced, "are a very bad man." A sneaky one, too. She'd had every intention of going home. Now what was she going to do?

Apparently she was going to have dinner with him. Ben insisted on it.

"I'm not leaving until I've eaten, so you might as well join me."

Escorted into the publike restaurant perched high on a hill above Naples, Tess gazed out the wide bank of windows across the farthest wall that afforded a view of Canandaigua Lake. Dark mahogany paneling surrounded the high-backed booths giving a modicum of privacy, but there were no romantic vases of flowers, no fluttering candles on the tabletops. There were pewter beer steins filled with pretzel sticks instead. Quiet elegance was clearly not what the owners had intended to recreate. Old Laurel and Hardy movies were shown on one wall. The antics of the Keystone Kops occupied another. There were frothy glasses of beer and upbeat music and raucous laughter. Tess read the motto on the wall above the bar that announced Good Time Charlie's The Name, Fun Is The Aim, and slowly let out her breath. She'd feared Ben would spirit her away to some place dark and dangerously romantic. She instinctively relaxed once she realized that seduction was clearly not what he had in mind.

It took her a while longer to figure out that teasing her was.

She first became suspicious when Ben asked blandly, "Would you like a Fuzzy Navel?"

Tess looked at him. Now how on earth, she wondered, do you answer a question like *that*? No thanks, I like mine just the way it is? Debating her options, she finally settled for "Would you?"

"No. Peach schnapps and orange juice isn't my thing." Ben's slow smile made her lungs stop working. "You're learning, sprout. You're learning."

No, she wasn't, Tess decided in despair. If she was learning anything at all, she wouldn't be here.

Tess played with her spoon. "Don't you take anything seriously?" she asked.

"Sure, I do." He covered her hand with his. "I take your stomping skills seriously. That's why I insisted on this particular table. It's a foot wider than the rest. You'll have to work to get at me," he confided.

Unfortunately he didn't have to work at all to get to her, Tess thought. She was becoming as receptive as a June bug in June. Her heart felt fluttery, her palms felt damp and she was generally physically aware of every single move he made. He couldn't even swallow without her noticing.

"You've never told me what you plan to do while you're in Denton Falls." As a conversational gambit, it seemed a perfectly innocuous subject, Tess figured, if there was such a thing around Ben Young.

"Didn't I?"

Just the way he said it informed Tess that he knew perfectly well he hadn't, and hadn't yet decided if he was going to.

Since he was so fond of putting her on the spot, Tess couldn't see any reason why she shouldn't return the favor. "So are you going to tell me? Or is it some big secret I'm not supposed to be privy to?"

Ben surveyed the relish tray the waitress had set between them. "You're not really interested."

"Yes, I am. I've never witnessed the return of a conquering hero before. It's been fascinating, to say the least."

Choosing a stuffed mushroom, Ben sat back in his chair. "I'm not a conquering hero. The furthest thing from it."

"Tell that to my female customers." Tess helped herself to a carrot stick. "You didn't come back just to see your mother, did you?"

"No." Ben hesitated before conceding, "Actually, I came back to mend and make amends for the sins I committed as a youth."

Tess tried to imagine what kinds of crimes Ben could have possibly perpetrated as a youth that would be serious enough to bring him back to Denton Falls to rectify them. "What kinds of youthful indiscretions are we talking about here? Crimes of passion, I trust."

Ben finished the mushroom and selected another. "Nothing so dramatic, I'm afraid. More like destroying park benches and not returning my library books."

This time Tess couldn't even pretend to be casual. "You came back to Denton Falls because of unreturned *library books*?"

"No, to make up for being a general pain in the derriere, to my mother as well as the community at large."

Tess still didn't know if she believed him or not. "Why?"

"Because as I lay in the hospital for weeks at a time it occurred to me that my life was a series of things left undone—or poorly done. A trail of loose ends the length of the Mississippi has followed me for years."

Besides that, Ben conceded, he'd wanted to return to the town of his youth to see how much it had changed, hoping it hadn't. As much as he liked lambasting it, Denton Falls had never held as much attraction for him as when he'd thought he'd never see it again.

Knowing he'd sounded uncharacteristically serious, he watched Tess frown even as she tried to keep things light.

"Wouldn't it have been easier to just send a check to the mayor?"

"Probably." Unable to stop himself, Ben reached out and caught her fingers with his again. "But then I wouldn't have met you, would I?"

And she wouldn't have met him. Tess realized that the thought disturbed her a lot more than she would have suspected a week ago.

Barely giving the menu a glance, Ben set it down and smiled at her. "Let's try something different."

Knowing she should disengage her hand from his, Tess left it where it was. "Everything with you is different. What did you have in mind?"

"Ordering something neither of us has had before."

Recognizing a challenge when she heard one, Tess shrugged. "Why not?" Determined to be as spontaneous as he was, if for no other reason than to hold her own with him, Tess perused the menu. "How about a squid salad?"

To her relief, Ben shook his head. "Too much like eating rubber bands."

"Soybean burger?" Tess tried again.

"Too—"

"—much like eating sawdust," Tess finished for him with a nod. Scanning the menu, she finally set it down. "Salamagundi," she decided. She knew she'd finally succeeded in surprising him when he sat back and gave her that pulse-pounding smile that made her want to do something even more reckless.

He turned her wrist over. "Shall we make it two?" He traced her throbbing veins as Tess tried to remember how to speak.

Settling for a nod, she watched as he shot the waitress a dazzling smile that guaranteed them very quick, excessively *personal* service. The girl could hardly get over to their table fast enough, Tess observed wryly.

Acknowledging her own thoroughly unliberated tendency to want to please him, Tess swallowed a sip of the dark beer Ben had urged her to try.

Watching her taste the unusual brew, Ben knew he had no right to be, but he was proud of her for throwing her natural caution to the wind, especially since it was so difficult for her. She'd come a long way today toward enjoying what life had to offer. Had stopped to smell the roses, as it were. Ben wondered if she knew how precious that commodity was. How few people seemed to possess it. How much he wanted to possess her.

"Have fun at the fair today?" he asked as their dinner arrived. He studied his plate, knowing that if he looked at her now, desiring her as he did, she'd be out the door in a flash.

With her mouth full, Tess nodded. "I had a wonderful time." She'd had, she realized, a superlative time.

"Surprise yourself?"

Puzzled at the huskiness in his voice, Tess nodded again, this time wryly. "Yes. Surprise you?"

"No. I knew you were a woman with spirit the moment I saw you."

"Spirit." Tess contemplated that. "Is that sort of like lack of common sense and inhibitions?"

"No. It's more like a love of life. The French call it *joie de vivre*."

Tess called it dangerously attractive, and so was he. She circled the rim of her glass with her finger. "Tell me more about yourself."

Ben settled back in his chair. "What do you want to know?"

"I don't know. Tell me what it's like when you're racing—what it's like to go so fast." If this didn't cure her of the affliction she seemed to have for him, Tess decided, nothing would.

Ben seemed to take the request at face value. "It's hard to describe. When you climb into the car and take the first few laps, it seems as if you're going a thousand miles an hour. But speed's relative. Once you get moving, your mind adjusts. By the time you're on the tenth lap or so, it doesn't seem fast at all, even though your pit board tells you you're going, say, 205. Everything seems to slow down. It's almost like slow motion." His mouth twisted suddenly. "It's easy to relax and get complacent, to lose track of how fast you're moving. Things happen fast at those speeds. There's not much room for error."

"It must be mentally grueling," Tess said, getting a sudden vision of hurtling down a track at 200 miles an hour.

"It's physically demanding, as well." Ben sounded relaxed and at ease. "The G-forces you pull in the corners put a lot of strain on your head, neck and upper body. You can get tense sitting in the same position for so long. And you get bumped all to hell. Even though you're strapped in tight, you're sitting on a hard seat. Even on a smooth track, you feel every jolt. After three or four hours of it, you start to feel like you've been in the ring with a heavyweight, taking body blows...."

"But you never get tired of it." Tess could hear the pleasure in his voice. The longing to get back to it.

Ben smiled faintly. "There's nothing like it in the world. It's a very sensory experience. What you feel, see, smell and hear going down a straightaway and into the corners—being in control of a finely tuned machine at high speeds... It's like great sex. Hard to describe."

But not hard to imagine. It was fast and dangerous. A reckless man's sport. Tess weathered a wave of dismay as Ben picked up his beer glass and studied her over the rim.

"How do you like the salamagundi?"

Trying to regain her balance, Tess considered the salami, egg, black olive and cheese concoction slathered on thick chunks of French bread as she wiped her fingers on her napkin. "I love it."

Ben's voice was rough. "You know what I love?"

Tess couldn't help it. Her heart ricocheted, her pulse quickened and her knees felt distinctly jellylike. "What?"

His gaze held hers. "The way you don't seem to care who I am."

Tess could feel her throat close. She picked up her glass of water and took a long swallow of the icy liquid. "Who are you?" she asked.

"See what I mean? You're totally unimpressed by my profession."

Tess shook her head. "Not totally." She was totally impressed by its danger and the fact that it was going to take him away from her—at best, for months at a time; at worst, permanently.

Trying to work her fear for his life into anger to protect her own, Tess asked, she hoped calmly, "When you said you'd come back to make amends, what did you mean?"

Ben played with her fingers. "I want to do something worthwhile while I'm here, make my life count for something."

"I'm sure you've entertained millions," Tess ventured. "That's something to be proud of."

Ben's smile was filled with self-mockery. "I'd like to be remembered for something besides my ability to push a car around a track at breakneck speed. Excuse me," he corrected dryly, "break-*leg* speed."

Sensing she was on the right track, Tess decided to pursue it. "So your accident made you reconsider the priorities of your life?"

Ben cradled her hand in his. "It's a funny thing about seeing your life flash before your eyes. Makes you see how small you are in the grand scheme of things. How unimportant material gain is. How important family and good friendships are. How precious community is. How it should be preserved at all cost. Denton Falls has fallen into something of a state of disrepair. I'd like to change the face of it for the better while I'm here."

Tess pulled her hand away, just to be safe. "What did you have in mind? Erecting a statue of yourself in the park?"

Tess knew her comment was inexcusably bitchy, but she was desperate. If Ben was angry at her, she reasoned, things might cool down between them.

To her dismay, he didn't seem to mind the remark at all. He even smiled. "I was thinking of something a little less...ostentatious."

"Like a small plaque?" Tess guessed. Knowing she was leaping over the boundaries of good sense and good manners, she told herself he couldn't possibly ignore overt rudeness. In fact, she decided, any man of sound judgment would be offended by her suggestions.

To her frustration, Ben simply looked bemused. "No. Like new swings, a climber or two. The park playground hasn't had new equipment added since I was a kid. Renovation is long overdue."

"I suppose this is your way of paying the city back for carving your initials into a park bench when you were sixteen," Tess surmised, searching for another opening to take a potshot.

"Actually it was two benches, and I was fifteen." Ben still sounded infuriatingly calm.

Deciding that if she was going to be offensive she might as well be *very* offensive, Tess acknowledged in a purposefully smug voice, "Guilt is a great motivator."

She knew she'd finally hit pay dirt when Ben sat back in his chair. "I wouldn't call it guilt, exactly."

Going for broke, Tess cooed, "What would you call it?"

"A positive turn of events." Ben tapped his fingers on the tabletop. "I'd like to wipe the slate clean. Do some of the things I didn't do before. Make up for some of the things I did do."

Tess knew she was playing with a loaded gun that was likely to backfire, but she couldn't seem to help herself. "Sounds like guilt to me."

Her eyes widened as Ben leaned over and put his hand gently over hers. "Call it guilt one more time," he threatened in a mild voice, "and I'm going to be forced to make you take that back."

Cool, Tess decided, was a word not found in Ben's vocabulary. Or in hers, either.

Feeling the spark of attraction burning brightly between them, she let her hand remain where it was, knowing it was foolish. "How?"

Ben gently traced a circle on her soft skin with his thumb. "I might have to do something rash."

"Like what?" She ought not to be encouraging him, Tess knew that. But she'd never felt this out of control, this reckless.

Ben leaned forward and whispered into her ear. "I might be forced to kiss you into capitulation."

Feeling the flames of desire flaring hot inside her, Tess licked her dry lips. "You wouldn't do that. We're in a public place."

"Wouldn't I?" Ben stroked the inside of her wrist with his thumb, extending the caress up the inside of her forearm. "A reckless man is likely to do anything."

And a woman without any sense, Tess reflected, making no move to pull away, was likely to let him.

Tess knew, feeling as she did, that it was going to be difficult for her to remain cool, calm and in control as Ben drove her back home. But she didn't know how difficult until he parked his Porsche in her driveway and quietly insisted on walking her to her door.

With every step, Tess could feel the tension mounting between them; the anticipation. By the time they reached her door, the air was rife with it. Nervous, Tess reached into her purse for her keys.

Taking her handbag away before she could locate them, Ben pulled her back into the intimacy of the shadows. "I enjoyed being with you today."

Such a simple statement. Why did it make her heart pound so frantically? "I enjoyed being with you, too," Tess whispered.

Ben reached around her and loosened her hair from its braid. "You're different when you relax. Softer. More open. I like it."

And she liked him, even though she knew that in a few weeks he would probably be gone again and forget all about her.

He speared his fingers through her hair, lifting and separating the silky strands. Tess had never before realized how sensitive her scalp was. Stunned by the tremors his ministrations were inciting, she heard her own quick intake of breath as his left hand settled on the nape of her neck. "Ben, I should go in—"

"Should you?" The words were softly mocking as he brought his lips to her forehead, stilling her instinctive protest.

Realizing her mind was no longer working properly, Tess wet her lips with the tip of her tongue as he lay a path of lingering kisses across her fevered skin. "I need to get to bed."

Ben extended the trail of kisses to her eyebrow, down her throbbing temple, across her cheek. "My thoughts exactly."

Ben's mouth found hers. Tess closed her eyes as he explored first the left corner, then the right, with excruciating thoroughness. Barely able to think, let alone reason, Tess searched frantically for what remained of her resolve. "I meant I have to get some sleep. I get up early—"

"Tomorrow is Sunday." Pressing her back against the smooth surface of the door, Ben traced her upper lip with his tongue. "You know what you're doing, don't you, Tess?"

Playing with explosives. Tess inhaled the tantalizing fragrance of his cologne, mingled with the even more enticing scent that was him. "What?"

"You're putting off the inevitable," he chided softly.

Tess found it impossible to breathe. "What's the inevitable?"

"You and me having a close encounter of the physical kind."

He was right. She was putting it off; because if they should ever become physically intimate, she knew she would never want to let him go. She didn't want to let him go as it was.

A tremor of desire, hot and swift and sweet, shook her as his palm slipped up inside her sweater to cup her breast. Dizzy with desire, Tess melted against him as his thumb gently circled the pink nipple. "Ben..." It came out a sigh.

"Yes, love." His voice was a smoky rasp as his lean hips moved against the softer curves of hers, making her exquisitely aware of his arousal.

"Please. Don't."

"Why not?" His mouth moved with aching slowness over hers. His breath was warm, his lips so very inviting....

Tess struggled for air. "Because."

He ran his tongue over her teeth, sending another wave of heat swirling through her. "Because why?"

Tess summoned up all her remaining strength. "Because," she forged on, "I don't want to get involved with you."

"I know. I don't want to get involved with you, either."

It took a second for it to sink in. Tess opened her eyes and found herself staring into the dark unreadable depths of his. "You don't?"

"No." His expression was calm, almost bland.

Tess felt as if he'd just dumped a bucket of ice water over her head. Ben allowed her to pull away without resistance.

"You don't want to get involved with me?" Tess watched in dazed disbelief as Ben shook his head.

"God knows, I'm physically attracted to you. But we're different people. Too different for anything really serious to develop between us."

The lie came out so smoothly, Ben was ashamed of himself. He hadn't lied to a woman like this since he was nineteen. But this was a special case: Tess was an exceptional woman; she was also a frightened one.

She wanted him, he knew that. But she was going to keep him at bay because of her perception of what he was: a reckless man. He certainly felt reckless at the moment. He wanted to make love to her so badly it gave him the shakes. He wanted to kiss that soft sweet mouth of hers until they both dropped from exhaustion, then haul her off to bed and make wild, passionate love to her for forty-eight hours straight.

He wasn't going to, of course. The situation called for careful handling or he was going to end up hurting her. Careful handling in this case, he acknowledged wryly, meant *no* handling.

He backed away from her with an effort, forcing himself not to touch her. "I think you'd better go in before things get out of hand, don't you?"

"Yes." Tess nodded, confused and uncertain. In spite of his obvious desire, Ben was pulling back and giving her the chance to retreat while she still could.

Accepting her purse, Tess closed her fingers around her keys and unlocked her door. Knowing the opportunity wouldn't be given twice, she took it swiftly, escaping into the safety of her house before she had a chance to change her mind.

Chapter Ten

She looked like a frowsy Marilyn Monroe.

Adding another layer of mascara to her already thickened lashes, Tess stared at her newly lightened hair in the mirror and let out a deep sigh. She knew what she'd done in the last hour had been the act of a desperate woman; but desperate situations, she reminded herself, called for desperate measures.

Ben had been honest enough to admit that he found her physically attractive but didn't want to get involved with her. Readily acknowledging her own inability to remember that she didn't want to get involved with him, either, Tess had decided that if she couldn't seem to resist Ben, then maybe she could make herself more resistible to him by becoming, at least on the surface, anything but innocent. She'd felt compelled to do *something*.

Still feeling unsettled about what had almost happened between her and Ben the night of the grape and wine festival, Tess dusted bright pink blusher on her cheeks. She still couldn't believe how badly she'd wanted him. She'd done everything but make love to the man on her porch, and *that* she'd accomplished later in her dreams.

He was on her mind, night and day. It didn't seem to matter that he hadn't come by the shop the entire week to supervise the installation of the exhaust fan and window awning, the hiring of an accountant and the completion of the wall mural. Instead of banishing him from her mind, his unexpected absence had only intensified her absorption with him.

She was like a woman possessed, Tess conceded in dismay. Even though she knew she was marching headlong into disaster, even though she wasn't sure how much he cared for her in return, she was falling head over heels in love with him.

It was time to take a gigantic step backward before it was too late.

Tess applied shocking-pink lipstick to her mouth and stood back from the mirror to assess the damage she'd wrought. She hoped she wasn't lobbing grenades at her own feet again; that she'd interpreted Ben's remarks correctly. She'd gotten the distinct feeling from what he'd said that, although Ben professed an interest in broadening her experience, what appealed to him most was her conservative small-town-girl image. That image was about to change—drastically.

Tess tugged on the lacy garters attaching the pink and black show-girl outfit she'd borrowed from Judith to the black fishnet stockings she'd finally located, after much effort, in a secondhand dress shop. Neither the bosom-revealing cut-to-the-navel décolleté style, nonexistent back nor the abbreviated length came within light-years of something she'd normally wear, even to a costume party. That was precisely why she'd chosen it for tonight's Halloween bash. It was as daring an outfit as she'd ever worn. It certainly didn't look like something a volunteer chaperon would show up in. She just hoped it didn't shock the rest of Denton Falls as much as she hoped it would shock Ben.

Half an hour later, Tess arrived at the high-school gym, which was redolent of sweaty socks and spiced apple cider. The rafters were hung with black and orange crepe-paper streamers. Surrounded by characters that ranged from the scarecrow in *The Wizard of Oz*, to Freddy of *Nightmare on*

Elm Street, she was halfway across the highly waxed hardwood floor when a blood-chilling chuckle sounded behind her.

Teetering in her strappy black heels, Tess whirled around to find herself face-to-face with the hideously deformed Freddy character. Grinning from ear to ear, the perpetrator quickly unveiled himself, revealing Robby Bellows, Fran's eldest.

"Hi. It's just me, Miss DeSain. Nifty outfit." He sobered at her startled expression, suddenly apologetic. "Hey, sorry if I scared you."

"I wasn't scared," Tess admitted. "I was terrified." She was still terrified. Four-inch heels were much harder to negotiate than she'd anticipated. "That's a very... effective costume. Is your mom here?"

"Yeah." The boy grinned, showing off artificially blackened teeth. "She's over by the back door, handing out doughnuts."

Tess spotted her friend Fran across the room and waved. When she turned back around, "Freddy" was waggling his eyebrows at her. "Care to boogie with a bogeyman?"

"Not just now, Rob, okay?" interrupted a very adult, very familiar smoky male baritone. "I've reserved the first dance."

"Wow. Sure, Mr. Young. No problem."

Promising herself she'd learn the meaning of *cool* if it killed her, Tess turned slowly. "Hello, Ben."

"Hello, Tess." Looking like a pirate in more ways than one, he gave her a long look that threatened to scorch her to her toes. "Glad you could come."

Tess struggled to remain unruffled and unaffected by the warmth in his gaze. At least, she decided, things were progressing between them. This time she wasn't surprised to see him. She'd not only expected Ben to be there, she would have been floored if he hadn't been. In fact, she would have been vastly disappointed, considering all the trouble she'd gone to.

So it wasn't his presence that dismayed her. It was her involuntary reaction to him that was giving her problems. Her heart was beating too fast, and in spite of her scant covering, her skin had a hot, flushed feeling she was sure wasn't due to an incipient illness.

Her only consolation was that she wasn't the only one affected. Robby Bellows appeared almost beside himself. His adolescent voice cracked under the strain of Ben's presence. "I forgot to thank you for coming to talk to our class the other day, Mr. Young. You were awesome."

"I was glad to do it, Rob." Ben seemed pleased by the compliment. "I've always found teaching to be a very...rewarding experience."

Oh, he did, did he? Suspecting he was referring to their driving lesson and the day, and night, it had eventually led to, Tess straightened her back, knowing it thrust her breasts out, putting them in danger of popping out of her underwired bra. She hoped Ben liked learning as much as teaching, because she planned to make the evening an enlightening one.

Ben's eyes slid to her like a magnet's to metal. "Bring a few friends by my place sometime," he told Robby, who was also—unfortunately, Tess realized in dismay—taking note of her form-revealing costume. "I'll give you a few pointers on racing."

"Hey, thanks!" Robby Bellows floated away on a cloud of ecstasy.

As soon as the awed teenager had left them, Ben deftly took Tess by the hand. "Where are you taking me?" she asked as he guided her to the middle of the gym's polished floor.

"I'm shanghaiing you. Pirates do that sort of thing, you know."

"Pirates must tell fibs, as well," Tess concluded as the band began to play. "I don't remember you reserving the first dance with me."

"That's not surprising." Ben's expression was impossible to read. "I understand the memory is first thing that goes when you fall in love."

Hoping her own expression was equally inscrutable, Tess eyed his outlandishly theatrical pirate costume, studying the billowing sleeves of his black satin shirt and the purple-and-pink polka-dot scarf jauntily tied around his head. "When does a person's sense of color go?"

Ben's quick smile did strange things to her heart rate. "Same time."

Concluding that he was teasing, Tess wondered how long it would take him to mention her outfit. She tensed in anticipation as he clasped both hands behind the small of her back and moved to the music. "You've changed."

Tess automatically straightened her arms to put more distance between her body and his. Of course, she'd changed. She used to be sane and sensible, and now she was totally confused. She prayed she wouldn't slide out of her costume, which barely covered her breasts. Remembering why she'd worn it in the first place, Tess tried to instill a sexy huskiness into her voice. "Is that a compliment? Or an observation?"

"Both." Rearranging her arms so that they lay around his neck, Ben rested his cheek against hers. "Is your hair lighter than it used to be?"

Yes, Tess silently conceded, and so was her head. Vowing not to melt into the warm bared V of skin exposed by his half-open shirt, Tess took a calming breath. "What do you mean by lighter?"

His bearded cheek scraped against her skin, sending her pulse rate soaring. "What do you mean, what do I mean? I mean lighter. Blonder."

Hoping her dangling rhinestone earrings didn't end up cutting and scarring one or both of them, Tess leaned away. "Does it look blonder?" she asked innocently.

"As a matter of fact, yes. By about two shades. You haven't fallen for the ad blitz about blondes having more fun, have you?"

"No," Tess purred. She was fairly certain being around him meant having more fun, however.

Removing her arms from his neck she planted her palms against his chest and tried not to think about how warm and inviting his skin felt under the sensuously smooth satin of his shirt, how fluid his muscles felt, how strong and masculine he felt, how it would feel to be loved by him—to make love with him—Tess frantically tamped down the thought.

"You look different somehow," he insisted, whirling her around.

She felt different. Judith had told her that lightening her hair would shed years. The use of peroxide seemed to shed inhibitions, as well. For the first time in her life Tess felt free of restraints, abandoned, almost wanton. Oddly enough, the fact that they were surrounded by other people, for once, only made it worse.

She knew from experience that Ben wouldn't attempt anything improper in a public place, but instead of calming her, all it did was incite her. Ben was under her control for a change. It occurred to Tess that her behavior could be as rash as her clothes; that this time, she could tease and be teased safely, without danger of it getting out of hand. When, *if*, the exchange got too intense, she could simply take shelter among her friends and neighbors. Refuge was a mere step away.

The power of it made her heady—and reckless.

Momentarily forgetting that her original plan had been to repel Ben, not to engage him in suggestive conversations, Tess found herself cooing, "When you say different, do you mean better, or worse?" Good grief, she realized, the way she'd said it had sounded almost . . . flirtatious.

"Neither."

Tess pushed away and frowned at him. "What do you mean, *neither*?"

Ben pulled her close again. She could almost feel him smiling against her tousled honey-gold hair. "I mean it looks good either way. You don't have to change, Tess. You were just fine the way you were. More than fine."

"This from the man who's compared me to everything from a nun to a baked potato," Tess reminded him, hoping that comment meant what she thought it did: that he liked the "before" better than the "after."

"I was incorrigible then," Ben told her. "I'm more reasonable now."

"Are you trying to encourage me?" she purred back. "Or discourage me?" She couldn't believe she'd said that!

Neither, apparently, could Ben.

"Keep this up," he promised, his smoky eyes on a level with her wide brown ones, "and I'm likely to show you. We're feeling plucky tonight, aren't we, love?"

Tess's blood sang with excitement even as she averted her gaze. "I don't know what you're talking about."

"Yes, you do. Did you bake the cookies for tonight? Yes?" His mouth curved as Tess nodded cautiously. She wondered if he was going to take her to task for making the donation when the shop still wasn't firmly in the black yet. Instead, he smiled slightly. "I thought so."

Unable to stop herself, Tess demanded, "Aren't you going to tell me I shouldn't be giving away cookies, I should be selling them?"

"Not me. Besides contributing to a worthy cause, it's a wonderful advertisement for the shop. Nobody bakes cookies like you do."

Determined to rechannel the conversation, Tess moved her hips so that they briefly brushed his. "Nobody eats cookies like you do." She teasingly traced a pattern on his satin shirt front with the tips of her inch-long artificial neon-pink nails, letting a sultry huskiness creep into her voice. "You must be a man of...huge appetites."

He was also a man with very expressive eyes. And at the moment they promised retribution. Ben's voice dropped to a soft growl. "Keep that up, and you're likely to find out, sweetheart."

The mild warning did nothing to lessen Tess's recalcitrance. If anything, it emboldened her. "Is that a promise?"

Ben's hands closed more tightly around her waist in response, sending sparks of excitement flashing through her veins.

"You're enjoying giving me a hard time, aren't you?" He sounded bemused, even confused. Tess took it as encouragement.

"I could give you an even harder time, if you like."

Tess wasn't sure what he thought she'd meant by that, but whatever it was, it effectively silenced him for close to a full minute.

Wondering how far she dared push him, Tess counted silently to sixty as Ben guided her around the crowded dance floor without speaking. He was attempting, Tess supposed, to give her a chance to regain control over herself—something she had no intention whatsoever of doing.

"What do you think of my decorations?" he finally asked.

"You did them?" Tess favored him with exaggerated amazement. "What?" she teased. "No cars, no wheels, no auto themes?"

"I tried, but I was outvoted. I seem to be outmaneuvered a lot lately."

He was acknowledging, at least in part, her ability to fence with him. Tess felt a rush of pleasure as the band started into a peppy reggae tune, "Don't Worry, Be Happy," that had been extremely popular the year before. It was how she felt at the moment: carefree and sassy—and bold.

She looked directly into his eyes and felt a warm sensation radiating all the way to her fingertips. She reveled in it even as she feared it. "Did you really talk to Robby Bellows's class?"

"That I did." Looking as composed as she felt nervous, Ben moved to the music with surprising grace, considering he was still limping slightly.

Unused to high heels, Tess concentrated on not stepping on his toes and crippling him for life. "What about?"

"Drinking and driving."

"Were you for it, or against it?"

Melding them together from the waist down, Ben dipped his head and nibbled her ear in mild rebuke. "What do you think?"

She thought they were ridiculously mismatched, and helplessly attracted to each other. Desire flared deep in Ben's gaze as he studied her with an intensity that stole her breath away. Fearing it mirrored the wanting in her own, Tess hastily looked away, only to be drawn back again.

The situation was beginning to look hopeless.

As two reasonably intelligent adults, Tess reflected, they both knew what was happening; they just couldn't seem to stop it. Ben, of course, wasn't trying very hard. She wasn't helping much at the moment, either, Tess recognized. She was clinging to the man like kudzu.

Attempting to repair the damage, Tess intended to desert Ben as soon as the music stopped. Instead, she found herself whisked off to the dance floor once again. "I came to work, not to dance," she protested.

"All work and no play makes Tess a dull girl," he chided.

"You're obviously not speaking from experience with that remark."

"You're right," Ben agreed peaceably. "I've never been a girl. Been close to a few in my time, of course..." The space between them thinned considerably as he spoke.

Tess sucked her stomach in to keep from coming in contact with him. "Aren't you supposed to be chaperoning?"

"I am. I'm chaperoning you. Everyone knows it's the sweet young things that always get themselves into trouble."

"I'm not that young," Tess demurred.

"But you are sweet."

And she was definitely getting herself into trouble. Around Ben, she concluded, it wasn't all that hard to do.

Holding her at arms' length, he devoured what little there was of her lacy costume with his eyes. "I love your outfit. You look so...authentic, so—disreputable."

She was acting fairly disreputably, at the moment, Tess recognized. And it didn't look as if things were going to improve much.

"You look fairly disreputable yourself," she lied, thinking she'd never seen him look so dangerously attractive, so in character. "Did you run out of razor blades?"

"The eleven o'clock shadow is part of my costume. It and the saber come off at midnight. Speaking of coming off..." He put his hand to one of the spaghetti-thin straps holding up her scanty outfit, and slowly slid it over her shoulder.

Tess's blood roared through her veins. "One more inch," she warned lightly, "and I'll use my authority to have you keelhauled out the door."

She didn't add that she had no authority. She had no sense, either. If he actually started to remove her clothes, in her present mood she was likely to help him, not hinder him.

Ben murmured something soft, and sensually Italian, in her ear.

Tess leaned away to look at him. "What was that?"

"I was just complimenting you on your costume."

Tess raised a wary eyebrow. "You barely said a word."

"Sometimes one word is all that's necessary."

It certainly didn't take much more than that to get yourself into trouble, Tess acknowledged. It didn't take much in the way of clothes to accomplish pretty much the same thing, either. Unfortunately, she'd worn the costume to get herself out of trouble, not into it.

"I don't suppose you'd be willing to teach me what you learned in Italy?" She averted her eyes from his mouth but she knew he was smiling.

"I don't think so. In spite of what you're up to tonight, you're much too nice a girl."

Which meant, Tess deduced, that she was going to have to work a little harder to prove she wasn't the nice, conservative, small-town woman he seemed to find so interesting.

By the time the party had shut down three hours later, Tess had racked her brains to no avail. She and Ben had bobbed for apples, served dozens of pieces of pumpkin pie, poured gallons of spiced apple cider and helped supervise an updated version of musical chairs. Ben cheekily called it "musical knees" since it involved the girls sitting on the boys' laps and vice versa as the music ended. For the truly unlucky, it involved the males sitting on the laps of other males.

For Tess, the evening was an unequivocal failure. Knowing that you couldn't get any more hopelessly "rural" than bobbing for apples together, Tess had hoped Ben would leave as soon as the party broke up, but as the gym emptied, he stayed behind and insisted on helping Tess clean up, since only three other people had remained for that purpose. It took her two seconds to figure out he was the co-chairman of the cleanup committee.

"I don't recall seeing you eat anything," he observed, calmly collecting a stack of soiled paper cups while Tess prayed for composure.

"I was too busy dodging you," Tess joked, tossing an empty pie plate into the trash. "I don't remember you eating anything, either."

"I was too busy chasing you," he mocked. He removed his head scarf. "What do you say we make up for lost time?"

Tess felt a crazy spiral of anticipation before she realized that all he intended to do was to feed her. Emptying two pie dishes and a relish tray, he handed her a plate piled high with food. "So much," she protested.

"They're just going to throw it out," Ben reasoned. "So you might as well eat. Besides, you earned it. Actually," he added on a thoughtful note, "you deserve more than just food after all you did tonight. A lot more."

Taunting her the way she'd taunted him all evening, he'd purposely made the remark ambiguous just to provoke her, Tess decided.

Wondering if she could stop him from stirring things up between them, she attempted to skirt around him as he guided her to a pair of folding chairs set against the back wall. "I'm really not hungry," she began.

"Aren't you? I thought you were dying to have someone take you in hand." Gently, he pushed her down onto one of the metal chairs.

She wasn't going to panic, Tess vowed as he sat beside her. Yet. There was still plenty of time for that—she hoped.

Ben ate a forkful of pumpkin pie. "Have fun tonight?" His voice was so bland it would have made TV's Mr. Rogers sound like a radical.

Figuring she might as well be hung for a sheep as a lamb, Tess ate a potato chip and confessed, "Yes. Did you?"

"I make it a point always to enjoy myself."

Tess wished she'd realized that before she'd put on the skimpy outfit. Out of the corner of her eye, she saw him flex the muscles in his right leg. "Tired?" She hoped he was. Because it had just come to her attention that they were suddenly alone. The gym was an empty cavern.

"A little. Stop looking so worried. My leg's fine."

It wasn't his leg that worried her. It was the rest of him. Now that the others on the cleanup committee had made their exit, she wished she hadn't been so brash before—so heedless of the possible consequences.

It was easy to forget yourself when you had loads of people around to protect you, she acknowledged. It was quite another thing to be sassy when you eventually had to pay the piper.

Of course, she reasoned, picking up another potato chip and munching it, she was probably worrying needlessly. Even now that they were alone, Ben probably wouldn't seek retribution—not in a school, and certainly not in the blazing glare of the gym's fluorescents....

A second and a half later, the lights clicked off.

For a moment Tess just sat in stunned silence while Ben murmured, "Right on time. Automatic timers are so wonderfully predictable." That and her stampeding heartbeat were the only sounds in the darkness.

Tess cleared her throat. "Ben?"

"Mmm?"

"You didn't take any of my earlier remarks seriously, did you?"

"I didn't?" Tess was aware of him moving closer to her in the dark. She felt the plate being taken from her hands, heard it being set on the floor.

"I suppose you thought I was being a little... capricious."

"I suppose I did." He pulled her to her feet. In the darkness Tess could barely see his face, but she knew he was close. Very close.

"I can't imagine what I was thinking of."

"Can't you? I can. I've been thinking the same thing for some time now." He led her to a small protected alcove where he pulled her gently, inexorably, into the circle of his arms. "We're alone now, Tess." His voice was soft and enticing, like fur on a cold winter's night. "There's no one here to stop you from doing what you want to do."

There was no one to stop him from doing what he wanted to do, either.

That fact probably should have frightened her, Tess reflected. But it didn't. It excited her. He excited her.

"I was only trying to get you going," she explained lamely. She could tell she'd said the wrong thing again just by the smile in his voice.

"Trust me. You've succeeded." His mouth was so close to hers she could feel his breath, sweet and inviting, on her lips. "You know what we're like together, don't you, Tess?"

Of course she did. Nitroglycerin in a saltshaker. One move and...boom! Something devastating happened.

"We're like fire and ice," he murmured, when she didn't speak.

"Who's the fire?" Tess realized her voice was husky with emotion.

She could almost see him smile again. "Let's see if we can find out."

"Shouldn't we see if we can find the lights instead?"

His hands slid up her bare arms. "I think I can handle this in the dark."

Tess trembled as he guided the skinny straps of her costume down off her shoulders. "Doesn't your leg hurt?" she asked in desperation.

Ben ran his fingers just inside the deep V on the lacy front, freeing her breasts from their flimsy confinement. "What leg?"

"The one that's where it doesn't belong—" Tess inhaled quickly as he eased her knees apart with his own. "Ben..." The word came out in a soft moan as he stroked her bared breasts with his thumbs.

"Yes, Tess?"

A flood of silver heat roiled through her veins as he tugged gently on her nipples. "Stop that."

"Why? Don't you like it?"

Of course she liked it. That was the problem. "We can't..." She moaned softly again as his hand moved around to her bared back.

"Can't what?" He explored the lower portion of her spine, vertebra by vertebra, slowly working his way down to the elasticized part of her costume that skimmed the small of her back.

"We can't do this—" Tess gasped as his fingers dipped inside "—not here in the gym, for goodness' sake."

Ben traced lazy patterns on the exquisitely sensitive flesh at the base of her spine. "Wise people make the most of their surroundings."

"If we were wise," Tess countered, "we wouldn't be in these surroundings." And she wouldn't be in such a pickle.

Tess sucked in air as she realized Ben had abandoned her back. Trying not to think of where his hand was, or of what it was doing, Tess swallowed dryly as he deftly undid the lacy garters attached to one of her stockings. "Shouldn't a custodian be coming by?" she asked desperately as the fishnet hose began sliding downward.

"Not this late."

Tess's eyes widened in alarm as she felt the other garter go, too. "Is that why you insisted on us eating before we went home?"

"Such a suspicious woman," Ben chided, slipping his fingers inside the highest point of the daringly cut legs of her outfit.

"Experience is a wonderful teacher," Tess responded unsteadily.

"Experience was what I was hoping to give you," he drawled.

"I thought what you were giving me was the business."

"That, too."

Tess closed her eyes as Ben gently circled her protruding hipbones with his thumbs. Lord, it was hard to be flippant when what you really wanted to do was abandon yourself to the moment. But if she did that, it would be committing herself to someone who hadn't made any declaration of intention—other than removing her clothes. He certainly hadn't made any declarations of love.

It wasn't until that moment that Tess realized how much she needed to hear him say something that would indicate the depth of his feelings for her. She wasn't the type of person to have sex without love, she acknowledged. What type of person Ben was, she still wasn't certain.

She was clearly about to find out.

Tess stopped breathing as Ben's fingers, following the lacy edging of her costume, moved closer to the core of heat between her thighs.

Panicking, Tess halted his progress with her own hand. "Stop."

Thwarted, Ben left his hand cupped maddeningly over her warmth. "Why?"

"I need to get home—"

He bent to kiss the cleft between her breasts. "I need you."

"Someone ought to be locking up the gym," she tried again.

"The doors lock automatically as you leave." He lifted his head and nipped her ear. "Stop changing the subject."

"I get nervous in the dark."

"I get turned on in the dark." His mouth captured hers, silencing her for a moment. By the time he finally allowed her up for air, Tess had forgotten how to breathe.

"I want you to stop that," she said with conviction. Before she did something she was going to regret in the morning.

"What do you want me to do? I'm receptive to suggestions."

And she was clearly receptive to him. Tess fought for breath as his hand subtly shifted. "That's just the kind of reckless thing I'd expect of you."

"That's not reckless." He pressed her back against the wall and held her there. "*This* is what I'd call reckless."

It was what Tess would have called incendiary. Her bare back up against the cool surface of the wall, she felt as if her body were on fire. She gasped in surprise and pleasure as Ben moved forward, molding his lean body up against the full length of hers, making her totally aware of just how physically aroused he was; how close to making love they really were. The hard shaft of his maleness pressed into her, filling her with longing.

"Ben . . ."

"Shh." Tess's heart hammered in her chest as his hand slipped around her nape. Tangling his fingers in her hair, he tugged gently, tipping her head back so that her face tilted up to his. Then, with a deliberate slowness that had her heart climbing into her throat, he lowered his mouth to hers, capturing her lips in a leisurely exploration so thorough it had her clinging to his broad shoulders for support. His lips never once leaving hers, he probed her kiss-softened mouth with his tongue, seeking entrance.

Tess instinctively tried to pull back and found herself stopped as his hand firmly squeezed her nape. "Open your mouth for me," he coaxed.

Knowing that if she spoke she was lost, Tess shook her head. It took her less than an instant to realize she was lost, anyway. Applying gentle but insistent pressure, Ben took his time, gradually easing her lips open. Tess moaned softly as his tongue slipped inside the warm moistness of her mouth, seeking out her tongue, demanding a response she was only too ready to give. Boneless and aching for more, Tess dropped her forehead against his bared chest—too sapped of energy, of the will to do anything more than murmur, "Beast."

His soft laugh stoked the fire within her, exciting her all over again. "You deserved that, and you know it. You've been asking for it all night."

Listening to his heartbeat—reassuringly steady in contrast to her own wildly erratic pulse—Tess sighed in acknowledgement. "I know."

"You shouldn't play with fire. It's dangerous."

"I wasn't—"

"Weren't you?"

Tess bit her lip at the mild rebuke. "I know it doesn't look like it," she admitted, "but I was trying to douse the fire, not feed it."

The hand on her nape tightened ever so slightly. "Throwing gasoline on a fire doesn't extinguish it, sweetheart. It just burns hotter and brighter. It can get out of control before you know it."

Something in his voice made her stop breathing. Her head came up. She looked into his eyes and saw the smoldering passion there—the danger.

Licking her lips, Tess tried to sound firm even though her heart was frantically trying to escape her chest. "Ben, I want—"

"What do you want, Tess?" His voice was dark and smoky.

Tess swallowed. She wanted him. And he knew it.

"Help me fight this," she whispered.

He released her nape and slid his hands down her bare arms, sending a shiver of awareness all the way down to her bare toes. "I'm not sure I can. I want you, Tess. Even more than before."

"I thought you said you didn't want to get involved with me?"

Tess had said it in desperation; hadn't, in truth, expected him to take her seriously. She wasn't even sure she wanted him to take her seriously. She was surprised when Ben slowly leaned away.

In the dim light his eyes were dark and unfathomable as he brought her hand to his lips, kissing her fingers. "So I did." Tess could feel him withdrawing, both physically and emotionally. "Come on, love. I think we'd better find a way out of here. Making love to you on a gym floor wasn't what I had in mind."

The moment of truth had passed, Tess realized. She didn't know how it had happened, but Ben's mood had swung from lustful to laconic.

Finding her own desire harder to control, Tess fought down a wave of disappointment as she and Ben felt their way slowly toward the green light over the exit.

Outside in the crisp October-night air, Ben seemed even calmer.

"You know," he said after a moment, "we ought to join forces on this."

Tess knew what she wanted to join with him: her body. Lord, it was hard to resist him. And she had to resist him, Tess knew, or there was nothing but heartache ahead for her. They were too dissimilar; too unalike in all the ways that mattered. They wanted different things.

Well, she amended, maybe not totally. Ben seemed to want her nearly as much as she wanted him, but that wasn't encouraging, either.

"What do you mean, 'join forces'?" she asked.

"You know, 'United we stand, divided we fall.'"

She'd already fallen, Tess reflected—head over heels in love with him. That was the trouble. No matter how hard she tried not to be, she continued to be attracted to him. More than attracted: besotted.

"If we work together on this," he continued, "we're more likely to be successful. What do you say we form a union?"

Tess swallowed. She knew what kind of union she wanted to form with him: the physical kind. "What did you have in mind?" she asked, afraid to look at him.

"We stop seeing each other, in or out of the shop. Start dating other people."

Tess felt her heart slide down to her knees. It was an eminently sensible suggestion; the kind of suggestion she hadn't thought he'd ever make. Why didn't it please her that he'd come up with it now?

Because her brain was starved for oxygen, obviously.

"Do you really think it'll work?"

"Of course, it'll work." Ben swallowed his own doubts and put as much reassurance into his voice as he could. "With a simple plan like this, what could possibly go wrong?"

Chapter Eleven

She hadn't seen him in a week and he was all she could think about.

Eyeing the capable repairman who'd arrived to replace Pele's heating elements and thermostat, Tess switched her attention to the two young men braving a cold rain to hang the newly painted Ye Olde Cookie Shoppe sign over the front of the shop. She let out a sigh of deep despair.

True to his plan, Ben had stayed away from the store for seven long days now, but his presence was everywhere. And if she'd been a desperate woman before, she was now a thoroughly distressed one. Unable to work up even the semblance of an interest in her stove's renovation, Tess found herself thinking more and more of Ben—wondering where he was, what he was doing. Two days ago he'd called to ask her permission to repair Pele rather than replace the erratic stove, and it had been all she could do to concentrate on his message and not just his voice.

Her brain had clearly atrophied. Unable to sustain her attention on the workmen outside her front window, Tess gazed at the colorful mural on the wall and knew she was in trouble. In the last day alone, she'd managed to burn four batches of cookies through sheer neglect, and had botched another two by forgetting to add sugar. All because of Ben.

He'd somehow become the center of her universe. That was enough to disturb her. But the worst part, Tess acknowledged, wasn't just that she didn't know what to do about the situation; what worried her most was that even if she could come up with a solution, she wasn't sure she would implement it, if it meant never seeing Ben again.

Unfortunately she voiced her desperation over her preoccupation with Ben in front of Judith and Cheryl during Sunday brunch at their house. Seeing their instantaneous interest, Tess attempted to retract her ill-advised remarks when it became apparent that her friends had decided to intercede.

"Stop sputtering. It's clear you need help," Judith decided, as she ate a black olive. "You just won't ask for it."

"All I need," Tess objected, helping herself to the green salad, "is Ben Young off my mind." And out of her heart, before he broke the latter.

"Not exactly. What you need is another man in your life—to get your mind off him." Judith paused and sipped her raspberry tea. "You aren't actually involved with him, are you, Tess? I mean, this isn't a case of the jitters or anything?"

"I have absolutely no romantic interest in the man." It was appalling how easily the lie had come out, Tess reflected.

Coming around the kitchen counter, Cheryl jumped into the fray. "Why not? Ben Young isn't sensible enough for you?"

"Would a man with any sense at all race cars for a living?" Tess countered. More important, would a woman with any sense fall in love with one who did? "He's everything I don't want in a man," Tess avowed. That much, at least, was true. Her mind repeatedly rejected him as wild and reckless, even if her body had no sense—or self-control.

"Look, Tess." Cheryl sat down at the teakwood table and placed her napkin on her lap. "There's no need to be so touchy on the subject. We know you don't need a man to feel fulfilled. And Lord knows, you don't need one to sup-

port or protect you. It's perfectly understandable to want
someone to share your life with. To have a family with. So
with that in mind—''

"What kind of man would you be interested in?" Judith
finished for her.

Having been in a troubled mood since the night of the
party, Tess took perverse pleasure in listing everything she
thought Ben wasn't. "Someone sensible. Stable. Practical.
Restrained." She elaborated on the theme through most of
lunch. She was even beginning to enjoy herself—until
Cheryl and Judith showed every intention of using the information against her.

"It would be criminal to let this data go to waste," Judith declared, "now that Cheryl and I are in business."

"Business?" Tess stared in confusion at them. "What
business?"

"We finally quit the glass factory," Cheryl confessed.
"We're now coowners and sole employees of DataMate."

"A computer dating service," Judith supplied in explanation.

"I don't need a computer dating service," Tess protested.

Judith ignored her, while Cheryl coaxed, "At least let us
match up your profile with our list of clients. The results
might surprise you."

"Stop muttering. What can it hurt?" Flicking on her
home computer, Judith punched Tess's vital statistics into
the keyboard.

"You don't have to date any of the men if you don't want
to," Cheryl added, curling up in a chintz-covered chair.
"Just look over the list and see how you feel. You'd be
doing us a favor," she added ingenuously. "We're still trying
to work the kinks out of the system. We need the practice."

And she clearly needed her head examined, Tess decided, for even considering going along with it.

Frustrated by her inability to forget Ben, Tess nuzzled one
of Cheryl's kittens as she considered the list of potential
candidates the computer spat out. Vaguely intrigued by the
choices Cheryl and Judith had presented to her, Tess
pressed by Judith to "eeny meeny" if she couldn't make up

er mind, finally agreed to date Marcus Amberg, a com-
puter-software developer who, on paper at least, appeared
o be a safe bet.

Actually Tess reflected, from his description, the man
ounded too good to be true. Which, as it turned out, was
xactly what he was.

"Well?" Cheryl and Judith cornered Tess in her shop the
norning after her date. "How did it go?"

Still wrestling with her conscience, Tess reminded herself
or the twentieth time that no one was perfect—herself in-
luded. "If I were writing a book about him," she con-
essed, "I'd subtitle it: 'Everything You Never Wanted to
now about Computers, but Were Afraid You'd Be Told.'"

Unfortunately, Tess realized, she'd revealed that to her
ate, too. Which was why her conscience was bothering her.

"Marcus wasn't very interesting," Judith surmised as
ess determinedly followed the recipe as she whipped up a
atch of cookies.

"You could say that," Tess agreed dryly.

You could also say that he had absolutely no sense of hu-
nor. Looking blank every time Tess had attempted to
hannel the conversation away from computers, the quiet,
alding man had spent the entire evening regaling her with
ales of algorithms. A normally patient person, Tess had
een bored to tears. Worse, the comparison between the ri-
iculously tedious Marcus and the infuriatingly intriguing
en had had her so thoroughly exasperated, she'd forgot-
en her manners.

"There's no need to look so devastated." Judith dug out
he computer list from her purse. "You've still got alterna-
ves."

"You can't let one man color your view of the entire male
opulation," Cheryl added consolingly.

Yes, she could, Tess decided. One already had. Ben had
nown her that a man could be attractive, funny, interest-
ng and exciting, all at the same time. And now, she real-
ed in dismay, she was having difficulty settling for
nything less.

"At least give the system another try," Judith urged. "Not all our clients are so limited in scope. Take Troy Cunningham, for instance. He teaches biology at the high school during the day, and woodworking to adults at night school."

"What does he do in his spare time?" Tess asked, not really interested.

Judith handed her the folded sheet of paper. "He's into gourmet cooking and he serves as a Boy Scout troop leader."

"I know for a fact that he doesn't know a blessed thing about computers," Cheryl added in encouragement.

"Think of it this way—" Judith smiled brightly "—after what happened on your other date, this time things are bound to be better."

They were wrong.

Tess knew instinctively they were wrong when, ten minutes before her date was due to arrive, Fran Bellows rang the doorbell. "Oh, Tess." With twins Kevin and Kiley in tow, Fran sighed in relief as Tess answered the door. "Thank God you're home." She and the two youngsters stepped inside as Tess beckoned them in from the cold. "I know it's a terrible imposition, but do you think you could watch the twins tonight? Frank's out of town on business, my usual baby-sitter has the flu, and I just got a call from the school about Rob."

"Has something happened?" Tess closed the door.

Fran nodded. "The bus that was taking Rob and the other kids over to Elmira for the football game slid into a ditch and they want the parents to come pick them up. Peter's no problem. He's spending the night at a friend's, but I hesitate to take the little ones. I don't know how long I'll be. Probably quite late. Oh, dear." For the first time, Fran seemed to notice Tess's high heels and dress. "You're all dressed up. Were you going out?"

"It's not important." Tess smiled encouragingly at her friend. "I'd be glad to look after Kevin and Kiley."

"But Tess," Fran said, looking distressed. "I might not get back to pick them until eleven or even later. None of the kids were seriously hurt, but they couldn't tell me if Rob needed to see the doctor or not—"

"It's no problem." Tess put her arm around Fran's sturdy shoulders.

"But Tess—"

"Look." Tess gave Fran a small shake. "You've got enough to worry about with Rob. Let me take the twins. In fact, I insist. And don't worry about picking them up. Let them stay overnight. You know they'd love it. Goodness knows, I've got room." Tess took the bulging diaper bag from Fran and peeked inside. "I trust you have pajamas in here?"

"Plus diapers and half their toys." Fran was known to be inordinately organized. "Tess, I can't ask you to stay home with them when you've got a date—"

"I really don't mind," Tess assured her. "In fact, having them here could be helpful. I've never met my date before. This will give me a good opportunity to get a quick look into his character. Anyway, I'm sure he won't mind. He's a teacher. He's used to being with kids all day. And after all," Tess said, gently coaxing Fran out the door, "everyone knows, any man worth his salt doesn't mind having kids around."

It was clearly not a universal law, Tess reflected wryly when her date arrived eight minutes later. Standing in the doorway, leather-clad Troy Cunningham took one look at the two-year-old twins tossing Cheerios all over her kitchen floor and gave Tess a considering stare.

"If those are yours, I trust your baby-sitter is here?"

"Actually," Tess replied calmly, after he'd refused her offer to take his jacket, "I'm their baby-sitter. I thought we could stay in tonight."

He shook his head. "Think again. I already have tickets for the wrestling match over in Penn Yan."

Oh, he did, did he? "I don't care for wrestling," Tess told him politely.

"You'll learn to appreciate it. Look—" he checked his wristwatch, a studded black leather affair that made Tess think of the Hell's Angels and manacles "—could you put a little speed on and get a sitter here? The first match starts in less than half an hour."

Already disliking the man enough to balk at crossing the street with him, Tess smiled sweetly. "Then you'd better hurry so you'll get there in time. You wouldn't want to be late."

He scowled at her. "I'm not joking. This is your last chance, and then I'm leaving."

Tess fluttered her lashes. "Is that a promise?"

His scowl deepening, Troy Cunningham took a shortcut through her flower beds back to his car. Leaving with a bad-tempered screech of burned rubber, he'd barely backed out her driveway when Tess heard a knock at her back door. In no mood to face door-to-door salesmen or overzealous candidates campaigning for local office, Tess marched briskly to the door. She discovered Ben standing on her doorstep.

"And what do you want?" she demanded.

Looking faintly taken aback at the way she'd practically unhinged the door in opening it, Ben smiled cautiously. "Sugar."

"Don't call me that," Tess huffed. "I'm not your sugar, or your honey or your sweetie. What I am, at the moment, is thoroughly irritated."

"I wasn't calling you anything." Ben's manner was as mild as hers was sharp. "It's what I want. Sugar." He held up a measuring cup.

Embarrassed, Tess felt her neck growing warm. "You want sugar?" she repeated.

"Actually, I don't." Ben's gaze met hers in amused apology. "My mother does. She wanted to know if she could borrow a cupful."

No, what Dorothy wanted, Tess mentally corrected, was to throw them back together, now that Ben had started avoiding her and the shop. And they both knew it. The trouble was, Tess realized, she wanted it, too.

The moment she'd laid eyes on him she'd felt as if the fuse on a keg of explosives had been lit and she didn't have the strength of will to extinguish it.

"You might as well give her what she wants," Ben said mildly, as Tess continued to block the doorway in indecision. "If you don't, she'll just think of something else."

Seeing the truth in that, Tess sighed and let him in. "It never occurred to you to just go to the store and buy some sugar?" she remarked dryly as he filled the bright yellow-and-white kitchen with his very male presence.

"Actually, it did occur to me. Tuesday night I picked up two five-pound bags of the stuff in anticipation of this sort of thing, but they've both mysteriously disappeared."

Searching the highest cupboard for the sack of sugar stored there, Tess stood on her toes. "How much sugar does your mother use in a week?"

Easily reaching over her head, Ben latched on to the sugar and handed it to her. "You'd be surprised."

No, she wouldn't, Tess decided, warming at his closeness. She was beginning to think that nothing Dorothy did would surprise her anymore.

"I like your dress," Ben said when she didn't speak. "Very much."

"Thank you." Knowing that what the ivory sweater dress lacked in color it made up for in clinginess, Tess calmly took note of Ben's white silk shirt, Tan suede jacket and softly worn jeans. The outfit was surprisingly sedate for him. The only spot of color was a crazy lavender-and-chartreuse paisley tie strung loosely around his neck.

Wondering if he'd put it on just to provoke her into remarking on it, Tess remembered what had happened the last time they'd shown an interest in each other's clothes. Praying that her face didn't look as hot as it felt, she asked, "Will one cup of sugar do? Or would you like to take back the bag, just in case?"

She felt awareness prickle across her nerve endings as Ben came up beside her. He leaned against the white counter. "I honestly don't think it's going to matter. It'll probably disappear within a matter of hours, anyway. Tess?"

Measuring out the sugar, Tess looked up to find him studying her with that direct gaze of his she still found unnerving. "What?"

"I know we agreed not to see each other anymore, but would you mind if I hid out here for a few minutes? If I zip right back she'll just think of something else she's in desperate need of."

Tess knew what she was in desperate need of: more sense.

"I promise I'll stay out of your way," Ben added. "You'll hardly know I'm here. Of course, if you're planning on going out?" His gaze skimmed questioningly over her dress, which clung flatteringly to her slim figure.

Tess had absolutely no intention of telling him that her date had already been and left with notable haste.

Knowing that if she had any sense of self-preservation at all she would hand him the sugar and shove him right back out the door again, she found herself saying instead, "I suppose you could stay a minute or two. If," she added pointedly, "you behave yourself."

His lazy smile told her he had no idea how to behave himself—and probably wouldn't, even if he did.

Disconcerted at the way he settled comfortably into her kitchen as if he belonged there, Tess scrubbed vigorously at the sink as Ben pulled up a chair. A handful of Cheerios flew out across his feet the moment he sat down.

Ben leaned over and peered under the antique oak table. "And what," he wondered out loud, "do we have here?"

"Twins," Tess told him.

Ben glanced up at her. "Isn't it more usual to feed them at the table, instead of under it?"

Resigned to being teased, Tess shook her head at him. "Very funny."

He eyed her in amusement, before turning his attention back to the giggling toddlers. "I don't think we've been formally introduced."

"Kevin and Kiley," Tess obliged, "meet Ben Young. Ben, meet Kevin and Kiley." Tess watched in amazement as Ben, in sharp contrast to her "almost date," showed an immediate rapport with the two youngsters hiding under her kitchen table.

Mindful of his mending leg, Ben squatted down to the children's height. "It's been a long time since I've had Cheerios. Care to share?" He opened his mouth.

After a swift assessment, the twins gleefully shoved Cheerios into his mouth—and down the collar of his silk shirt. When the supply of cereal had apparently been exhausted, Ben rose.

"Cute kids," he noted as Kiley, always the more adventurous of the two, attempted to unbuckle his belt. "Yours?"

Flushing at both the comment and Kiley's preoccupation with Ben's belt buckle, Tess replied, "Of course not. They're Fran Bellows's. Don't be ridiculous."

"Why is that ridiculous?"

"Because I'm not, and never have been, married."

Ben's gaze melded with hers. "That wouldn't stop a lot of women."

But it would stop her, Tess acknowledged. As much as she wanted children of her own, she wanted a normal home for them even more. *Normal* meaning one that stayed in one place, with a mother and father who came home every night.

Ben sat on the edge of the table. "You're a very traditional woman, aren't you, Tess?"

Aware of the subtle shift of mood, Tess grabbed a dish cloth and began wiping down the kitchen counter. "You mean quaint and old-fashioned."

"Now Tess," he mocked. "Don't go putting words in my mouth."

"I couldn't." Tess calmly watched him eat Cheerios. "There's no room. Would you like something to drink with those?"

"Sure." Ben popped another one into his mouth. "What have you got?"

Tess peered into the fridge. "Apple juice, apple juice or apple juice."

Ben pretended to ponder the choice. "I think I'll have . . . apple juice."

"Smart move." As Tess poured it, Kiley, giving up on Ben's belt buckle, spotted a pack of chewing gum peeking out of his shirt pocket. "Gum?" she asked hopefully, tugging on his sleeve.

Smiling, Ben squatted down to the child's level and gave Kiley an amused look. "Are you supposed to have gum, young lady?"

"No," Tess answered for her. "They swallow it."

Kevin, not brave enough to approach Ben as directly as his sister but eyeing the gum pack with avid hope, had wandered over to Tess's side.

"I guess I need a magic wand up my sleeve," Ben said. "I don't seem to have anything else I can give you."

"How about the business?" Tess said. "You're pretty good at that."

Ben shot her a quick, bright look that told her he saved "the business" for her, and she could expect more of it in the near future.

Ben distracted the twins from the gum by building them cereal towers. A minute later, he lifted his arms from the table and asked easily, "What have I got on my elbows?"

Carefully keeping her distance, Tess handed him the glass of juice. "What color is it?"

"Pink, I think."

"Then it's probably strawberry yogurt." Tess estimated the cost of the suede garment and hoped it wasn't permanently damaged. "I'll do what I can to remove it if you'll leave the jacket when you go."

"That's not necessary. It was my fault for not looking before putting my elbows on the table."

Slipping off the jacket and hanging it on the back of his chair, Ben continued making towers of Cheerios for the twins, to their obvious delight. Tess watched the three of them for a moment, then found herself saying hesitantly, "I don't suppose you'd care to stay for dinner?"

Ben didn't hesitate at all. "I'd love to."

Tess wondered if she was heading for trouble—again. And decided she probably was. "Before you say that," she told him, "you ought to know it's fish sticks and French fries."

"My favorite," Ben swore solemnly.

Tess raised a disbelieving eyebrow. "I would have thought chateaubriand and champagne were more your style."

"That," Ben scolded, as she served the twins, "is because you jump to conclusions a lot. Here, I'll do that. You've got enough to keep you busy."

Obviously comfortable with children, Ben insisted on cutting up the children's food, and was careful it had cooled down before he let them touch it.

"Ah, a catsup man, are we?" Catching on to Kevin's likes faster than Tess thought he had any right to, Ben picked up the squirt bottle and made a smiling face with it on the boy's plate.

"You're awfully good with kids," Tess noted. "Have any of your own?"

Ben grinned at her. "That was subtle. No, Tess. I don't have any kids. Like you, I'm traditional. I believe in getting married first."

Tess ate a French fry. "So, why aren't you? Married, I mean."

Ben helped himself to two more fish sticks. "Because I never met a woman I wanted to wake up next to every morning." He glanced up. "Does that embarrass you?"

Knowing that just the thought of him in bed had put color into her cheeks, Tess responded, "I wish you'd stop insinuating that I'm some sort of prude."

"I don't think you're a prude. I think you're the kind of woman a man takes home to meet his mother. Speaking of mothers, mine is looking out her window at us."

"Don't you dare grin like that," Tess warned, clearing the table. "Your mom's hard enough to discourage without us looking like we're enjoying ourselves."

His voice was softly scolding. "Aren't you enjoying yourself, Tess?"

As a matter of fact, she was. Which definitely meant she was getting into trouble again.

Ben insisted on helping with the dishes while the twins played at their feet. Cheerios and French fries were rampant underfoot.

"You need a Dustbuster," Ben told her, skirting the worst of the debris.

"Or a dog," Tess agreed, scraping squashed cereal up off the floor.

Ben wiped a bowl and put it away before locating the broom. "Would you settle for a helpful man about the house? For the evening, I mean."

"There's no need for you to do that," Tess protested, making a grab for the broom. "I can manage."

Ben held it out of reach. "Look, it's clear you've got your hands full with these two. Anyone would. Where's their mother, by the way?"

"Fran had to go out of town tonight at the last minute."

"And you had a date, didn't you?"

Tess had wondered if he'd seen her date leave. Embarrassed, she said with false cheer, "Not for long."

Ben swept with surprising efficiency. "He didn't like the kids?"

"No," Tess concurred. "How about you? Have you been dating?"

"No."

Pleased far more than she knew she should be by the admission, Tess turned away and chirped to the twins, "Time for baths."

Ben put away the broom. "Let me help."

Tess tried to sound firmly decisive. "Really, Ben, there's no need."

"Sure, there is." He ignored her protest and scooped up Kevin. "They're tired. And so are you. Come on. We'll get it done with twice the fun, then relax over a cup of coffee together. I even promise to keep my hands to myself. Deal?"

"Deal," Tess agreed reluctantly, partly because she was exhausted and partly because it was as plain as day that the twins were having a ball with Ben around.

Filling the tub and getting both children settled in it, Tess, leaving Ben in charge—at his insistence—had just gone to grab two clean towels from the clothes dryer when she heard Ben's surprised "Hey!" from down the hall. Heading for the bathroom at a trot, Tess rushed in to discover that Kevin, apparently feeling braver than usual, had splashed soap and water all over the front of Ben's white silk shirt.

Tess was torn between chagrin and laughter. Laughter won. "Oh, Lord!" She swallowed a giggle. "I'm sorry...."

"Don't be. That's what I get for wearing prissy clothes into a combat zone. I should've remembered what little boys are like. I was one myself."

Yes, she supposed he had been, though it was hard for Tess to imagine.

"You're hovering. Go rest." He pushed her out the door. "I can handle it from here on out."

Warmed by his insistent good nature, Tess sat in the living room and listened to the twins splashing in the bathtub while Ben sang, "Oh, Susanna," subbing "A banana on my knee" for the usual "banjo."

Kevin and Kiley chortled with glee and squealed, "Nana!" They were clearly enamored with Ben's unusual rendition—and enamored with Ben, as well. And so, Tess admitted, was she.

Ben insisted on reading the twins a bedtime story. Snugly tucking them into her spare bed afterward, Tess expressed her regrets again at Kevin's attack on Ben's shirt.

"Stop apologizing," Ben scolded. "I'll just wear a vinyl raincoat next time."

Next time? Tess absorbed the remark in alarm. What next time?

Standing just outside the kitchen, Ben glanced at his soiled jacket. "I don't suppose you know of any dry cleaners that have experience getting yogurt out of leather?"

"I don't have the faintest idea who to take it to," Tess confessed. "I've never had anything leather cleaned."

Ben feigned shock. "How unsanitary!"

"I meant I've never owned a leather coat, and you know it."

Ben, insisting on teasing, feigned blankness. "How should I know if you've ever owned a leather coat? For all I know, you wear avant-garde leather lingerie."

Tess knew better than to discuss her lingerie with him. As Ben stood grinning at her, she held out her hand. "If you slip off your shirt I'll rinse it in cool water before it's stained."

For the first time Tess could remember, Ben looked hesitant.

"What's the matter?" Tess joked. "Don't trust me with silk? I admit I don't have lots of experience with that, either, but—"

"It's not that." Ben's voice had a strange toneless quality that was unfamiliar to her.

Puzzled, Tess watched him turn away from her. "What is it, then?"

Crossing the room, Ben stood with his back to her. He put his hands in his jeans pockets and studied a mauve and blue Monet print on the wall. "I don't think I should take my shirt off."

Tess studied him in confusion. "Why not?"

He rocked back on his heels. "I don't think undressing in front of you is a very good idea."

He didn't? She'd have thought he would consider it a terrific idea, right up there with her undressing in front of him. What was the matter with him? Tess frowned as he continued to stand with his back to her. She'd never seen him so reticent about anything. He certainly wasn't what anyone in their right mind would call shy. So why was he so obviously embarrassed? "Why isn't it a very good idea?" she persisted.

Ben's steady gaze met hers in the mirror over the fireplace mantel. "I don't want to floor you."

Did that mean he thought she was going to be affected if he removed his shirt? Apparently so, she decided, as he continued to stall.

Tess put her hands on her hips and gave his reflection a cool stare. "Look, you narcissistic oaf. I think I can handle seeing your bare body without going into a girlish faint—"

Without another word, Ben unbuttoned the white silk shirt and slipped it off. It whispered to the carpet.

Tess willed herself not to follow it to the floor; willed herself not to stare, although the latter was just about impossible. She'd had no idea how extensive his injuries had been. He'd never told her his back had been burned.

Tess swallowed dryly. Speech was beyond her. Thought was beyond her. How could she not have realized? But she hadn't. She knew he'd broken at least one leg, but she'd had no idea how seriously he'd been hurt. Except for his limp, his wounds weren't immediately apparent.

"Well?" Ben's voice was challenging. "Are we going to faint, or no?"

Tess wasn't sure. She tried to get her brain to function, but her mind remained a void.

Turning to face her again, Ben bent down to pick up Purrfect, the latest kitten Cheryl had talked her into. Tess watched him stroke the vibrating cat and wished she could think of something calm and reassuring to fill the awkward silence that stretched between them. But she couldn't. She couldn't think of anything at all. She was so afraid of saying the wrong thing, so afraid he'd mistake her stunned reaction for revulsion—

"You could have told me," she finally managed, knowing it was inadequate but would have to do.

Ben's gaze held hers. "I suppose I could have."

"Why didn't you?"

"I didn't know what to say. Or how to say it."

Same problem here, Tess conceded as she licked her dry lips.

"I'm disappointed in you," he said.

Already feeling criminally inadequate under the circumstances, Tess felt as if her heart had just been squeezed in a vise. "You are?"

"Of course. I thought I'd get at least a small swoon."

Tess stared in disbelief. Good grief, he was teasing!

Knowing it was her cue not to take the moment too seriously, Tess laced a lightness into her voice she didn't feel as she replied, "How about if I just dropped to my knees and genuflected instead? It's so awkward trying to prostrate oneself in a dress."

Ben solemnly considered the suggestion. "One knee or two?"

"Two." Tess forced herself to speak, although her throat felt tight. "This dress has a snug skirt. I don't want you to think I'm a woman of high hemlines and low morals."

"I know exactly what kind of woman you are," Ben said, thinking, *The kind men cherished. The kind they protected. They kind they loved.* And that, he realized, included him.

Chapter Twelve

Needing time to absorb the sudden revelation of the extent of his feelings for Tess, Ben set down the cat, using the motion to retrieve his shirt. He was no longer just attracted to Tess, or simply intrigued with her; he knew that now. He'd fallen in love with her.

The funny part was that he wasn't even sure when he'd made the jump to light-speed. But he recognized the exact moment the change in attitude had become clear to him: when he'd realized she'd taken him at his word and started dating other men. He'd felt positively homicidal toward the man leaving her house tonight.

The irony of that hadn't escaped him, considering they'd never actually *dated* each other. She'd fought that kind of attachment. Still fought it.

Ben recognized the emotions flitting over her face. She was afraid of hurting him now that he'd laid himself bare to her. She was even more afraid of getting involved with him. The former was something he feared he was probably going to use against her—the latter, something he intended to remedy as soon as possible. He'd lied to her when he'd said his mother had sent him over for sugar; he was the one ho'd needed sweetening in his life. When you got down to , he needed Tess, period. Especially right now. He needed touch her and be touched. He needed to know that she idn't find him physically repulsive. "Come here, Tess."

Tess felt heat surge through her veins at the husky timbre f his voice. "Why should I do all the work? You've got two egs." An injured leg. She wiped the thought from her mind efore it showed on her face.

"So I do, but if you don't come here, you'll force me to ome after you, and I don't trust myself to do that calmly t the moment."

"Oh, well . . . if you're going to be that way about it—"

Afraid to rock the boat lest he go and get touchy on her fter all, Tess concentrated on putting one foot in front of he other until she was standing before him. He'd slipped his hirt back on, but it hung open down the front. Tess found erself focusing on the smooth muscles of his chest, the atin texture of his skin.

She took a deep breath and inhaled the exotic fragrance f his after-shave, along with the erotically male scent that vas his own. Feeling the fires of desire flaring within her, he said in desperation, "If there's anything I can do—I nean, for your burns—"

Ben took her hands in his. "My burns are the least of my roblems."

Tess latched on to the new subject like a drowning woman eeking any available handhold. "All right. Go ahead and orce me to be reprehensibly nosy. What's the most of your roblems?" She hoped it wasn't terminal.

He contemplated her long enough to make her uncomortable. "I've lost peripheral vision in my left eye. I'm not ure yet how much it will affect my racing—whether or not 'll get worse in the future."

It wasn't terminal. Tess felt overwhelmed with a sense of elief. It must have shown, she realized, because he immeiately picked up on it.

"That strikes you as good news, does it?" His tone was aconic.

"Considering some of the alternatives, yes. You scared me. I thought you were going to tell me you were dying of cancer or leukemia or something."

There was a potent moment of silence. Then, suddenly unexpectedly, he laughed. Not loudly, but in soft surprise "That's what I like about you, Tess. You have a way of simplifying things into good and bad. There's black and there's white, but never any shades of gray with you."

"I wasn't trying to offend you."

"I know."

Tess tried to gauge his mood. "Do you mind talking about it?"

"I'm not sure." His eyes never left her face. "I've never done it before."

"If I ask you about it will you think I'm snooping?"

"Probably."

Tess decided to take that as encouragement. "So what happened?"

"Detached retina, caused by a severe blow to the head." He sounded clinical, almost like a medical textbook. "I hit my head during the accident."

Tess felt almost physically ill as she visualized Ben in a car careening out of control while going two-hundred-plus miles per hour. "I thought all race drivers wore helmets."

"I was wearing a helmet." His voice was as dry as the Sahara. "That's why I'm still alive. Like a Timex, I took a licking, but I'm still ticking."

Reminding herself that his career was why she couldn't afford to get involved with him, Tess licked her lips as he let go of her hands. "I'm still willing to rinse out your shirt— if you want me to, I mean." She was willing to do a lot more than that, she realized in dismay. A lot more.

Ben unbuckled his belt. "You're irresistible when you're contrite."

He was so close she couldn't breathe. "I'm not contrite. I'm..."

"Stunned." Ben finished for her. "I know. Most people are. Don't be so nervous." As he spoke he tucked his shirt back into the loosened waistband of his jeans.

Tess's pulse hammered in her ears. She wasn't nervous, she was appalled—by his behavior and hers. His scars were a vivid reminder of what he had been, of what he was: a man who liked flirting with danger; who liked flirting, period. She watched Ben calmly rebuckle his belt.

"You," she decided, "are a terrible tease."

"Terrible," he agreed. "Come sit down. My legs are giving out on me."

So were hers. Pulled down onto the couch, Tess fiddled with her watch. "It's getting late," she remarked.

Ben sat beside her, leaving half an inch between them. "So it is."

Tess tried not to think about how muscled he was. "Aren't you tired?"

"A little." But he made no move to leave.

Tess glanced sideways in his direction and found him watching her intently. He was waiting for her to make the first move, she realized. Tess considered her options, and went for the safest one: conversation.

"Ben?"

"Yes, Tess."

That sensual purr did terrible things to her composure. She swallowed dryly. "Can we talk?"

"I can think of more exciting ways of spending our time together."

So could she. That's why she wanted to talk. Tess dried her damp palms surreptitiously on her dress, which she suddenly wished wasn't quite so clingy. "You were burned in the accident, weren't you?"

Two seconds passed before he answered. "Yes."

Tess forced herself not to jump off the cushion as he rested his arm across the back of the couch. "I thought racers wore flameproof suits."

"They're flame resistent. They're meant to give a driver time. They don't protect you indefinitely. Nothing protects you indefinitely, Tess."

Not even keeping him talking, she thought wryly. "Do you want to tell me more about what happened, or shall I just continue to use my imagination?"

"There's nothing much to tell."

"Fine." Tess busied herself punching a couch pillow into shape.

Ben remained silent. Tess had counted up to thirty-six before he finally expanded on his reply. "I was trapped. The car was smashed all to hell, both my legs were busted. They couldn't get me or the fire out, at first."

An appallingly vivid vision of what it must have been like, trapped in the twisted wreckage of his car, surrounded by the intense heat of the fire, made Tess's throat close. "I would have been terrified."

"I wasn't feeling too cool and calm myself. For a while there, I thought I was going to end up like a cheap diner special: very well-done." He didn't tell her he still woke up at night with his sheets drenched in sweat. He was having enough trouble getting her into bed with him as it was, he observed wryly.

"I don't see how you can joke around like that. You almost died."

Ben snagged her gaze with his. "I learned a very important lesson. Until the accident, I always thought I was indestructible—Superman on wheels. Now I know I'm mortal."

"Well," Tess responded, "being mortal isn't so bad."

"Not when you consider the alternative." Ben lifted her hair off her neck. "Don't feel sorry for me, sprout. I'm luckier than some. I lived."

"I'm not feeling sorry for you." It was a lie. She wanted to comfort him, do things for him, make it up to him for his having suffered so much.

"Yes, you are."

"No," Tess insisted, trying for a little more believability. "I'm not."

"Prove it."

Tess felt her heart begin to pound. "How?"

"Let me wait on you for a change." Giving her no time to protest, Ben disappeared into the kitchen. He wasn't gone more than three seconds before Tess dashed into her bedroom. Searching her closets and drawers for something nonseductive to replace the clingy dress, she finally settled for a pink sweater two sizes too large and a pair of sweatpants.

Ben emerged from the kitchen ten minutes later. He stood in the doorway and surveyed her. "What the hell have you done now?"

Ensconced at one end of the couch, Tess flushed at the laconic remark. "I put on something more comfortable."

"I hate to tell you this, but when they say that in the movies, they aren't referring to sweatpants." He handed her one of the coffee mugs.

Ignoring his amusement, Tess tasted hers, then remarked in surprise, "How did you know I like cream and no sugar in my coffee?"

Ben gave her a slow smile. "I didn't. I made it the way I like it."

That wasn't what she wanted to hear. She didn't want to acknowledge that they had anything in common. Tess shook her head at him. "You amaze me."

Sitting a millimeter away, Ben played with her hair. "You amaze me, too. Successful businesswoman, devoted friend and baby-sitter, gourmet cook..."

Tess was almost starting to believe he was serious until that last bit. "I make the very best fish sticks," she agreed dryly.

"Actually, you do. They were nice and crispy. Who was the guy who left as I arrived?"

"I don't think the who is as important as the what," Tess told him.

"Okay, I'll bite. What was he?"

"A misguided effort on the part of my friends." Reluctant at first, Tess ended up confessing that Cheryl and Judith had arranged a computer date for her. Ben appeared sympathetic, which didn't surprise her. He was, after all, the object of similar interest from his mother.

"You need to learn to say no," he chided.

"So do you." Tess attempted to lean away. "To your mom."

Ben held on to a lock of hair, stopping her. "It's hard. I owe her. You know, not too many women would put up with this as long as you have."

"You fiddling with my hair?"

"With my mom playing matchmaker."

"Maybe I'm dumber than most," Tess joked.

Ben caressed her nape. "Maybe. Then again, maybe you're nicer."

Tess, still trying to keep it light, quipped, "Well, you know what they say about nice girls."

Ben ran a finger down her cheek. "I could tell you what some of my racing teammates have to say about nice girls." He studied her pinking cheeks with apparent fascination. "Good Lord, you blush easily. So, what do most normal people say about nice girls?"

Sorry she'd brought it up, Tess quoted, "Always the bridesmaid, never the bride."

"Lord, don't say that around my mom," Ben teased. "She's bound to take this whole matchmaking thing really seriously. I'm starting to take it seriously myself." Ben reached past her to click off the lamp.

Caressed by moonlight, Tess felt the sinewy muscles of his shoulder and forearm close around her, gently trapping her in their curve. "Ben—"

He slipped his wrist under her chin, urging her mouth up to meet his. "Yes, Tess."

Tess's heart fluttered wildly in her chest. "You're not thinking of doing anything crazy, are you?"

He pulled her still closer, coaxing her forward until her lips were within a whisper's distance of his. "What's your definition of crazy?"

He was. "Ben, please. I—"

His lips brushed over hers, slowly, sensuously. "Stop panicking." His voice was low and intimate. "All I want to do is kiss you."

Tess wished that that was all she wanted. She let out a soft moan as he nipped her lower lip—playfully at first, then with clearer intentions. "Ben—"

Ben traced her mouth with his tongue. "Yes?"

"We can't do this."

He explored her mouth with his, slowly, thoroughly. "We *are* doing this."

"I mean we can't do it here on the couch," she protested.

"Sure we can." He pressed her back until she lay on the blue and mauve cushions beneath him. "See?" He nuzzled her neck, trailing kisses down her throat to the small hollow where her pulse throbbed.

"Fran might come back. The twins might come in—"

He silenced her with a lingering kiss that curled her toes. "The twins are sleeping like logs. I checked on them while you were in your room."

"You're just saying that because you're trying to seduce me," Tess declared, supremely aware that his knee had just slipped between her legs.

He rested his weight on his elbows and gazed down at her. "I'm saying it because it's true."

"So, you're not trying to seduce me?"

Ben's smile was as dangerous as an open flame. "Did I say that?"

It wouldn't matter if he had said it. Actions spoke louder than words. Somehow—Tess wasn't sure exactly how—he'd managed not only to remove her shoes, along with his own, in the span of two short minutes, but one of her crew socks was missing as well.

"You promised to keep your hands to yourself if I let you stay," she reminded him in desperation, wondering where his hands were at the moment—and what they were doing.

Ben guided her arms out of the way, so that their bodies touched from waist to toe. "So I did. But I didn't say anything about the rest of me."

The rest of him was doing terrible things to her body's thermostat. Steaming inside her heavy sweater, Tess gasped as Ben used his teeth to pull the thick garment up out of the way so their bare midriffs could meet. "It's amazing what you can do without hands," she managed.

"I'm a man of many talents," Ben confided. He was also a man with many tricks up his sleeve; and he was going to use every one of them, if necessary, to make her realize they were meant for each other.

She was right in recognizing that they weren't the same as each other, he acknowledged, but what she didn't seem to

see was that they were different in the very best ways. Like
yin and yang, their personalities fit together like opposing
pieces of a puzzle; and so did their bodies.

He allowed himself another lingering taste of her mouth
and was rewarded with Tess's deep shudder of response. "I
want you, Tess."

Wondering if her need for him was as obvious as his was
for her, Tess fought to keep some semblance of sanity. "I
know."

"Tell me you don't want me," he murmured against her
throat, "and I'll be out of here so fast your head will spin."

Her head was already spinning. Tell the man you don't
want him, a silent voice of reason insisted. But she
couldn't—because it was a lie. She did want him. She
wanted him so much that it was a physical ache.

She took a deep, shaky breath. "I don't want you to
leave."

"I think we may be making progress here." He shifted his
weight. The heat of his body seared her through four layers
of clothing. As Tess rose in alarm, Ben gently pushed her
backward until she was stretched out fully beneath him.
Before she could protest, his lips fastened on hers, stealing
her breath away, robbing her of the will to speak and the
ability to think. Tess moaned deep in her throat as his
tongue sought out hers, dueling briefly with it before inti-
mately exploring the moistness of her mouth.

"Is Fran coming by for the twins tonight?" he murmured, finally freeing her mouth in favor of her throat.

"Fine time to ask," Tess managed, shuddering as his lips
traced a heated path down to the hollow at the base of her
throat and back up again.

"Yes—" he gently nipped her earlobe "—or no?"

"No." Tess felt her insides quiver as he pressed his hips
against hers. He explored her ear with his tongue. "She
didn't think she'd be back until late, so I insisted on keeping the twins for the night."

"Why did you want me to think she was coming back?"
He moved his quest to her other ear, taking his time to explore it at length.

"I thought it might save me from a fate worse than death."

"You've obviously got a lot to learn about sex," Ben scolded.

Tess swallowed dryly. "I suppose you're going to give me a quick lesson, you being an experienced man of the world and all."

"I'm sure as hell considering it." He slid his hands under her sweater. "I didn't think you lied. I thought you believed in total honesty."

Tess sighed. "It seemed to be the right thing to do at the time."

"So is this." His mouth captured hers. The heat they created together seared her down to her toes. "Tess, I don't want to spar with you anymore."

Tess inhaled the familiar, exotic scent of him. "No?"

"No."

"What do you want to do?"

He leaned away so he could look deep into her eyes. "I want to love you—the way you were meant to be loved: gently, thoroughly." His slow smile made her heart thump. "Immediately."

Tess fought to salvage her self-control, but it continued to elude her. It had been so long since she'd wanted anyone the way she wanted Ben.

Actually, she admitted, she'd never wanted anyone the way she wanted Ben; had never felt quite this way before. Tess struggled for coherent thought as Ben's hot, lingering kiss stole it away. She'd never realized how devastating desire could be. How consuming... How exciting... He could ask her to do anything, anything at all, and she would do it.

"This is the moment when you're supposed to say, 'I want to love you, too, Ben,'" he chided. "Or you inform me it's time for me to get lost."

Fighting for air, Tess managed, "I don't want you to get lost."

"Could you be a little more positive? After all, when a man says he loves you, he needs a little reassurance that he's not barking at the moon."

Tess, realizing he was keeping her talking to keep her from thinking, gave him a cool look. "You didn't say you loved me. You said you wanted to love me. Not quite the same thing."

Ben pressed his lips to her forehead. "I warned you I wasn't articulate. You sure you aren't a frustrated librarian at heart?"

Tess shook her head, hoping in vain it would clear it. No, she was just frustrated. She wanted him so badly her knees felt weak.

Ben brushed his knuckles across the softness of her cheek. "Don't be afraid of me, Tess. I'd never hurt you."

Yes, he would. Eventually he would leave Denton Falls and her, looking for new challenges. In her heart she knew that, and yet she still desired him.

She still loved him.

"I want you, Tess—" he brushed his lips across her throat "—the way I haven't wanted a woman in a very, very long time."

"Why?" Tess whispered. "Why me?"

It was a question that had been bothering her for almost as long as she'd known him. Why her and not someone who was far more like him than she was? He could probably have any woman of his choosing. Goodness knew, enough females did everything but throw themselves at his feet. So why had he zeroed in on *her*?

"Because you're special." He traced her mouth with his fingers. "Because you're fresh and honest. You're everything I've ever wanted."

And he was everything she'd always told herself she didn't want in a man: a rover, an adventurer, a man addicted to action and new experiences. A man who would break her heart—if she let him.

He held her face in his palms so that she was forced to look at him. He waited for her lashes to flutter open, meeting her questioning gaze with his very direct one. "Tell me what you see," he commanded gently.

"A handsome man?" Tess answered, trying desperately for some semblance of sanity.

"A frustrated man," Ben corrected, "looking at a beautiful woman." When she dropped her gaze again he lifted her chin. "A beautiful woman," he repeated, "full of intelligence and humor and generosity, with high principles and high morals, whose only real faults are too much modesty, too much humility and an unfortunate tendency toward martyrdom."

Not sure how to respond, Tess said, "You're getting personal again."

Ben smiled, and this time her heart stopped beating. "That I am. And I intend to get a whole lot more personal. You can count on it."

Gently opening her lips with his own, he devoured her mouth, seeming to dissolve Tess's bones, sending her adrift in a stormy sea of emotion. Caught in the maelstrom, Tess clutched at his shoulders. "Ben," she whispered tremulously.

"Yes, love." His voice and touch were gentle as he slid his strong hands over the swell of her hips.

"I've got cold feet."

"Give me a few more minutes and that'll be cured, I guarantee you."

Tess had never known a man who could tell jokes while making love. Finding it nearly as irresistible as the brief, nipping kisses trailing down her throat, Tess sighed. "I mean, I'm nervous. I haven't done this in a while."

"Me either." He coaxed her sweater up and over her head and tossed it to the rose-colored carpet. "Looks like we both need some practice."

"When I say 'a while,'" Tess forged on, "I really mean only once before." With Randall, who hadn't been considerate or patient, or, in truth, a very good teacher.

Ben kissed the throbbing hollow of her throat. "I'm not much better. Looks like we both definitely need more experience."

Tess closed her eyes as he extended the kisses down to the cleft between her breasts. "I'm trying to tell you, I'm not very good at this sort of thing."

Ben abandoned her breasts in favor of the soft skin of her stomach. "I don't believe you. You'll have to prove it to me."

She caught her breath as Ben's fingers found the elastic waistband of her pants. "I'm serious," she insisted, close to tears of frustration.

"So am I." Tess closed her eyes as she felt her sweatpants deftly being removed. "Tess, you're not worrying about the 'after' as much as the 'during,' are you?" Ben asked as she involuntarily pressed her knees together when he showed every indication of consigning her lacy pink panties to the same fate.

Unable to voice her fears, Tess simply nodded.

"That's what I figured." His hands stilled momentarily. "I know it may be hard to believe," he said, his voice genuinely serious for the first time that Tess could remember, "but I'm responsible and reliable when it comes to something as important as this. You don't need to worry."

Not sure if that meant he'd been sure of the evening's outcome, or was simply prepared for any eventuality, Tess settled for a polite "thank you."

His slow smile warmed her and reassured her. "You're welcome, sprout. Now that we've got that out of the way..." He pulled her to her feet. Reaching around behind her back, he swiftly discarded her bra, after a momentary tussle with the back clasp. "Damn hooks and eyes," he murmured, laying a kiss on the curve of her bare shoulder.

"The modern version of the chastity belt," Tess joked, more nervous than she'd ever been in her life.

"It goes along with the modern version of the noose." Ben guided her hands up to the colorful purple and green necktie that had somehow become hopelessly knotted around his neck. "Help me get this damned nuisance off," he coaxed. "It's always giving me grief like this."

Balanced on shaky legs, Tess untangled the offending tie with equally shaky fingers. "If it's always giving you trouble, why did you wear it?"

Ben unbuckled his belt. "I was trying to get your attention."

"Trust me," Tess managed as his hands undid the metal clasp. "You've got my undivided attention."

And in a moment he was going to have the rest of her, too.

Tess knew in her heart that it was what they both wanted. Anxious to end the heart-stopping tension that was all but paralyzing her, she reached out shyly, intending to help him shed his shirt.

Ben captured her hand in his, stopping her. "Not so fast." His low laugh of surprised pleasure excited her even more. "We have the whole evening. Let's make this last more than two seconds."

With her palm pressed against his chest, Tess resisted the strong urge to smooth it down the arrow of dark hair that stopped at the top of his jeans. "I thought you liked fast women."

"Did you, now?" The look in his eyes made her heart pound so wildly, she was certain it would escape her chest. "I hate to disappoint you, but that was a lie made up by a reporter who thought the real me wasn't quite exciting enough for publicity purposes."

"I think you're exciting enough…for any purpose," Tess whispered.

"I think you're pretty damned exciting, yourself." He pulled her closer, until she was standing toe-to-toe with him. The sensation of her bare feet touching his was unbelievably erotic. "Undress me. Slowly."

Suppressing her urgency, Tess slipped the necktie from around his neck, then pushed off his shirt. Both dropped unnoticed to the floor.

Willing to let him set the pace, even though the anticipation of what lay ahead sent both excitement and fear rushing through her veins, Tess mustered up all the calm she possessed. "Now what?" she asked.

Her eyes met Ben's as he slowly lowered the zipper on his jeans. Her heart leaped to her throat as he shucked them and his dark briefs and kicked them to the side. "Now," he said softly, "we light the match."

Reaching out for her, Ben circled her in his arms. The light dusting of soft hair on his chest tantalized her sensitized breasts as his tongue teased her lips, wrenching a shudder from deep within her.

"Oh, Ben." As her knees buckled, Tess melted against him, reveling in the hard maleness of his lean body. Ben's hands slid down over her back to cup her bottom, pulling her up into the cradle of his hips, pressing her against his arousal and driving home his physical need for her.

When neither of them could stand it any longer, Ben lowered her back to the couch, stretching himself over her on the firm cushions.

"God, Tess. You're so beautiful."

He pushed her hair back, gently stroking her face with his fingers—first her cheeks, then her chin, then her throat, extending the caress to her softly rounded breasts, teasing the pink tips with his thumb. Tess moaned softly in pleasure as he smoothed his palm over her abdomen, then moved his caress to trace circular patterns first around her navel, then the slight protrusions of her hipbones. He followed the same path with his lips, kissing her throat, exploring her breasts with his tongue before moving lower, down to the soft skin of her stomach and then farther to the pulsating heat between her legs.

Tess held her breath as he lingered there, and curled her fingers into his muscled shoulders. "If I start to do anything you don't like," Ben said, his voice a rough smoky rasp, "you tell me to stop."

At the moment, Tess couldn't imagine not liking anything he did. He could probably bash her over the head and she'd love it, she was so enamored of him, so much in need of him. And he needed her.

As her smooth legs tangled with his longer, rougher ones, Tess felt a surge of desire and love for him so hot and so sweet she felt as if they'd both been plunged into a caldron of heated honey. After rolling them over so that they lay on their sides, Ben explored every curve, every hollow of her body in intimate detail until she was nearly crazy with desire.

Struggling to breathe, Tess moved against him in wild impatience, seeking release from the tension building inside her. "Ben, please... I'm going crazy... I can't wait...."

"Neither can I, sweetheart." Moving so quickly that Tess gasped in surprise, Ben slid up and over her, joining them together at last, eliminating all the barriers between them.

Cupping her face in his hands, not allowing her to look away, he waited until her lashes had fluttered open again before he spoke. "I'm not going to let you be an innocent bystander, love." His voice was low and intimate, sending a spiral of excitement shimmering through Tess's veins. "This time I'm going to do everything in my power to ensure you're a participant." And then, he did. Spinning her into the whirlwind of his love, pulling her into the mad dance that was desire, he stroked her slowly at first, then faster, faster, until all gentleness was gone.

Unable to get enough of him, Tess inhaled the jungle-musk scent that was him, unable to believe how wonderful he felt; how wonderful he made her feel. Loving him heightened all her senses. Nothing had ever felt so good. Nothing had ever tasted so good. The air had never been so sharp and clean. The dark had never been so mysterious, so enticing.

All her pent-up desire was released, all her hunger unleashed. Wanting to please him, to touch him, Tess speared her fingers through his dark hair. The strands were clean and thick and soft. He tangled his own hands into her golden mane and held her still so that he could taste her mouth again and again, exploring its soft, sweet moistness.

Her arms and legs entwined with his, Tess reveled in the sleek hardness of his body as the thrusts grew faster, harder. He was a considerate lover. He took nothing, but he asked for everything, encouraging her to shed her old staid image of herself, renewing her, coaxing her with gentle words of praise until she was wild and free and abandoned, meeting him caress for caress, kiss for kiss, touch for touch, until finally they both collapsed, exhausted, in the wake of the storm.

Chapter Thirteen

Spent emotionally and physically, Tess lay in the warm circle of Ben's arms and tried to make sense of what had happened. Ben, she knew, was peacefully content with what had just transpired between them.

Tess was panic-stricken.

She hadn't meant it to happen; had meant to keep it from happening, because she knew it was just going to complicate both their lives and eventually make one or both of them miserable. She already regretted it more than she could say. It was like laying a foundation for disaster.

Of course, she told herself with conviction, things could always be worse—though, at the moment, she couldn't seem to think how....

Weighed down by dismay, Tess stared up at the shadowed ceiling. There must be something terribly wrong with her, she decided. The man had as much as told her, flat out, that he desired her body but wanted no permanent involvement with her. So what did she go and do? She gave herself to him, body and soul, knowing perfectly well that for her, at least, it was the deepest kind of commitment. All she'd wanted to do was to not get hurt. Yet what she'd done, she suspected, had just guaranteed it.

"I suppose this comes under the heading of 'making love, not war,'" she finally managed as Ben remained silent.

Ben tightened his arm around her waist and nuzzled her hair. "I suppose it does."

Tess closed her eyes as he extended his exploration to her throat, kissing and caressing the soft skin with his lips. "I don't understand how it happened," she said truthfully.

"Don't you?" Ben's voice was lazy and amused. "Want me to start over?"

Tess swallowed as he moved closer, the very physical evidence of his desire pressing against her hip. He was clearly willing and able to make good his offer—more than willing. Just one word from her, Tess knew, and he'd roll her over and make mad, passionate love to her all over again.

Astounded at how just the thought threatened to liquefy her bones, Tess abruptly sat up, shivering as Ben ran his hand caressingly down her bare arm. "I know *how* it happened." Tess forced a calm into her voice she didn't really feel. "I'm just not sure why it happened." Or what she was going to do about it, now that it had.

Tess pushed her hair out of her eyes and looked around the room. She was mortified by the fact that Ben was taking the entire incident in stride while she was at her wits' end.

At least she would be, if she had any wits left. She supposed it might help if she got some clothes on. Gazing around the living room in search of her pink sweater, she finally located it draped over the end of the couch.

As she reached for it, Ben captured her wrist in his long fingers. "It happened because we are, and always have been, attracted to each other. And you know it."

No, Tess reflected, it had happened because she'd forgotten for a moment who he was, what he was: a man who risked his life for a living.

Carefully extricating her wrist from his grasp, Tess tugged on her sweater and yanked it down as far as it would go over her bare thighs.

Uncharacteristically still, Ben watched her as she rose from the sofa and started searching for her underwear. "You're upset."

Tess jerked the rising sweater down again. "Of course, I'm upset!"

"Why?"

Ben's calm seemed to stretch her own nerves to the breaking point. "Because this wasn't supposed to happen, that's why." Because Ben had never made any secret of the fact that he didn't plan to settle in Denton Falls. And now she didn't think she could stand it if he left. "Seven short days ago we agreed it would be best if things cooled off between us, remember?"

Ben rose to rest on one elbow so he could see her face as she felt under the couch. "So we did." And now she was plainly wishing they could take a gigantic step backward. Damn it, why?

Throwing his bare legs over the edge of the couch, Ben ground his teeth in frustration as Tess determinedly avoided looking at him. Because she was still frightened and uncertain—that was why. She was clearly wondering what their lovemaking meant to their relationship; how it would affect their futures.

He was beginning to wonder the same thing himself.

Torn between wanting to give her time and space and wanting to make hot, sweet love to her all over again, Ben forced himself to sit still on the couch as Tess abandoned her search for her elusive panties and pulled on her sweatpants. He honestly wasn't sure if she needed reassurance or silence at this point. The wrong words at the moment, he suspected, would send her scurrying for safety. In any case, what could he say when he wasn't sure himself if they'd taken the wisest course?

Most women pined for declarations of love and devotion to justify sexual involvement, but Tess wasn't like most women. Far less predictable than he'd first assumed, and infinitely more complex than he'd ever imagined, she might be inexperienced, but she was nobody's fool. It was as plain as day that she realized, as he did, that their deepening relationship wasn't without its drawbacks, so his saying he loved her wasn't likely to reassure her. More likely, she wanted to hear him say it was all a terrible mistake; for him to promise that it would never, ever, happen again.

Although he could lie like a trooper when necessity dictated, Ben felt he couldn't do it this time. He cared for her too much. The trouble was he wanted and needed her, too.

"So," he said, deciding for once in his life to play it safe. "What now?"

If she said, "It's time for you to get lost," he didn't think he was going to handle it well. He'd gone and fallen in love with her. He hadn't thought he would. He didn't even think it was wise. And if he could undo it now, he probably would. He really didn't need any more complications in his life at the moment, and their growing involvement was becoming one very large complication. It seemed so right for them to be together—and yet so wrong.

She was firmly ensconced in her community. Unfortunately it was the same community that he intended to improve and then leave. Unless they came to some sort of understanding, soon, something was going to hit the fan. Likely him, he conceded, if the expression on her face was any indication. She looked as if she couldn't decide whether to love him, or murder him.

"I think," Tess said dully as she retrieved her crew socks from under a chair, "that it's time for us to revamp our original plan."

Ben counted slowly to three before managing calmly, "What do you mean? What plan?"

"Our plan to keep from getting romantically involved when we're so obviously attracted to each other." Tess slipped her socks on as she talked. "Avoiding each other hasn't worked. Dating other people obviously hasn't worked." She refused to look at him when she said that. "So now..."

Ben didn't realize he was holding his breath until she paused.

"So now?" he prompted.

"So now..." Tess paused again. "I don't know," she admitted in confused dismay. "What time is it?"

"A quarter past ten," Ben answered, glancing at his watch.

He'd recently replaced the Rolex with a Mickey Mouse Seiko. It was one of those crazy things she loved most about him, Tess admitted: his sense of the ridiculous. What kind of man would spend over a hundred dollars for a watch with a children's cartoon character on it?

"I suppose you'd better leave." Discomfited and anxious to send him on his way before she changed her mind again, Tess handed him his shirt and jeans, which she'd collected, and waited for him to put them on.

Naked, and planning on staying that way at least for the moment, Ben settled back on the sofa. He had no intention of leaving just yet. He needed time to decipher exactly what, if anything, they could do that would help them extricate themselves from an impossible situation. "Tess?"

"Yes?" Tess had finished putting on all her clothes that she could find and was starting to straighten the living room.

Ben tried to choose his words carefully. "What would you think about us jumping in with both feet?"

He knew just from her stillness that she was going on guard all over again. "Doing what?"

"Don't look at me like that," he scolded, although she'd yet to focus in his direction. "I'm not suggesting anything kinky."

Shifting a chair that probably hadn't been moved in a month, Tess continued to look everywhere but at him. "I'm not sure what you mean."

Ben quashed an urge to cross the room and wrestle her back onto the couch so she would sit still. "It's really very simple." Actually, nothing between them was ever simple, Ben realized, or without complications. But since he was desperate, he decided to plunge ahead before the plan's pitfalls became glaringly obvious. "We go ahead and get involved."

Tess put down the chair cushion. The air around them suddenly seemed too thick for her to breathe. "You mean, become lovers?"

Ben sounded calm, thoughtful. "Not necessarily. We simply stop fighting the attraction. We start seeing each other—exclusively, regularly. We get whatever it is we have for each other out of our systems."

Tess felt as if she were suffocating. It was a suggestion that sent fear, dismay and excitement shooting through her veins. "That's a ridiculous idea. It would never work."

"Have you tried it?"

Tess licked her dry lips. "No."

There had never been the need. She'd never felt so impossibly attracted to anyone as inappropriate as Ben. And even if she had been, no one but Ben would ever suggest such an outlandish solution.

"Look at it this way," Ben urged when she continued to hesitate. "We both acknowledge that we're all wrong for each other. In fact, we probably would never have met a second time if my mother hadn't had her hand in it. And we certainly would never have become partners on our own. Correct?"

Tess nodded slowly.

"If nothing else, this plan will finally get us some peace. My mom isn't likely to keep setting us up if we're already seeing each other," he reasoned. "And we both know that we're better off controlling our own lives than being manipulated by her. Right?"

Tess nodded again.

"So what have you got to lose?"

Just her heart, Tess thought. The more she was around him, the more she fell in love with him, wanted to make love with him. Purposely letting him into her life was, in her view, akin to walking on hot coals with her bare feet and daring something awful to happen.

Something awful was already happening, Tess realized as she glanced out the front window and saw Fran's Pontiac turning into her driveway.

"Oh, dear Lord." Tess hurriedly closed all the drapes.

Sensing her alarm, Ben sat up. "What's the matter?"

"Fran's come for the twins!" Turning the lamp on low, Tess stared at Ben's nude form in horror. "You've got to get dressed and get out of here!"

Ben stood up from the couch. "I thought you said she wasn't coming back for them tonight."

"I didn't think she was! She must have picked up Rob and gotten back to town sooner than she expected." Tess winced as she heard one of the Pontiac's doors slam. "Will you *please get dressed*?"

Ben gathered up his jeans and shirt, but instead of putting them on, he held them against his chest. "Just as soon as you agree to see me tomorrow."

Tess opened her mouth, then snapped it shut. "That's extortion!"

Ben studied her. "What, exactly, is your definition of extortion?"

Tess heard Fran's wooden clogs clomping across the asphalt driveway. Her eyes widened in pleading. "Can't we talk about this later?"

"It's now or never, Tess. We haven't got time for indecision."

She knew that! Furious and frantic, Tess started pushing him, clothes bundled against his bare chest, across the room into the hall. "All right!"

"All right, what?" Ben dropped his briefs as he resisted her urging.

Tess picked them up and jammed them into his hands as she continued to shove him out of the living room. "All right! Yes! I'll do anything you say. Just get yourself dressed!"

"Anything?" Ben stood calmly in the hallway as Fran rapped softly on the front door.

"Yes, anything!" Tess pushed him into the bathroom and slammed the door shut two seconds before Fran knocked again and cautiously peeked in.

Tess checked on him five minutes later, as Fran bundled up the sleeping Kevin and Kiley and carried them out to the Pontiac. Dallying just long enough to start her on a case of ulcers as she opened the window and silently pointed for him to leave, he shook his dark head. "Not quite yet."

"What do you mean, not yet?" Tess hissed back at him. "You promised!"

"I promised to get dressed. Nothing was said about me leaving."

Longing to strangle him, Tess gave him a deadly glare. "What's it going to take to get you to leave? My firstborn child?"

Raising both eyebrows in total innocence, Ben finished buttoning his shirt. "Would I blackmail you?"

"You already have," Tess pointed out. Tapping her foot, she ignored the feeling of quicksilver rushing through her veins as he zipped up his jeans and rebuckled his belt. "I agreed to see you tomorrow. What else do you want?"

Ben stood so close that his breath ruffled her already tousled hair. They both spoke in low voices. "I want a firm time, so you don't try to weasel out of it by saying you'd forgotten about a previous engagement. Tomorrow at five."

"Morning? Or afternoon?" Tess sniped, thoroughly exasperated at him.

"Afternoon, of course. Right after you close up the shop. I need your help with the renovation I'm doing on the old Weston place." He smoothed back her tangled locks. "It'll be our first official date."

"I'm not going to be your lover," Tess vowed, trying to sound firm.

"I'm not asking you to be. All I'm asking is that you see me on a voluntary basis so we can work on getting this infatuation we have for each other out of our systems. With luck, we'll end up as good friends." He smiled slightly as Tess eyed him with suspicion. "Shall we shake on it?"

Afraid to touch him lest she get herself into trouble all over again, Tess hung back as he took her hand in his. Just the touch of his skin on hers set her blood aflame.

"Being a careful woman, I'm sure you believe in insurance," he added softly, pulling her wrists around his waist and holding them there. "Let's seal the bargain with a kiss."

"Friends," Tess managed, "don't kiss. They help each other in need."

Ben whispered against her lips. "I'm in need...of a kiss." Silencing Tess's automatic protest, he captured her mouth in a soul-searing embrace that had Tess clinging to his shoulders. "I'll pick you up at the shop tomorrow at five," he promised. "Be there."

And then he silently exited through the window.

"Friends help each other when they're in need," he reminded her the next evening after whisking her, protesting all the way, to his new home.

She needed a brain transplant. Wishing she'd had the courage and good sense to leave the shop at four forty-five, before he'd arrived, Tess stared at the spruced-up cobblestone mansion, whose front windows were no longer boarded up with plywood. "Are you fixing it up to live in it?" she asked, determined to keep her distance from him until she'd figured out just how he planned on them ridding each other of their apparent infatuation.

"I'm already living in it," Ben told her. "I have been for weeks now." He took her hand in his and played with her fingers. "I know you can wield a mixing spoon with a vengeance. How are you with a paintbrush?"

Supremely aware of how small her hand was compared to his, of how lean and strong and masculine he was, Tess reconsidered her plan to try to slip away when he wasn't looking. "You never said you needed decorating skills. I thought all you wanted was advice."

"I need advice—and decorating skills."

Chastising herself as a coward, Tess studied the rambling structure as Ben led her down the slate pathway to the front door. "Why don't you just hire someone to finish renovating it for you? You can afford it."

Ben led her inside the marble foyer. "I have hired help. A BOCES crew is doing most of the outside," he told her, referring to the local vocational school. "I'm helping with the inside. I don't want people to think I'm too lazy to do things myself."

"Do you really care what other people think?"

"I care what *you* think," Ben told her truthfully.

Tess considered him. "I think you're—"

"What?" Forgetting he'd promised himself he wasn't going to touch her, that he was just going to talk to her for now, Ben found himself clinging to her hand.

"Entertaining," Tess conceded.

Closing the heavy oak door, Ben resisted the urge to lock it, knowing it would justifiably alarm her. "What else?"

"Provoking. Attractive." Irresistible.

"I thought you despised my clothes." Ben damned himself as he slipped his arms around her waist.

"Do you want the truth? Or tact?" Tess asked.

Watching her nervously lick her lips, Ben forced himself not to let his tongue follow the same path. "Truth."

Tess eyed his green and orange sweater. "You'd look better in blue."

"That was tact," Ben scolded, pressing his mouth against her hair.

"Actually, it was both." Tess cleared her throat as he moved closer. "You're not forgetting that we're not going to be lovers, are you?"

"Of course not." Ben brushed his lips against her left cheek. "Worried things will get out of hand?"

Tess swallowed dryly. "No. I'm worried you might get out of hand."

She wasn't too sure about herself, either. She still thought Ben's plan to extinguish their infatuation for each other was about as safe as playing with a loaded cannon.

Two cannons. Ben had just unknotted her braid and was burying his face in her loosened hair.

He inhaled deeply. "God, you smell wonderful. What are you wearing?"

"Cinnamon." Feeling her knees start to buckle, Tess automatically put her arms around his waist. "I bake cookies for a living, remember?"

"How could I forget?" Pressing his palms against her shoulder blades, Ben pulled her still closer. "It's how we met."

Yes, it was. Tess still didn't know if she was glad that had happened or not. She tensed as he coaxed her hips closer to his. "What are you doing?"

"Trying to warm you up. You looked cold."

Not anymore, she wasn't. "I don't think this a good idea," she murmured.

Ben kissed her forehead. "Why not?"

"Because the last time we got this close, we ended up making love. That's why not."

Ben planted a kiss on her nose. "We did, didn't we?" He didn't exactly sound displeased. "You can't expect to banish the attraction if we never touch," he chided.

"I realize that, but—"

Ben touched his mouth lightly to hers. "A kiss doesn't have to lead to anything more serious."

"I know that," said Tess, considering a kiss plenty serious enough to worry about, knowing she was likely to want a whole lot more.

"Some intensive kissing and touching might be just what it takes to nip this thing in the bud," Ben reasoned. His hands dropped to the snap on her jeans. The sound of it coming undone was accompanied by Tess's quick intake of breath. "You are interested in a quick cure, aren't you, Tess?"

Tess latched on to his wrist as he deftly lowered her zipper. "Ben, no. Someone might come in. One of the workmen—"

"The BOCES crew went home an hour ago." He slid his hands inside her jeans to cup her small bottom. "No one's going to come in."

And then, with perfect timing, his mother appeared in the doorway. "Oh, dear." Tess heard the surprise in the older woman's voice. "I am sorry."

"Hi, mom." Removing his hands from Tess's jeans, Ben sounded ridiculously calm to Tess, considering the circumstances. "What are you doing here?"

Dorothy sounded as mortified as Tess felt. "I brought over a casserole. I wasn't sure you were eating the way you should. I didn't mean to intrude."

"Dorothy, this isn't what it looks like," said Tess desperately, fairly sure her being half unclothed was a compromising position, no matter how you looked at it.

"I'm sure it's not, dear. Don't worry about it." Dorothy gave Tess a look of apology before facing her son. "I'll call you later, Bennett," she told him, setting down the casserole on a nearby hall table, "when you're free."

It was at least two minutes after Dorothy left before Tess could speak again. When she finally did find her voice, it was riddled with accusation. "You knew she was coming.

You wanted to make sure she knows we're seeing each other outside the shop again.''

Ben looked genuinely injured. "I didn't. I'm innocent. Scout's honor.''

"You," Tess exclaimed, "were never, ever, a Boy Scout." He wasn't innocent, either. Tess pointedly rezipped and resnapped her jeans.

Possessing a keen sense of survival, although she sometimes forgot to utilize it, Tess would have gone home then, but Ben insisted on her staying for dinner. "Why go home and cook? This chicken casserole is big enough to feed ten armies," he pointed out, shoving it into the microwave. "Besides, we'll never get sick to death of each other if you keep running away, will we?''

Tess knew she'd been around him too long when that last part actually made sense to her.

Determined to rid herself of her infatuation for him, she agreed to stay for dinner, standing to the side as Ben tossed together a green salad and doused it with homemade Italian dressing. After she and Ben had finished half the casserole and the better part of a bottle of Chardonnay, Ben, insisting Tess behave like a guest, stacked the soiled glassware neatly in the kitchen's new dishwasher before he took her by the hand. "The BOCES crew and I have been busy little bees. Come see what we've done.''

Given a guided tour, Tess marveled at the changes. With a fair amount of work and money poured into it, the old mansion had taken on the air of a well-tended dowager. After being led up the mahogany staircase, Tess wandered in open wonder through the series of airy rooms. Elegant and well cared for, with polished wood banisters and gleaming chandeliers, the home was everything she'd always imagined it could be, and more.

The only thing that puzzled her were the furnishings. The elaborate Victorian sofas and love seats weren't at all what she considered to be Ben's style. Remembering the huge commercial stove, enormous refrigerator, and banquet-size dining table accompanied by at least twenty chairs, Tess swiftly deduced that the house was meant to handle a large number of people. When they got to the bathrooms and she found specially positioned chrome bars installed near the baths and toilets, she couldn't think of anything to say.

Ben was clearly amused by her puzzled silence. "Kinky, eh?"

"Why," Tess asked, "do I get the feeling you've been leading the entire town on, all this time?" Rumors had run rampant about Ben's plans.

Ben leaned a shoulder against the doorjamb. "Who, me?"

"Yes, you. You purposely let us all think you were creating an East Coast equivalent of the Playboy Mansion, when all the time you had completely different plans in mind, didn't you?"

"I just love watching people jump to conclusions," Ben confessed on a sigh.

"You're donating this as a senior citizens' center when you're through, aren't you?" At the moment, the local center was temporarily located in a chilly, cramped church basement, inaccessible to the handicapped.

Ben smiled. "Have I told you how quick you are?"

"Not lately. Have I jumped to any other conclusions I shouldn't have?"

"Not that I'm aware of." Taking her hand, Ben led her into the vaulted-ceilinged library that apparently served as his living room and bedroom. Tess knew from the thoroughly modern furnishings, racing mementos and colorful clothing scattered high and low that they were his personal belongings.

"Come sit down." He guided her to an oversize leather sofa.

Tess sat ramrod straight as he settled next to her. When it became obvious that he had no intention of touching her—had, in fact, moved to the opposite end of the long couch—she allowed herself to relax.

"You're a lot nicer than I'd originally thought," she decided. "You're certainly doing more for Denton Falls than I could ever hope to."

Toeing off his shoes, Ben put his feet up on the oak coffee table. "I've got a lot to make up for."

"Your misspent youth," Tess surmised with a nod.

"My misspent youth," he agreed. He rested his head on the back of the sofa and closed his eyes.

Feeling secure for the moment, Tess slipped off her own shoes and tucked her feet beneath her. "You've indicated you were a royal pain in the neck when your mom remarried."

"The neck and a few other places." He rolled his head and looked at her. "My one real regret was that I never told my stepdad how I felt about him, how sorry I was for being such a donkey's behind. He was a good man, Tess—the best thing that ever happened to my mom. And I almost spoiled it for them. Would've spoiled it, if he hadn't sent me packing. I understood that later, but I never had the chance to tell him. He died last year. I can't tell you how much I regret never telling him."

Tess traced the patch she'd sewn on her jeans since her cat-rescuing mission. "I'm sure he knew."

"Maybe," Ben acknowledged.

"No 'maybe' about it." Tess shook her head. "He knew."

"You don't have to try to comfort me. I can face reality, Tess."

"Good. Face reality now. He knew how you felt about him."

Ben let out an impatient sigh. "You don't know that."

"You're obviously forgetting something."

Ben gave her a look that was both bemused and wary. "Oh? And what's that?"

"That I knew him. He was a good customer of mine. We talked a lot."

Ben laid his arms across the back of the love seat. "So?"

"So, let me set your mind at ease. He knew how you felt about him, and I'd venture to say he felt the same about you. He was very proud of you. So proud that, frankly," Tess admitted, "I thought he was your father."

Ben looked unconvinced as he pushed a lock of dark hair off his forehead. "You're just saying that to make me feel better."

"No, I'm saying it because it's true. Besides," Tess declared, "I could come up with better ways than that to make you feel better."

Shocked at herself, Tess wondered what her blood-alcohol level was as Ben lay back and smiled at her. "Pray tell? How?"

"Well, there's this." Surprised at her audacity, Tess told herself she was only working on ridding herself of her infatuation for him as she eased his sweater over his head and slowly unbuttoned the front of his shirt.

"What else?"

Stunning herself further, she leaned closer. "This." She kissed him in the hollow of his throat, reveling in the irregular pulse she found there.

Ben's voice was husky. "Have any other treatments for whatever might ail me?"

Tess felt her own throat go dry with wanting. "What ails you?"

"My wrist aches." He pointed to the scraped bone peeking out from under his long sleeve. "Here."

Convinced she could cure herself of him if she just tried hard enough, Tess kissed the spot. "What else?"

"It sort of hurts here." Ben indicated an area on his left cheek.

Tess obediently kissed it. "Anything else?"

"I bit my lip at breakfast. Here." Ben pointed to a spot on his mouth.

Telling herself she was definitely on the right track, Tess leaned over and kissed that, too. "Feel better?" Her breath mingled with his.

Ben entwined his fingers with hers. "I feel . . . slightly out of control."

She didn't. For once, Tess thought in wonder, she felt in control. Ben, in his own way, had come to her aid when she'd needed him. And now she wanted to do the same for him.

She wanted to touch him, heal him. She wanted to soothe away his pain, his worries, his fears, his guilts. Just for this moment, she wanted them both to forget who they were.

"Does this hurt?" Removing his shirt, she guided his head into her lap and trailed her hands lightly across his back.

"No."

"You seem . . . tense." Waves of tension rolled off him.

"I don't want to repulse you."

"This from a man who's been wearing T-shirts that would make most people's teeth ache," Tess chided gently.

"I offered to take them off," Ben reminded her.

"I seem to remember you offering to take off more than just your shirts."

"I was trying to impress you with my quick wit," Ben defended. "Tess, you don't have to do that."

Tess smoothed her palms over his back in an effort to make him relax. "I know that."

"I wouldn't think any less of you if it repelled you."

"Would you think any less of me if I confessed that lavender combined with chartreuse repelled me?"

"I suppose this is a reference to the tie I own that I wore to your house last night?"

"The tie you used to own," Tess corrected, gently tracing his spine. "You left it in my bathroom after you insisted on blackmailing me. I donated it to the Salvation Army this morning."

"That wasn't very nice of you."

"I know." Tess sighed. "They'll probably have to look at it lying there on a table for months before someone buys it. But it was that or throw it away, and I couldn't see the sense in upsetting my trash man."

"I don't suppose you've ever seen anything quite like it."

"Your tie?"

"My back."

"I've seen burns before," Tess replied honestly. But never anything like Ben's. It made her wonder how he'd lived through the fire.

"You probably think I'm being a little oversensitive."

"I think you're sexy as hell," Tess confessed.

Rolling over, Ben pulled her face down, closer to his. "I think you're pretty damned sexy yourself. A little prickly at times, of course . . ."

"A little prickly?" Tess repeated. "Is that anything at all like crabby?"

"It's a lot like crabby. Now that I've offended you, you want to fight?"

"Why should I want to fight with you?"

"So we can kiss and make up, of course."

Not waiting for her answer, he kissed her deeply, teasing her lips with his tongue, nibbling at her lower lip with his teeth.

"You know what makes me crabby?" she whispered.

"Men who call you crabby?"

"Men who insist on teasing," Tess corrected breathlessly, "when they have absolutely no intention of following through..."

Ben rolled her beneath him on the couch so swiftly her head spun. "You shouldn't say things like that, when you know I'm a man who can't resist a challenge."

And she, Tess realized, eagerly coming to him, couldn't resist him.

She was never going to get him out of her system if they made love ten times a day for the next hundred years.

Tess lay on the couch alone the next morning, thinking about it.

She didn't care if Ben was a little more adventurous than she liked. She didn't care if, on the surface, they were all wrong for each other. She loved him. And she wanted to be with him, and have children with him—lots of them. And that wanting wasn't going to go away.

Tess was absorbing that new realization when she became aware of Ben standing in the doorway, shirtless. Tess felt excitement singing through her veins at just the sight of him. She sat up and pushed her hair out of the way.

"We never seem to make it into a bed," she observed wryly, realizing they'd yet to get off couches.

"Nonconformists rarely do the expected," Ben answered.

Ben never did, Tess acknowledged. She frowned suddenly as he came to sit on the edge of the sofa. He was too quiet, too still. Tess felt a frisson of alarm skim over her flesh. "Is anything wrong? Did I hurt you?"

"No." Ben smoothed his hand over the afghan covering her bare legs. "I'm afraid it's me who might have to hurt you."

"Hurt me? How? By jilting me now you've twice had your way with me? I've heard the third time is the charm." She'd been kidding, but Ben didn't even smile.

"Not exactly."

"All right, then." Tess clutched the knitted blanket. "What, exactly?"

"I had a phone call this morning—from my racing team. They've got a car ready for me. They want me to come back."

The time had come, Tess realized. She'd always known it would. And now it was here.

Trying to be brave, Tess forced herself to sound enthusiastic. "Ben, that's . . . wonderful for you. You must be so excited. When will you leave?" Proud of herself, Tess even managed to joke, "Not this morning, I trust."

"No." Ben's voice was calm. "Tomorrow."

Chapter Fourteen

He was leaving tomorrow.

Hardly able to breathe, Tess willed herself not to lose her composure as she pulled the blue and red afghan up over her bare breasts. "Morning?" she finally asked. "Or afternoon?" As if a couple of hours would matter!

"Morning," Ben told her quietly. "I'll be leaving early so I can get down there by tomorrow afternoon. It's a long drive."

"Where are you going?" Another irrelevant question, Tess realized. What did it matter where he went? What mattered was that he was going.

"The car and crew are waiting for me in Miami. I have to go, Tess."

"I know you do," Tess blinked madly, refusing to use tears to persuade him to stay. She'd known he was going to move on, sooner or later. He'd never lied about his intentions. He'd never promised her anything.

She'd put the blinders on herself, hoping things would somehow miraculously change; knowing that they wouldn't.

"We both knew this was coming," Ben said.

"Yes." Tess acknowledged that truth with a nod.

"I never tried to pretend it would be any different."

"No, you didn't." Unable to look at him lest he see the moisture swimming in her eyes, Tess located her sweater and put it on.

"Is this to be a temporary arrangement? Or a permanent one?" Tess was fairly sure she already knew the answer to that one, but just in case...

"Permanent," Ben answered. "After the bugs in the car are worked out, we take it to Europe. I won't be coming back to Denton Falls except to visit."

"Then I guess it's time for us to say goodbye." Tess had never realized how much words could hurt physically, but these seemed to sear her throat.

"I guess it is. Unless you want to come with me."

The very calmness of the words stopped her. Tess looked at him then, but his expression was unreadable. "I'm not sure what you're saying. Are you asking me to come with you to Florida? And then...to Europe?"

"Would you come if I did?"

Tess tried to think through this new equation, but her mind felt wrapped in fog. "You mean leave Denton Falls with you? For good?"

"Yes."

Tess felt her throat closing as what he was asking of her sank in. "Ben, I couldn't leave permanently. I have friends here. A business." Her mother's business, which she'd promised to keep going, whatever the cost. "It's my home."

"Home is where the heart is."

No, Tess reflected, home was where you set down roots and made a life for yourself—just as she'd done here. Didn't he know that?

"Ben, I couldn't just leave my shop on twenty-four hours' notice." She wasn't yet certain that she was willing to leave it at all—

"My mom would probably be willing to take over until we figured out something more permanent. It wouldn't be hard to sell, if it came down to that. It's a profitable enterprise now."

Yes, it was, thanks to him. The irony of that hadn't escaped her. Ben was the miracle she'd prayed for to get her shop back on its feet again. And now that he'd done it, he was going to break her *heart* in two....

"Look." He ran his hand through his unruly dark hair, trying to bring some order to it. "I understand how you feel about the shop...about Denton Falls. Try to understand my point of view. I can't stay in upstate New York indefinitely."

At his unexpected terseness, Tess lifted her chin in open defiance. "Why not? You could do a lot worse than Denton Falls."

"And I could do a hell of a lot better. So could you."

Bristling at the criticism, Tess jumped to her hometown's defense. "I like this town the way it is. You're the one who's wanted to change it from the second you came back, not me."

Ben's impatience was beginning to grow visibly. "I wasn't knocking Denton Falls. I was trying to point out that you could relocate if you wanted to. You wouldn't have to give up your career if you left here."

Tess felt her own temper rising. "Meaning I'm being obstinate and selfish by not leaping at the chance to go with you."

"That's not what I meant."

"Isn't it?"

"Okay," he conceded, "maybe it was, in part. I can't race cars here. You can start a new business some place else. Make of that what you want."

"What I want doesn't seem to matter a whole heck of a lot, apparently. And you're getting very personal again."

"How the hell can I be impersonal on this? I want you with me, Tess. I don't want to leave without you."

But he would if he had to. Tess knew it, and so did he. She knitted her fingers together in her lap. "Maybe we could compromise somehow."

Ben's mouth twisted. "You know what compromise is, don't you, Tess?"

Tess bit her lip at his look of bleak amusement. "What?"

"A situation where everyone's unhappy."

She was already unhappy. Desperately so. "Ben, I don't want to leave. I like it here. I feel a part of things—"

Ben cut her off. "You can make a home anywhere you want to."

"How would you know? You've never stayed in the same place for more than two months." Tess realized she was getting personal herself, but she couldn't help it. He was asking her to drop everything and go with him, to chase around the world after him while he risked life and limb. And for what? Excitement? Trophies? Fame and fortune?

"That was the choice I made when I took up racing." His voice went flat, cautioning her. "Just like this is the choice I'm making now."

"Without thinking about how it affects anyone else," Tess replied bitterly, realizing she was more upset by the fact that he was returning to the dangers of racing than she was about him simply leaving.

Ben stood with his hands jammed in his pockets. "I'm thinking about how it affects you and me. Are you?"

Tess tensed. The question sounded threatening—and somehow ominous. "Am I what?"

"Thinking about how your decision to stay here affects us."

"Is there any 'us'?"

"I guess that's what we're trying to find out here, isn't it?"

Tess tried to swallow and couldn't. "I thought it had already been decided. You were the one who said you didn't want to get involved."

"And now you know why. This is exactly what I knew would happen. What I wanted to avoid." He sat down on his heels so that he could look her in the eye. "Look, I never intended for us to get so close. I didn't want to hurt you. I hadn't counted on us falling for each other like this. I'd undo it all if I could."

She wouldn't, Tess realized. No matter how painful this was clearly going to be, she was glad they'd met; she was grateful for having known him. He'd opened whole new worlds for her, and now her life would never be the same. She would never be the same. "There's no need for you to feel guilty. It takes two to tango. I knew what I was getting myself into."

"Call it guilt one more time," he warned, obviously trying for levity to ease the tension rising between them, "and I may have to do something drastic."

In no mood to be cajoled, Tess gave him a cool look. "Like what? Stay?"

"Would it make you happy if I stayed? Is that what you want?"

Tess considered the softly spoken demand. Would she be happy if he stayed, knowing how he felt about racing? Knowing what he'd have to give up to be with her? "I don't want to see you die racing," she answered truthfully. "Just thinking about you getting into a car again scares me half to death. If you knew me the way you think you do, you'd know that."

"You really hate me for being who I am, don't you, Tess? What I am."

No, she didn't. She loved him. It was what he did for a living that she despised. "What do you care, so long as you get what you want?"

She knew just from his expression that she'd hurt him deeply. "I care. If I didn't I wouldn't be bothering to explain why I have to go. Damn it, don't you think I know it was selfish of me to allow this to happen?"

"I hope you're not looking for an argument from me on that point," Tess said, knowing her only salvation lay in anger, "because you won't get one."

Ben's temper quickly matched her own. "Arguments I get from you without asking. What I'm looking for now is a little reason. Do you always have to think of just yourself? Couldn't you at least consider seeing a viewpoint other than your own, for a change?"

Surprised by the attack, Tess challenged, "Couldn't you? Other people manage to work things out without blowing each other's lives to smithereens. Why can't we?"

"Because I don't believe in long-distance affairs," he stated flatly. "They take too much of a toll on both parties."

Tess's spine stiffened. "Now what are you saying?"

"I'm saying I'm not interested or willing to be a part-time lover. I won't settle for one day with you here, two days with you there. I want you with me all the time. I won't settle for anything less than a full-time partnership. I don't do anything halfway. It's all or nothing, with me. It always has been. It always will be.''

Tess felt her heart constrict. "That smacks of an ultimatum.''

"Does it? Maybe it is, then.''

Sick and angry, Tess surveyed him. "What happens if I refuse to go with you? You never darken my door and I never hear from you again. Is that it?''

Ben looked at her for so long, she could hardly swallow. "Are you refusing to go?''

"I hate it when you answer a question with a question.''

"I hate it when you can't see past the nose on your face.'' He made a grab for her as she got to her feet. "Where the hell are you going?''

Tess snatched her hand away. "I'm going home. Since, unlike you, I have one.''

Ben watched her with narrowed eyes. "You're running away again.''

"No.'' Tess yanked her jacket on and headed for the door as she spoke. "You're the one who's insisting on flitting from place to place. I'm just the one who's getting in your way.'' Tess slammed the door on her way out, hoping it would vent her anger. It didn't. And nothing, she suspected, would ever make the hurt, or the anger, go away.

The next day came all too soon for Tess. She watched from her front window at first as Ben kissed his mother goodbye and prepared to leave. Tess came out her back door just as Ben threw his suitcase into the Porsche. In two minutes he was going to exit her life forever. She knew it. And she didn't know what to do about it.

Wearing the same designer jacket he'd had on the day they'd met, and with his hands in his jeans pockets, he turned toward Tess as she approached.

Tess fought a terrible urge to throw herself into his arms and beg him not to go as Ben watched her with a closed expression she'd never seen before. Finally he said, "I have to go.''

No, he didn't. He wanted to go. Unable to speak, Tess remained silent.

"Come with me. Scout things out. See how you like it. Most people find racing exciting, especially when they know the drivers."

Tess considered reminding him that she already knew more than enough about racing to keep her up nights worrying herself sick about him, then rejected the thought. It didn't matter, because it really wasn't the issue. The issue was his refusal to even consider a compromise. "I can't. Unlike you, I have other people to consider besides myself."

Ben remained calm in the face of the accusation. "You could close the shop temporarily. Your customers would survive for a day or two."

Tess shook her head. Even if she could accept the danger he put himself in every time he stepped onto a racetrack, if she closed her shop to follow him every time he raced, she wouldn't have any business to come back to—something Ben either didn't understand or couldn't accept.

"I love you, sprout."

Tess knew he did. And that made it all the worse. He loved her, but he was still leaving; because as much as he loved her, he loved racing more. "If you say so."

"I do say so." This time he did take her stiff body into his arms briefly for an embrace. He kissed the top of her head when she refused to look at him. "I know you're mad at me—"

No, she wasn't. She was disillusioned and sick at heart.

"And I know you probably think this is the worst thing that's ever happened to you."

She didn't think it. It *was* the worst thing that had ever happened to her.

"But our going our own ways is really the best thing for both of us. You'll see. Hell, you'll probably forget all about me before I'm even out of the county."

No, she wouldn't. She would never forget him, though she suspected he would soon forget her. He would flit about from continent to continent racing, she would stay in New York to keep the shop going, and they would see each other

n passing maybe once a year when he came to see his mom.
t was all she could hope for, all she could expect from him.
And it was breaking her heart.

After he left, Tess dove into her business with a vengeance. She was going to be all right. What was it her
mother had said after Tess's own father had left? "I got
along without him before I met him. I can get along without him now." Except that Tess didn't think she could get
along without Ben. But what could she do?

Her desire to put down roots just didn't mesh with Ben's
need to race. Even if she'd been willing to leave Denton
Falls, her need for security was at odds with his choice of
careers. Racing was inherently dangerous. No matter how
careful he was, there would always be risk involved—the
kind of risk she couldn't accept.

A week later, Tess scrambled eggs for Sunday breakfast,
disgusted with herself because she was still thinking of Ben.
What was he doing now? Probably soaking up sun on some
sand-strewn beach. She looked out the window at the gray
November sky. The thermometer read twenty-three degrees.

Bored and restless, Tess found herself turning on the TV,
searching for the news. She got the national weather fore-
cast: sunny and warm in Florida—perfect for racing.

Tess dumped the half-eaten eggs in the sink and turned on
the garbage disposal, wishing she could consign Ben's race
car to the same fate. Another woman she could tackle on
human terms, but how in the world did you compete with
the smell of engine grease and the roar of the crowds? She
despised racing for taking Ben away from her. The seduc-
tress was her nemesis. She probably required psychological
care, the way she was giving it almost human qualities.
What was the word? *Anthropomorphizing.*

Tess immediately thought about the day she and Ben had
aspired to be "wine snobs" at the Grape Expectations fair,
and she felt a shaft of pain spear through her. Things would
never be the same without him. There was no use pretend-
ing they would be. But she'd manage.

By the end of the week, she'd almost succeeded in convincing herself of that—after all, she still had her friends—when Dorothy came by to see her.

Stopping by the shop to help out, as had become her custom after the day Ben had spirited Tess off to the fair leaving Dorothy and Cheryl in charge, Dorothy put her arm around Tess.

"Don't look so miserable, dear. I know it's hard to believe right now, but things will work out. They always do. Bennett will be back. You'll see."

Tess shook her head as she pulled away. "I don't think so, Dorothy."

"Of course, he will. You two were meant for each other. Your mother and I knew that from the time we first met." Dorothy smiled slightly. "You know, your mother was so very dear to me. We were very close. She wouldn't have wanted you to sacrifice your happiness for the shop. She left it to you to sustain you after she passed away, not to keep you from pursuing your happiness. That's partly why I gave you the money, dear. Your mother and I promised each other we'd look after each other's children in case anything happened to either one of us."

Trying not to think of what that investment had eventually done to her peace of mind, Tess kissed Dorothy on the cheek. "I couldn't have asked for a nicer foster parent. You've been like a mother to me."

"I plan to continue being like a mother to you, dear—" Dorothy's gray eyes twinkled "—for a very long time to come." She was clearly in a spritely mood.

Too happy, under the circumstances, Tess realized after a moment. With her own thoughts focused on Ben, Tess totally missed the cues at first, in spite of the obvious hints Dorothy was dropping all over the place.

"Tess, dear." Insisting Tess stop for a cup of coffee, Dorothy filled the glass case with cooled chocolate-chip cookies, browned to perfection by Pele's new thermostat. "You're so good with whipping things up. Do you think you could make a cake?"

Barely listening, Tess, thinking Dorothy was referring to some sort of birthday cake, shrugged. "Of course, Dorothy. What kind? Flat or tiered?"

"Tiered, I think. Most wedding cakes are tiered, aren't they?"

A birthday cake was obviously out. Thinking Dorothy was perhaps considering getting remarried—she had, after all, been seeing a very nice gentleman named Donald—Tess asked sensibly, "How many people should it serve?"

She was even more confused when she'd clearly caught the older woman off guard. "How many people? Well, I'm not sure yet. I suppose I'll have to check with the bride and groom."

Tess, more confused than ever, queried, "Who is it for?"

This time Dorothy smiled seraphically at her. "Don't be silly, dear. Why, you and Ben, of course."

Tess was certain she'd heard incorrectly. "Me and Ben," she repeated.

Dorothy smiled again, that infinitely charming smile her son had inherited. "Well, of course. Who else would it be for?"

"Who else?" Tess agreed hollowly. She honestly didn't know what else to do or say. For heaven's sake, hadn't Ben said anything to his mother about their parting on less than amicable terms?

"What do you think of peach for the bridesmaids, dear?" Dorothy, having caught up with filling the case, had begun paging through a bridal catalog. "It's such a nice warm color."

"Peach is a nice color." Thinking of strangling Ben—if she ever saw him again—for the inexcusable omission, Tess tried again to bring her attention back to what Dorothy was saying, but it was almost impossible.

"Would you like a traditional service? Or did you and Bennett plan on writing your own vows?" Dorothy asked.

"We haven't really discussed it," Tess said truthfully.

"Would you prefer punch?" Dorothy persisted. "Or champagne?"

"I prefer champagne," Tess answered, not believing for a second that any of Dorothy's fervent planning was ever going to be needed. Ben was gone. He wasn't coming back. Even if he did return briefly, it certainly wouldn't be to marry her, as long as they hadn't worked their problem out. She wasn't sure she would marry him, in any event, she was so peeved at him for not telling his mother that his absence was a little more than temporary.

"Do you prefer pink? Or the regular kind?"

"The regular kind." Tess absently looked over her supply of cookies. Three dozen pecan chocolate-chip. Five dozen oatmeal-raisin. Two dozen granola clusters. She'd baked all morning and most of the afternoon.

For seven days now, Tess admitted, she'd run her bakery shop like a taut ship, trying to bring some normalcy back into her life. She'd always enjoyed baking. Normally the day-to-day running of the shop gave her a great deal of pleasure. But the truth was, Tess admitted, it wasn't half as much fun now that Ben was no longer there to give her the business....

"Brut? Or extra, extra dry?" Dorothy asked.

Tess stared at the older woman for a moment, trying to remember what they'd been discussing.

"The champagne, dear," Dorothy prompted. "Would you prefer brut? Or extra, extra dry?"

Since it didn't matter anyway, Tess picked one at random. "Brut."

Dorothy nodded in satisfaction. "I'm not sure about guests yet. You'll have to let me know who you'd like to have present, but we simply have to invite Ben's favorite Uncle, Fred, to the ceremony. We ought to invite Marc, as well, don't you think?" she asked thoughtfully.

"Who," Tess asked cautiously, "is Marc?"

"Ben's favorite cousin," Dorothy explained. "The two of them were like peas in a pod as boys. Marc would be terribly hurt if he wasn't invited to the wedding. Tess, darling—" She stopped suddenly, her face filled with concern. "Are you well? You seem pale."

"I'm a bit under the weather." Tess told herself Ben would appreciate that comment, considering the sky above her was filled with thick gray clouds. That was one of the things she loved most about him: his ability to see the ridiculous, the funny, the absurd . . .

Dorothy—not surprisingly, considering whom she'd parented—immediately understood. "Considering our weather, that's not unusual. Which is another reason why I popped over to talk to you. I've decided to follow nature's idea, at least temporarily. I'm going to join the birds."

That proved it, Tess concluded. She was becoming mentally unstable. "Join the birds," she repeated.

Dorothy smiled. "The snowbirds, dear. I've thought it over and decided that Bennett's right. With my arthritis, there's no reason for me to stay here and freeze all winter long. So I'm going to spend summers here and winters down in Florida."

Tess couldn't speak. It was bad enough that Ben hadn't told his mother they were as likely to murder each other as marry. It was bad enough he'd gone off and put his life on the line again, but now Dorothy was leaving, too.

"What do you think, Tess?" Dorothy asked.

Disinclined to inform Dorothy of what she thought, Tess managed, "I'm sure you'd enjoy Florida."

Dorothy appeared satisfied with Tess's answer. "It's settled then. I suppose I'd better get busy making arrangements."

Still reeling, Tess pulled the lids off bins and measured out the flour and brown sugar. What was Ben doing now? Eating? It was already late afternoon, but Ben wasn't noted for keeping to schedules. He had a tendency to overlook things like good nutrition taken at regular intervals.

Part of Tess hoped he was eating. Part of her hoped he missed her too much to eat.

And part of her, she conceded, was so mad at him she hoped that if he was eating, he choked.

Two days later, Tess was in the midst of baking more cookies when Cheryl and Judith stopped by her shop to bolster her spirits. "You look surprisingly cheerful," Judith stated bluntly.

Cheryl looked equally amazed. "We were afraid we'd find you down in the dumps, what with Ben gone and all."

"I've been thinking about what I'm going to do to Ben, if and when I next see him," Tess answered truthfully. "How's the dating business?"

"In a word," Judith confessed wryly, "going nowhere."

"That's two words." Cheryl pointed out.

"It doesn't matter. It's still going noplace." Judith turned to Tess. "It would help if some of our friends gave us a little support now and then."

"Judith," Tess warned, "don't start."

"Start what?" Judith gave her a look of pure innocence. "I was simply telling you how business was. After all, you did ask." She stirred sugar into the cup of tea Tess had placed before her. "You know, it's amazing how many interesting men there are here, considering the size of this town."

But none of them, Tess reflected, could be half as interesting as Ben, half as sensitive, half as much fun. Where was he now?

"Successful," Judith went on. "Full of enthusiasm. Interested in pursuing a long-term relationship."

"Judith." This time Tess frowned in sterner warning.

"I can't help it," Judith protested. "We've just signed up the perfect man for you." She smiled in satisfaction. "Haven't we, Cheryl?"

"I've given up finding the perfect man," said Tess. "There's no such animal."

"Not *The* Perfect Man," Cheryl corrected. "The perfect man for *you*. Everyone's idea of a perfect mate is different."

And hers, Tess thought, was in Florida.

"His profile matches up with yours in a way you wouldn't believe," Cheryl added.

Cheryl was right, Tess reflected, she didn't believe it.

"At least give him a chance," Judith persisted.

"No." Tess shook her head adamantly.

"Why the dickens not?"

"Because there's no point."

"Come on," Cheryl coaxed. "What's it going to hurt? Just one date."

Tess shook her head again. "Watch my lips: *N-O*."

Judith frowned in reproval. "You're just being stubborn."

"No," Tess countered. "I'm being sensible."

"Take a well-intentioned suggestion and be a little less sensible."

Tess frowned. "That sounded like something Ben would say."

"Well, maybe he's right once in a while. Have you ever considered that?"

No, but she'd considered murdering him. She still couldn't believe he'd been so unreasonable. First he'd expected—no, *demanded*—that she all but dismantle her life to chase after him. And then, when she couldn't, he hadn't even bothered to inform his mother they'd permanently parted ways.

He couldn't have made her madder if he'd tried—

If he'd tried. Everything around her seemed to come to a halt as Tess stopped in midthought. Ben was no dummy. He was as shrewd as they came. What if making her angry was exactly what he'd intended to do?

Tess considered the novelty of the thought. Ben knew how she felt about Denton Falls. Did it make sense that he would just assume she'd drop everything to follow him around the world, especially when he knew how much his racing upset her?

And then there was the subject of her shop and all it meant to her.

Would a man who'd asked her, straight in the beginning, if any changes to her shop would go against her late mother's wishes, later insist she totally relinquish the same shop without question? Was it logical he'd help her make the shop a success, then expect her to desert it?

Tess felt as if her lungs would never work again as the thoughts pressed in on her. What if Ben had told her the truth? That, deep down, he hadn't wanted to get involved with her because he'd known his day for parting would eventually come and he hadn't wanted to hurt her?

How would he try to save her from hurt when it looked inevitable?

By making her angry?

By demanding the impossible?

By leaving abruptly so she'd have no time to reconsider? All of the above?

Tess came back to attention as Judith tapped her foot in impatience. "Well?"

Tess raised an eyebrow. "Well, what?"

"Are you going to date this fellow?"

"No. It wouldn't be fair to him."

"He's willing to take the chance," Cheryl responded.

"That's brave of him." Tess scowled. "But I'm not."

"Not brave?" asked Judith. "Or not willing to take the chance?"

"Both."

"Be optimistic," Cheryl urged. "He could be the man of your dreams."

"No, he couldn't." He was in Florida. And if she'd been braver and not so cowardly, she probably would be with Ben now, instead of just wishing she were. It had taken her long enough to realize it but she recognized, now, that even the shop meant little to her compared to him. Still, she didn't want to give it up. If only she could find someone interested in running it for her, Tess reflected, so she wouldn't have to abandon it. Not Dorothy, obviously. She was planning on spending the winters in Florida. If only there was someone else—someone she trusted....

"This is our last shot at this sort of thing," Cheryl confessed. "We're getting out of the dating business and thinking of going into something else."

Tess focused her attention on Cheryl. "How about a cookie shop?"

Judith looked perplexed, but Cheryl's interest immediately perked. "Are you thinking of selling?"

"I'm seriously thinking of taking on a new partner," Tess confessed. "A managing partner for when I'm not here."

Judith and Cheryl exchanged a quick look. "Do you expect not to be here?"

"I don't know yet," Tess confessed. Even if she was willing to leave Denton Falls, even if she could figure out a way to keep her shop going without her, she knew it was only half the solution. She wouldn't leave if Ben couldn't meet her halfway—if he continued to put his life on the line.

"Would you be interested in taking over the shop if I wasn't here?" she asked.

"I'm definitely interested," said Cheryl. "Judith probably will be, too, once she realizes this computer-dating business was a harebrained idea."

"I heard that," Judith interjected. She turned to Tess. "Your future here isn't exactly what I'd call set in concrete yet. Are you going to give this man we've lined up a chance, or not?"

"Not." Refusing to be badgered into it, Tess positively declined to take part in the computer date. Which was why, when she heard a car pull into her driveway at dinnertime and then heard a knock on her door, she steadfastly ignored it. Whoever he was, the man would eventually get the idea and go away, she told herself.

Only he didn't. He persisted and persisted. He even came around to the side door when she didn't answer the front one. Dismayed and embarrassed, Tess ignored the fourth knock and the fifth.

Tess had gone so far as to turn up the TV and was about to ignore the sixth knock when she glanced out the kitchen window. Her heart skipped rope as, in the dim light of her porch light, she saw a head of unruly dark hair, a wildly patterned black-and-white jacket and a neon-yellow T-shirt.

There was only one man she knew of who was confident enough, or crazy enough, to wear bright summer clothes in the Northeast in the dead of winter.

Chapter Fifteen

Ben." Tess knew she was staring, but she couldn't help herself. She couldn't seem to get enough of him. Her eyes wanted to drink him in. She wanted to reach out and touch him, absorb him. Her heart felt stuck in her throat, which seemed to have shrunk to the size of a reed.

"Hello, Tess." Ben's smile was cautious, his eyes watchful. "How are you?"

How was she? Good question. Confused, excited, fearful...

"Surprised," she managed. "I didn't expect you." She hadn't expected to see him ever again, except briefly in passing. "Shouldn't you be in Florida or somewhere racing cars?"

For a second, Ben simply looked into her innocent brown eyes and wondered if she had a mean streak he hadn't guessed at, after all; if he'd totally misjudged her. And then he realized: she didn't know. She honestly didn't know, in spite of all the publicity and hoopla accompanying his recent retirement. What the hell was he going to say to her? He could tell her a partial truth: that it was hard to race professionally when you had a leg pinned together with assorted bits of metal; that pressing an accelerator with it was like kissing a woman through plastic wrap—you knew what you were doing, but it just didn't feel quite right.

He could tell her he'd proven he could still drive a car; he just couldn't compete. He could tell her that he no longer had the stamina, the kind of single-minded focus it took to win.

He could say it. And, at least in part, it would be the truth. But that wasn't what had brought him back. Tess had. His feelings for her had.

It wasn't until he'd buckled himself back into a car and taken a few laps that he'd realized how much he'd changed. Even without the accident—even if his vision had been one hundred percent, even if his body and mind had been unscarred—within minutes he would have known that racing could never be the be-all and end-all of his life again.

He'd lost the necessary edge. He'd started thinking of something besides what car was on the track with him, how the machine beneath him felt, how fast his lap times were. He'd started thinking about something besides himself. He'd started thinking about Tess; and when that had happened, he'd known it was time to hang up his racing helmet.

Afraid that if he told her, she'd automatically, wrongfully, take the blame for his shortened career, he needed all his self-control to keep his voice calm as he answered, "My racing days are over."

At first, in his more self-pitying moments, he'd felt as if his life were over. It wasn't that it had never occurred to him he wouldn't race forever. He was enough of a realist to recognize that all good things must come to an end. He just hadn't expected the end to come quite so soon.

He'd turned thirty-two last January. With any luck, he still had most of his life ahead of him. He'd quit while he was still on top. It wouldn't be difficult to get started on something new. None of it, he knew, would mean anything to him if Tess wasn't there to share it with him.

Ben's gaze drifted from her hair to her mouth. "Were you napping? It took me a while to get your attention."

Afraid she was hearing only what she wanted to hear—that he'd decided to retire from racing, after all—Tess found herself confessing, "I was hiding out."

"From me?" he queried softly.

Even in her muddled state of mind, Tess heard the pain in his voice. "No." She swallowed, then admitted, "I thought you were my date. I can't seem to convince Cheryl and Judith I'm not interested in computer dates"—that the only man she cared for, would ever care for, was him. "Would you like to come in?" Her voice, she realized, was a rusty croak.

Ben's was hesitant. "I have something important to tell you first."

Tess felt as if her heart were being squeezed in her chest. Here it comes, she thought: the end. She fought down a horrifying urge to cry her eyes out on the spot. "What is it?" Her voice still sounded appallingly like a creaky door hinge as she forced the words out, but she couldn't help it. She'd had so much time to think, to realize that she couldn't live without him. She could survive, but she wouldn't really *live*. Nothing could ever take his place—not friends, not the shop. So if he'd come back simply to make a clean break, she didn't think she could stand it.

Ben rocked back on his heels as he confessed, "I'm your date."

For one long moment, all Tess could do was look at him. "You're my date?" she finally repeated, trying to make sense of what he'd just said.

His breath fogged in the chill air. "I'm afraid so."

"You had Cheryl and Judith set you up as my date?" she asked, still struggling for comprehension even as she remembered her friends' exceptionally bland expressions earlier that day.

Ben nodded.

"Why?"

Ben smiled faintly. "Because I wasn't sure you wanted to see me again. I thought you might be more likely to let me in if you thought I was a reliable, boring, no-risks, no-thrills kind of man."

"I guess that shows how much you know," Tess managed.

"I guess it does." His direct gaze warmed her to the core. "Now that you know it's me and not some sane, sensible stockbroker, do you still want to hide out?"

"I don't care for stockbrokers, sensible or otherwise. Anyway, I think it's a little late for that," Tess acknowledged. But what was he doing here? If he'd really come to sever all ties, he wouldn't have gone to all this trouble just for entry into her house—would he?

Granted, he didn't like leaving loose ends, Tess conceded. For all she knew he was probably still on his wipe-the-slate-clean campaign. But there were probably much easier ways to end a relationship.

Ben shivered visibly in his lightweight jacket. "Can I come in now? It was eighty degrees in Orlando when I left, and I forgot a coat. It's chilly out here."

Forcing her unresponsive legs into motion, Tess moved back so he could enter. Her knees and brain felt curiously wooden, but she was determined to match him quip for quip. "Aren't you afraid it might be chilly in here, too?"

As Ben walked into her kitchen, he gave her that slow, lazy smile that made her heart do silly things inside her chest. "I'll take my chances." Once inside, he swung the door shut and pulled her gently to him.

"What are you doing?" Tess breathed.

"Saying hello, of course." Bringing his lips down to hers, he kissed her slowly, thoroughly, like a man deprived of water suddenly coming to an oasis and drinking his fill.

Tess drank in his kisses like a woman similarly deprived.

When he finally released her mouth, he laid a steamy path of kisses to her ear. He nibbled on her lobe, savoring it, then whispered in a husky voice, "Hello, Tess."

Tess had to swallow before she could speak. "Hello, yourself."

The shakiness in her voice seemed to spur him on. He nuzzled her throat, kissing the soft flesh with hot, hungry lips. His breath came out in a long exhalation. "God, I missed you, Tess."

"I missed you, too," she admitted. It had only been less than two weeks, but it had seemed like a year. "You're looking good," she added.

It was a lie. He looked better than good. He looked terrific. Even more attractive than she remembered, he was tan, lean and fit.

"You look good, too, Tess." His gaze was almost a physical caress. "Very, very good. And you still feel as good as you look." His lips found hers again. Finally releasing her mouth briefly, he murmured, "We need to talk."

"Yes." Overwhelmed by emotion, it was all Tess could manage.

"We need to do a few other things, too," he added.

"Like what?"

"Like make up for lost time." He kissed her again. And then again.

Tess matched him kiss for kiss, caress for caress.

It was as if she would never get enough of him. She'd thought that if she ever saw him again she would be cool and calm and dignified. But after just one look from those smoky green eyes of his, she was putty in his hands.

And she was definitely in his hands. Tess sucked in air as his palms slid over the gentle swell of her hips. "Have you really quit racing?"

"Yes, love. I've really quite racing." He extended the caress up her sides and then up and down her back.

"Why?"

Ben considered his options. "It was time." His hesitation was so brief, he knew she hadn't noticed it. "Aren't you going to ask me what I'm going to do, now that I've retired?"

"I'm afraid to. You might tell me you've decided to take over the cookie shop, after all."

Ben kneaded the taut muscles at the center of her back. "Actually, I've been thinking about starting a business of my own." He'd been toying with the idea for nearly a week now.

Reassured by his tone, Tess all but purred under his ministrations. "Does it have anything to do with racing?"

"In a way. Racing is the only thing I have any real expertise in. That," he added, "and getting you going."

Tess leaned against him, mentally bracing herself. "Where would it be?" If he said Afghanistan, she wasn't sure what she would do.

"Central Florida."

Tess knew, just from the careful way he said it, that he was testing the waters, seeing how she responded to the idea of leaving Denton Falls. Considering that her feelings were always so transparent to him, Tess realized that he likely already guessed she would leave the shop in order to be with him, as long as she had someone she trusted to watch things for her—and as long as it didn't involve her sitting and watching him risk his neck racing.

"Florida is a nice place," Tess commented neutrally, knowing that Ben, for all his apparent cynicism over that option, was searching for a compromise. He'd given up racing—possibly for her, possibly not. What was important was that he'd come back and was trying to find a middle ground where they could be together, where they could both be happy.

"That it is. Especially this time of year." He closed in on her again. "Of course, maybe you aren't interested in taking up a new challenge. Maybe you don't want to leave the shop. Then again, maybe you've decided you don't want me around driving you crazy in the Florida sun."

Tess decided she wasn't going to let him off the hook quite so easily. "Maybe I still want you driving me crazy here."

"Wouldn't surprise me. I still want you here—" he kissed her nose. "There—" he embraced her chin. "Everywhere." He savored her mouth.

"You know what I mean." Tess was breathless.

Ben refused to be dampened. "Yes, love. I know what you mean. Compromise is difficult at best, but nothing good ever came easy. And I warn you, I'm a very determined man. I've come back with all sorts of new ammunition. I'm bringing out the big guns this time," he confided solemnly.

"What kind of big guns?" Tess managed as he backed her up to the wall. The man definitely had a thing about walls, she decided.

"Well." His smile was pure Young as he pressed his body against hers. "There's this." He kissed the left side of her mouth. "Then there's this." He kissed the right side of her mouth. "Then, of course, there's this." His lips found hers in a soul-wrenching meeting that had Tess struggling for breath. "That's called the Bennett Special," he informed her.

"You don't play fair," Tess whispered.

"All's fair in love and war."

"Which are we involved in now?"

"Let me show you."

Reveling in his warmth, lost in a world of sensation, Tess was brought back to the real world with a rush as muffled noises coming from down the hall grew closer.

"What the hell?" Ben's head jerked up as Fran's twins started clamoring for their share of attention.

"I forgot to tell you," Tess said dryly. "I'm baby-sitting."

"Ben!" the youngsters squealed in unison as they scampered toward him.

"It's your fault for singing to them," Tess told him as four chubby arms reached up for a hug. "They never could resist a good tune."

"If I thought it would have the same effect on you," Ben murmured as he kissed her once again, "I'd be singing all the time." His gaze promised that the parting was going to be temporary as he let her go and gave his attention to the twins. "Hello, princess. Hello, sport." Ben dropped down to their level. "You been taking care of Tess for me?"

Kevin nodded solemnly, then gave Ben a bear hug around the neck that threatened to cut off his air supply.

"Good boy." Ben ruffled the boy's hair. "How about your sister? Have you been watching out for her, too?" Kevin nodded again.

"As if we women needed tending," Tess commented without rancor as Kiley latched on to Ben's left leg.

"You and I are going to have a long talk about tending," Ben promised, "right after we get these two to bed." Ben hugged Kevin before putting the small boy back down on the floor. He turned his attention to Kiley, gently coaxing her away from his knee. "What's the story, princess? Are you keeping your brother under control for me?"

Kiley, having no idea what Ben was asking, simply turned toward him and buried her head in the voluminous folds of his jacket.

"Ah," Ben noted sagely, "the inscrutable female. You never know what they're thinking."

"She's been asking for you, wondering where the devil you've been," Tess said. She'd been wondering the same thing herself.

"I was looking for my brains," Ben said, kissing the little girl's blond curls and receiving a tightly clutched, thoroughly wrinkled lapel in return. "I seemed to have lost them—at least temporarily."

Tess shook her head at him. "You shouldn't say that. Kids take things very literally. They're probably going to want to help you look for them."

Sure enough, Kevin, having grown braver in Ben's absence, insisted on a "brain search," leading Ben into the living room. Giving the twins the attention they, and Tess, had sorely missed during his absence, Ben finally persuaded the toddlers it was time for sleep. After tucking them into bed, he joined Tess in the kitchen where she was making a pot of coffee.

Tess handed him two tissue-wrapped packages. "The twins made you something at the shop last week while you were gone."

As Ben smiled and unwrapped the handmade treasures of clay, Tess brought out the three dozen pecan chocolate-chip cookies she'd stashed in the freezer. "So did I. Actually, I have something else for you, too." Reaching into the top drawer of the small desk in the hallway, Tess approached him. "I was down at the high school the other day," she explained, "and since they hadn't gotten around to giving you well-earned credit for all your talks to the students warning against drinking and driving, I suggested they get with it and do so. So they did. This is the result." She handed him a leather folder that contained his longtime-wished-for diploma.

For once, Ben looked genuinely speechless as he took it from her hand. "I don't know what to say."

Remembering his remarks about her manners, Tess quipped, "How about 'Thank you'?"

He brushed her hair back from her flushed cheeks. "Thank you. Tess, you didn't have to do this."

"I know that. But friends help friends in need." She paused. "We are still friends, aren't we?"

"I'd like to think so." Ben's gaze warmed her to the core. "I'd like to think we're that and a lot more. I brought you a present, as well." Going outside to his car, he brought in three boxes of oranges, one at a time.

"So many." Tess gave a soft laugh and shook her head. "Crazy man."

"You do like oranges, I trust?"

"I love them. What the heck—I love you," Tess confessed.

Ben put his arms around her. "I love you, too. Surprised to have me back?"

"Yes," she said truthfully. "I wasn't sure I'd ever see you again."

"Is that why you told my mom you'd bake our wedding cake?"

Tess flushed. "I thought she was talking about a birthday cake when I said yes to that."

"My birthday isn't until January."

"Not yours, idiot. Mine. It's in a couple of weeks."

"Really?" Ben's breath warmed her face. "How old will you be?"

Tess wrinkled her nose at him. "None of your business."

"Thirty," he immediately guessed. "Don't worry, Tess. You're not getting older. You're getting better. Blonder, too."

"I was going to change that back," Tess confessed. Her hair was still at least two shades lighter than the original brown. "But I've sort of grown accustomed to it this way."

Ben kissed her forehead. "I've sort of grown accustomed to you. I'd like to continue this discussion," he added, his lips against her temple. "There's only one small problem—"

Tess sighed at the scuffling noise coming from down the hall, indicating that the twins weren't quite asleep. "Actually, I think there are two small problems and both their names start with *K*."

"Maybe we'd better move into another room," Ben suggested.

"Which other room?"

"Any other room. Unless you've got a desire to make love on the kitchen floor amid twins and Cheerios."

"I swept up the Cheerios," Tess explained. "There are only a few strands of spaghetti scattered around at the moment."

"Does that mean you do have a penchant for making love on kitchen floors amidst spaghetti and little kids?" He nuzzled her throat.

"No. It means I object to your assessment of my kitchen floor." Tess sighed. "I have a penchant for making love with you, alone, in my room."

"I think we'll need to work on the 'alone' part," he said solemnly as the twins pranced down the hall toward them, "before we can get busy on the making-love part."

Half an hour later, with Kevin and Kiley snugly tucked into bed once again, Ben guided Tess into her bedroom and firmly closed the door.

"Maybe we should talk some more before we both get out of control," Tess suggested as he indicated he had every intention of loving first and talking later.

"I'm already struggling for control. What do you want to talk about?" Ben asked, continuing to unbutton her blouse.

Tess fought for coherent thought as he leaned over and kissed her exposed breasts. "About me and you. About us being together. About our future, in general. You do have some sort of plans?"

"I have some plans," Ben admitted. "An old racing buddy of mine wants me to help him start up his own performance driving school. He's asked me to be his partner. It's in a good location with a great population-density ratio. The area's still growing. It's a popular place for racing.

There's good weather year-round. And since it's near Orlando, it's also near other attractions, and that's always a drawing card."

He was putting an inordinate amount of enthusiasm into his voice, Tess noticed, almost as if he were afraid he still needed to convince her.

"Orlando's where you'll be developing this project of yours?" she asked.

As Ben slowly nodded, Tess felt herself tense instinctively, then relax. Her father lived just outside Orlando with his second wife, the former flight attendant, whom Tess had yet to meet.

"What does it involve, this performance driving school of yours?"

"My friend Dane and I plan to teach would-be race drivers basic skills and help them decide if they have potential. We also plan to teach professional chauffeurs evasive techniques."

"It sounds perfect for you," Tess admitted. A way to have his cake and eat it, too. Being involved with racing, without having to race.

"Nothing's perfect," Ben contradicted, "unless you're with me. I did a lot of thinking while I was gone."

"I did a lot of thinking while you were gone, too," Tess confessed.

"What did you decide?"

"Less than five hours after you left, I decided you meant more to me than the shop did. But I never got the opportunity to tell you." She gasped as he bent his dark head and caught one of her nipples in his mouth. "You didn't have to stay away so long, you know. A day or two would have done just fine. The least you could have done was phoned. Why the devil didn't you?"

"I was afraid you'd tell me to get lost."

"I'm the one who's been feeling lost—without you." She moaned softly as he abandoned one nipple for the other. "Ben?"

"Yes, love."

"I still don't know if it'll work out. Cheryl and Judith have indicated they'd like to take over things at the shop.

And I know your mother will help when she's here. But I'm not sure I'd be very good at starting things from scratch."

"No one ever knows how things will work out." Ben swirled his tongue around the pink circle of exquisitely sensitized flesh. "You can plan till you're blue in the face, then...pow! Something comes along to change things."

Tess sighed with pure pleasure as he continued his tender attention to the cleft between her breasts. "I suppose you're right. It's just... I don't know about you racing when it's so dangerous."

"Living is dangerous. Loving is dangerous. Besides, I won't be racing." Ben extended his surveyal to her flat stomach.

"Excuse me. *Teaching* racing is so dangerous. The only thing worse than a professional driver racing around a track at breakneck speed," Tess concluded, "is an *amateur* racing around a track at breakneck speed."

Ben explored her navel. "I promise to screen the candidates carefully. No hot dogs. No suicidal maniacs. Just serious contenders with talent."

"Promise?"

"Promise."

"Lord, there's the twins—again." Tess let out another sigh, this time of exasperation, as four tiny hands began pounding on the other side of the bedroom door.

"Remind me to install dead bolts in our new house," Ben murmured, "when we have kids."

Afraid to take anything for granted, Tess wanted to clarify things before either of them misunderstood. "Ben, I definitely want children," she said carefully.

"I realize that." Ben traced a path down her breastbone, exploring the valley with his tongue.

Tess moaned in pleasure, then frustration as the twins' pounding became increasingly louder and more impatient. "It might get tiresome at times." Times like now, she reflected, when they'd like just a little time alone.

"I realize that," Ben repeated, moving his attention to the hollow of her pulsing throat.

"It's one thing to entertain someone else's child for an hour or two," Tess plowed on, determined not to have any misunderstandings between them. "Quite another to take on the responsibility of your own for twenty years or so."

Ben raised his dark head and put his nose on hers so that she couldn't have looked away even if she'd wanted to. "What, exactly, is it you're afraid of? That I don't like kids?"

"That you might find kids amusing on a temporary basis but not on a permanent one."

"Let me tell you something." Ben cupped her face in his palms. "Number one: Kids don't bother me, on either a temporary or permanent basis. Number two: Not only do they not bother me, I'd definitely like some of my own."

"Truly?"

"Truly. There's something else perhaps even more important I should tell you."

"What's that?"

"My mother is absolutely crazy about children. She's been pestering me to provide her with grandchildren for nearly ten years now."

Tess considered that. "Really?"

Ben nuzzled her neck. "Really."

"You're just saying that to make me feel better," Tess replied. Her heart began to thump at Ben's slow smile.

"Lord, Tess," he purred, pulling her down and stretching out on top of her on the bed. "Give me some credit here. I've got lots better ways to make you feel good than that." And he proceeded to demonstrate, turning his full attention to the project.

Tess moaned softly as he gently kissed her throat, then each of her breasts, extending the tender exploration to her ribs, tracing each in turn with his lips, before turning his attention to her navel, circling it with his tongue before proceeding to the soft skin below.

"Have I succeeded yet?" he asked in a husky voice that made Tess's heart beat even faster.

"Succeeded in doing what?" Tess managed, weaving her fingers into the soft clean strands of his dark hair.

"Convincing you I mean business here. Please say no," he added, in an even huskier voice.

"Why?"

"So I can persuade you some more, naturally."

Tess didn't doubt that he would have in any case, but he was prevented from doing so when the pounding on the door became louder. Tess groaned as it became obvious that Fran's twins weren't going to be put off any longer. "Is your mother really crazy about little children?"

Ben rubbed his mouth against hers. "Absolutely."

Tess, basking in his love and wanting him all to herself, quipped, "I don't suppose she'd care to 'borrow' Fran's twins for the evening?"

Tess saw the light dawn in his eyes as he, too, realized it was a way of killing two birds with one stone. It would at least temporarily satisfy Dorothy's love of babies, and it would give them some much-needed time alone.

"I think she'd love the idea," Ben answered, smiling.

"What do you think we should do?" Tess asked.

"Ideas like this don't just come along every day," Ben predicted solemnly as he helped her to her feet. "I think we should grab the little rascals before they batter down the door, run them around the block a hundred times or so, then bundle them over to my mother's while they're too tired to do anything but be on their good behavior."

"As if you'd recognize good behavior," Tess murmured.

"I heard that."

"Good." Tess gave him a sassy grin. "Saves me having to say it again."

Ben's eyes promised retribution of the loving kind. "Before we start taking advantage of my mother, there's something else I'd like to take advantage of first." His voice was soft and intimate and full of love.

Tess felt her pulse quicken all over again. "What's that?"

Ben brought his mouth to hers. "You, of course."

Chapter Sixteen

It had taken two more days for Ben to convince her that her joining him in Florida was the right move, Tess reflected, but both of them had enjoyed every minute of it. Ben was nothing if not persuasive.

Not without a qualm or two, Tess stifled her ingrained reticence and went ahead with plans to start up Ye Olde Cookie Shoppe near where Ben and Dane Morgan were opening their performance driving school. As much as Tess both liked and feared the challenge of starting a new shop from the ground up, she wasn't about to let Ben off without making a few concessions himself.

"If I'm going to agree to temper my natural caution," Tess said, "and move thousands of miles for you, what are you going to do for me?"

"I'm going to try to cultivate a bit of prudence to balance my natural bent for adventure, of course," Ben promised.

Touring Disney World with Ben and Dorothy, Tess, walking hand in hand with Ben through the Magic Kingdom, wondered exactly what his definition of "prudence" was. So she asked.

"Prudence is exercising sound judgment, of course," Ben chided.

"What do you consider exercising sound judgment?" Tess persisted.

"Loving you, naturally." Ben kissed her soundly on the mouth. "Speaking of exercising sound judgment, have you done anything about seeing your dad and stepmother, now that we're here?" Ben had insisted Tess not make the same mistake he had in his youth when his mother had remarried, pursuing the subject until Tess had finally agreed to phone her parent.

"I met with my stepmom yesterday," Tess told him. And she'd had a long talk with her father afterward.

"At the risk of being nosy, what happened? Did you get along with her?"

Tess grimaced. "Actually, I did. A lot better than I thought I would. Dad's a lot calmer than I remember," she admitted. And his new wife had turned out to be a sensible woman of thirty-five who seemed to know exactly how to curb Duke DeSain's natural bent for adventure.

"He seemed perfectly normal to me," remarked Ben, who had surprised Tess by seeking out her father first and having a long, apparently enlightening discussion with him. "How the hell did he get a name like Duke, anyway?"

"He gave it to himself. Like you, he thinks he's John Wayne." Tess crinkled her eyes as Ben did his best to appear as innocent as a newborn lamb. "Dad offered to fly me up to New York whenever I want to see Cheryl and Judith," she added in amazement. "He never would have taken the time to do that a few years ago. He was always too busy trying out something new and crazy." In fact, his thirst for danger had been what had pulled him and Tess's mother apart—something Tess had finally confessed to Ben the morning she'd flown down to Florida with him.

Ben squeezed her fingers reassuringly. "People change."

"Some do. Some don't." Still not totally convinced that what Ben considered caution was the same thing she considered caution, Tess tested him occasionally. "What did you have in mind for this afternoon?"

"Well, I have a friend who's taking up a small jet for a test run, and I thought I'd go along." He dodged as Tess aimed a jab at his ribs. "Only kidding. How would you like to go on Space Mountain with me?"

"Roller coasters in the dark do strange things to my stomach."

"How about retired race drivers in the dark?" Ben drawled.

They did strange things to her heartbeat—one in particular. Tess shook her head in reproval. "And I thought pushy business partners were hard to manage."

"The new business is all yours. Cheryl and Judith are my business partners now," Ben reminded her.

"So they are. You know, you didn't have to buy a new refrigerator-freezer for them. Cheryl could hardly speak on the phone, she was so stunned."

"I enjoyed doing it. I make a habit of enjoying myself," he told her, sliding his hand down her back.

He also made a habit of getting her into trouble.

Tess laced her fingers through his so she knew where at least one hand was. "We ought to be making firm plans for the wedding," she remarked, catching sight of Dorothy, "before we're outvoted. I know it's too much to ask for *you* to try to curb your exuberance, but do you think you could convince your infamous Uncle Fred to behave himself?"

"My Uncle Fred hasn't the faintest idea how to behave himself. The rest of the family just ignore it and pretend he's normal."

"How can you ignore someone juggling bowling balls?" Tess wanted to know, sitting down on a vacant bench.

Ben joined her. "Don't forget the cymbals."

"What cymbals?"

"He bangs them between his knees while he juggles the bowling balls."

Resigning herself to being married in a circuslike atmosphere, Tess sighed. "So we seat him in the back row and hope for the best. Remind me to make sure nothing breakable is near him." Tess rested her head against Ben's shoulder in contentment.

Ben rubbed his cheek against her hair. "I love your outfit."

Tess glanced down at her hot-pink Minnie Mouse sweatshirt, then at Ben's wildly patterned, wildly colored Mickey attire. "I still can't figure out why your mother told me you were actually a very conservative dresser."

"I can. She lied. She was afraid my wardrobe would scare you off."

Tess glanced at his outfit again. "A very natural fear," she murmured. "I don't suppose there's any way I can talk you into not wearing chartreuse for the wedding ceremony?" she asked sweetly.

Ben tweaked her ear. "I don't suppose there's any way I can talk you into wearing chartreuse so we match?"

"Let's compromise and wear chartreuse underwear," Tess suggested.

"Let's compromise and wear no underwear."

"You're hopeless."

"You'd better take me in hand," Ben agreed. "How about we go back to the hotel now, so you can start?"

Tess gave him a mockingly stern look. "How about you trying to behave yourself? For a change. What on earth is your mother doing?"

Ben glanced in the direction Tess indicated. "Buying more Mickey Mouse T-shirts for Fran's kids, I suspect."

"They already have three each."

"Then maybe she's buying them Minnie and Mickey dolls. They only have two of those each, so far—counting Rob, who probably would have preferred something a little more adult."

"She's a wonderful woman," Tess confessed, "even if she's spoiling Fran's kids terribly at the moment. I don't know what we'd do without her."

"No need to wonder about it, since she'll be near us most of the year." Ben paused. "Does that bother you at all?"

"No," Tess replied honestly. "I love the idea." Tess shook her head as she watched Dorothy approach the cash register. "You're right. I think she's buying those kids more stuffed animals. But what in the world is that baby shirt in her hand for? Fran doesn't have any infants."

"I imagine she's buying it for our baby," Ben said calmly.

Tess felt a curious thrill race through her. "What baby is that?"

"Considering it's my mother we're talking about here, the one who isn't conceived yet." He kissed her hair. "How do you feel about that?"

Tess snuggled up to him. "About your mother getting pushy again?"

"About us having a baby right away. And," he added wryly, "my mom getting pushy again."

"I feel...happy, lucky and loved. But most of all," Tess decided, linking her fingers with his, "I feel...Young at heart." She pulled him to his feet.

Ben raised an eyebrow. "Where are you taking me now, wench?"

"Where do you think?" Tess laughed softly and tugged on his hand. "Space Mountain, naturally. But there's only one small problem..."

"And what might that be?"

Tess sighed. "You may need to hold on to me the whole time. Do you think you could put up with that for four minutes or so?"

"I think I could manage it." Ben pulled her closer to his side as they began to walk. He planned on holding on to her for a lifetime.

* * * * *

COMING NEXT MONTH

#595 TEA AND DESTINY—Sherryl Woods
Ann Davies had always taken in strays—but never one as wild as playboy
Hank Riley! She usually offered tea and sympathy, but handsome Hank
seemed to expect a whole lot more....

#596 DEAR DIARY—Natalie Bishop
Adam Shard was falling hard for his childhood pal. But beneath the
straightforward, sardonic woman Adam knew so well lay a Kerry Camden
yearning for love...and only her diary knew!

#597 IT HAPPENED ONE NIGHT—Marie Ferrarella
When their fathers' comedy act broke up, impulsive Paula and straitlaced
Alex grudgingly joined forces to reunite the pair. But after much muddled
meddling by everyone concerned, it was hard to say exactly *who* was
matchmaking whom...

#598 TREASURE DEEP—Bevlyn Marshall
A sunken galleon, a tropical isle and dashing plunderer Gregory Chase...
Could these fanciful fixings finally topple Nicole Webster's decidedly
*un*romantic theory on basic biological urges?

#599 STRICTLY FOR HIRE—Maggi Charles
An accident brought unwanted luxury to take-charge Christopher
Kendall's fast-paced life—a lady with a limo! And soon bubbly,
rambunctious, adorable Tory Morgan was driving him to utter
amorous distraction!

#600 SOMETHING SPECIAL—Victoria Pade
With her pink hearse, her elderly companion and her dubious past, there
was something mighty suspicious about Patrick Drake's new neighbor,
beautiful Mitch Cuddy. Something suspicious, something
sexy...something pretty damn special !

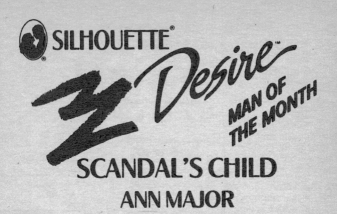